NEIL ALBERT

BURNING MARCH

A Dave Garrett Mystery

A SIGNET BOOK

SIGNET
Published by the Penguin Group
Penguin Books USA Inc., 375 Hudson Street,
New York, New York 10014, U.S.A.
Penguin Books Ltd, 27 Wrights Lane,
London W8 5TZ, England
Penguin Books Australia Ltd, Ringwood,
Victoria, Australia
Penguin Books Canada Ltd, 10 Alcorn Avenue,
Toronto, Ontario, Canada M4V 3B2
Penguin Books (N.Z.) Ltd, 182–190 Wairau Road,
Auckland 10, New Zealand

Penguin Books Ltd, Registered Offices:
Harmondsworth, Middlesex, England

Published by Signet, an imprint of Dutton Signet,
a division of Penguin Books USA Inc.
Previously published in a Dutton edition.

First Signet Printing, March, 1995
10 9 8 7 6 5 4 3 2 1

 REGISTERED TRADEMARK—MARCA REGISTRADA

Printed in the United States of America

PUBLISHER'S NOTE
This is a work of fiction. Names, characters, places, and incidents either are the product of the author's imagination or are used fictitiously, and any resemblance to actual persons, living or dead, events, or locales is entirely coincidental.

To my wife, Linda.
Who knows where the time goes?

AUTHOR'S ACKNOWLEDGMENTS

I would like to express my gratitude to the following persons for their kind assistance in the preparation of this manuscript: Suzanne E. Sipes, of the Disciplinary Board of the Pennsylvania Supreme Court; the Lancaster County District Attorney's Drug Task Force; and Adrianne Sekula-Perlman, M.D., of the Philadelphia Medical Examiner's Office. Every mystery writer needs a good pathologist, and she's a great one. I also thank Craig Schroll, of Firecon, Inc., for his expertise in fire scene analysis; Richard Nuffort, my partner, for his help in understanding the mysteries of corporate filings; Nancy Fornoff, my firm's office manager, for her help in explaining our bookkeeping system; Robert K. Weaver and Timothy Weaver, for their insights into the problems of the disabled; my agent, Blanche Schlessinger; mystery aficionado Jack Ebersole, and my writing coach, Roberta Strickler, for their suggestions and criticisms; and Donald Deibler, without whom nothing would have been possible.

Your time and efforts are very much appreciated.

Chapter One

Tuesday, 10:00 A.M.

I didn't know the receptionist, which was a relief. It was difficult enough being back at my old firm without seeing someone right away who remembered me. When I'd left, we'd been using a stout mother of five who spoke with a South Philadelphia accent and transposed phone numbers. I wondered if she'd been one of the hundreds of thousands of Philadelphians who'd fled to the suburbs in the last couple of years. The woman behind the desk was one of the new breed of city office workers—young, black, probably still single, and very likely still living with her parents. The clothes and jewelry didn't look like they came out of a budget that included a rent check.

"My name is David Garrett. I'm here to see Emily Voss."

I didn't get the reaction I expected. She just looked at me, her mouth slightly open. She started to say something, but it trickled away after a couple of syllables. Then she recovered enough to put some words together. "Uh . . . do you have an appointment, sir?"

"Yes, I do."

"Please—just have a seat for a minute." She picked up the

phone, but hesitated a long time before punching the buttons.

The room was just the same as when I'd last seen it, more than two years ago. Dark wood paneling, scarred by contact with the backs and armrests of the wooden chairs. A couple of dim lamps. A low table with magazines. I noticed that they were still making the same mistakes with the reading material—what kind of impression did *Law Office Economics* make on the clients? I remember telling Emily it gave me a funny feeling that we set out *Conde Nast Traveler* for a clientele that included shabbily dressed young couples filing bankruptcy. "It'll give the kids something to shoot for," she said in a voice that left no room for disagreement, and I'd let it drop.

The last time I'd been in this room was the day my disbarment took effect, the day before Thanksgiving. Somebody at the Pennsylvania Supreme Court had a hell of a sense of humor, picking that date. The next day I couldn't think of much to be thankful for. I remember boxing up my things with the help of my secretary and carting them down to my car. It was an awkward day, and the strain showed in everyone's face. Attorneys clogged the hallways and the door to my office, mostly being silent, sometimes offering help or encouragement. The partners I'd been closest to took me out for a last lunch. If we'd been daytime drinkers we might have achieved the atmosphere of a good Irish wake, but we weren't. One of them, not thinking through his words very well, suggested that since I wasn't a lawyer anymore I could go ahead and get as drunk as I wanted, which didn't help the atmosphere much. There was simply nothing useful to be said, and by the end of lunch our table was completely silent. People were afraid to face me. When we returned we saw that Tom Richardson, the senior partner, had signed himself out to "Legal Research—Law Library." We all knew that he hadn't been to the law library in twenty years. He never came back the rest of the afternoon.

"Dave, I'm glad to see you again."

The voice was warm and rich, and a little scarred by forty

years of smoking. I looked up; Tom was standing at the doorway that led back to the private offices. He was stout and short, with just a dark wisp of hair left at the temples.

"Tom, you haven't changed a bit." I offered him my hand but he came forward and embraced me instead.

"We've missed you, Dave."

"It's good to see you again, Tom." We released each other and I got a good, close look. He was wearing trifocals now, instead of just bifocals, and his skin looked a little more flushed, but the most important thing was his eyes, which were baggy and almost glazed over with fatigue. I was looking at a very tired man. I lied a little. "You look just the same as ever."

"That's the advantage of being bald and fat, not much more can go wrong." But his tone was flat and he didn't even try to smile.

"I was here to see Emily, actually."

"That's what Denise told me." His tone became more clipped. "Dave, we have to talk. In my office. Coffee?"

"Thanks. Black, no sugar."

I had some time to look around while he ordered coffee. It was an old man's office, full of the smells of pipe smoke and furniture oil. His desk was an immense oak affair, darkened by the years and covered with books and piles of legal documents. In one corner was a photograph of his wife, dead before I'd ever joined the firm. One wall was taken up with a decaying set of nineteenth-century Pennsylvania Supreme Court decisions, which gave off a faint musty smell. The leather chairs smelled of sweat, from the days before offices were air conditioned. A state-of-the-art dictating machine sat on a table across the room, still in its factory plastic.

"Still dictating to Margaret?" I asked.

He glanced at the machine briefly, as if he was surprised it was there. "Never could figure out what was supposed to be the advantage of those damned things. It takes me the same amount of time to dictate no matter if she's here or not. And if

I make a mistake or leave something out, she's right there to ask me about it."

"And if she takes it down herself you know that she'll do the typing herself and not the office pool." It was an argument that had gone on the whole time I'd been a partner.

"And so what? Being the managing partner ought to have some perks, shouldn't it?"

An unfamiliar secretary brought in coffee—evidently Margaret had reached the stage in life where she could delegate such things—and quickly disappeared. "You won that fight a long time ago, Tom." The dictation system had been my idea, five years before, and before I'd ever presented it I had known that an exception would have to be made for him.

I saw him looking at my ringless left hand as I held the cup of coffee. "Things didn't work out with Terry, I suppose," he said.

"They'd been rocky for a long time anyway. She lost her license, too, you know."

"You're a generous man. She's the reason you're not a lawyer now."

I sipped my coffee. I appreciated his concern, but talking about it didn't help. "So what's going on with Emily? Isn't she in yet?"

He avoided my question. "When did she call you?"

"Last Friday. She wanted me to come down to talk about something. Monday was bad for me, so we set it for this morning."

"What did she say she wanted to see you about?"

"What's going on here, Tom?"

"Do you know what happened to Emily?"

"Happened?"

"She's dead."

"When?"

"Late last night or early this morning. There was a fire in her apartment."

"Jesus, I didn't know anything about this. When did you find out?"

"The police called the firm's answering service about four this morning. I've been up since."

"I liked her. She sent me a nice note after I left."

"We're all going to miss her. The reason you don't see Margaret is because she's taken the day off. She came in and left right away when she heard the news. They were close, you know."

"You look like you could stand to bag it, too."

"There's too much to do." His voice was worn and thin. He'd never looked younger than his age, but now he looked a lot older.

"When's the funeral?"

He shook his head. "She left instructions she didn't want a burial, just a memorial service, and cremation, and the ashes scattered on the ocean. I'll be taking care of that, since there's really no family. She wasn't very close with her sister, and the woman's all the way across the country."

Neither of us said anything for a moment, and I had a feeling where the conversation was going to go next. But I wanted to let him take the lead.

"What did she want to talk to you about?" he asked.

"I wish I knew, Tom. She just said that she wanted a consultation, to decide whether or not the firm needed an investigator."

"To investigate what?"

"She didn't give me any idea. It wasn't a long conversation. The main points were that it involved the firm, and that she hadn't made a decision to hire me, she was just checking out options."

"She was an employee. What gave her the idea she could make a decision like that?"

"I don't know." But I had a hunch that whatever she wanted to talk to me about, she hadn't felt comfortable sharing it with any of the partners, at least without talking to me first.

He drummed his fingers on his desk. "Her calling you. This is very . . . disquieting, Dave."

"Did she say anything to you last week?"

"Just the usual day-to-day things. She certainly didn't mention you. Or why we'd need an investigator."

"What about yesterday?"

"She wasn't here."

"Oh?"

"She called in first thing in the morning and said she was ill, that she wouldn't be in the rest of the day. The fire took place late last evening or very early this morning." He frowned. "She was hardly ever sick. I can't remember the last time she'd taken a day off, except for vacations."

"You sound like you've already done some checking."

"Well, the illness was real enough. I saw her on Friday, and she had a cold. I talked to her family doctor, got him out of bed at six this morning. He saw her late Friday afternoon and gave her some pills. I talked to her briefly on Saturday afternoon and she said her throat was sore, that she was feeling worse."

"Did she mention whether she'd be in Monday?"

"No, it wasn't discussed."

"What did she say when she called in?"

"She left a message with the answering service; no one here talked to her. The message was just that she would be out Monday but would be in Tuesday. This may be none of my business, Dave, but had Emily ever called you before last Friday for anything?"

"No. And I'll save you the trouble of saying it. The call to me, and her death—it may be a coincidence, but I'm not convinced. I'd like you to fill me in on what you've learned."

"I haven't seen the report myself, but the medical examiner's office read me the highlights over the phone just a few minutes ago. They say that the fire was accidental."

"Hold on a minute. How does the ME get to that conclusion? That's the fire marshal's job."

"I'm sorry. This isn't my field and I'm getting things a little confused. The fire marshal said that it was a kitchen fire. They said that they would be suspicious only if it was shown that she died before the fire. In other words, that she was killed and then the fire was set to cover up a homicide. And the medical examiner says she was definitely alive at the time of the fire."

"How did they determine that?"

He swallowed. "They said they found smoke and soot particles in her bronchial tubes. It shows she was still breathing during the fire. Does that sound right to you?"

"Sounds plausible to me, but this is a little out of my field."

"I thought you were the fire expert."

I shrugged. "I handled some fire cases when we used to do subrogations for Prudential, but I don't know about cause of death issues. The fire marshal's theory is that she put something on the stove and forgot about it?"

"Basically, yes."

"As I recall from Christmas parties, she drank, didn't she?"

"Not heavily."

"The pills the doctor gave her, were they some kind of antihistamine, that she shouldn't have taken with alcohol?"

"I have the names from her doctor; I haven't had time to look them up yet."

"What if she took her pills, put something on the stove, had a nightcap or two while waiting for her dinner, and just went out?"

"And what if she didn't?" It wasn't really a question.

"Tom, come on. You should hear yourself."

He turned away from me and looked at the rows of books on the far wall. He chose his words carefully. "I knew this woman very well. In twenty years the books were never off by a penny. Do you think she'd ignore a warning about mixing alcohol and medication? And what would she be doing up in the middle of the night cooking a meal? She practically never cooked—she lived where she did because there were enough all-night restaurants and takeout places around that she didn't need to. And even if she took a day off, can you imagine her not checking in, to see if everything was all right?"

"There's nothing in what you've said that isn't explained by her illness, except the cooking. And as far as that goes, we don't have to assume she had an urge to play Julia Child at midnight. She could have been just heating up some takeout, or a doggie bag. You said yourself she had no great experience in the kitchen; maybe with some pills and a couple of drinks in her she didn't realize the danger of leaving food unattended."

"So explain why she was cooking in the middle of the night."

"She'd slept all day and her sleep patterns were screwed up."

He sighed. "You're giving me quite a hard time."

"That's because you're a friend."

He looked at me impatiently. "So do something other than cross-examine me."

"Assuming, just assuming, that her death is suspicious, do you think there could be any connection to the firm?"

"What do you mean?"

"A lot of money passed through her hands."

"So?"

"Perhaps she was diverting funds."

"I don't believe it, not for a second."

"Just assume."

He moved uncomfortably in his seat. "All right. I'll entertain the idea. How does that explain a murder?"

"Maybe she was stealing on instructions from someone, or to pay a blackmailer, and they leaned on her too hard."

He snorted. "Emily being blackmailed? What on earth for? That sounds pretty silly."

"Can you think of anyone who meant her harm?"

"Not a soul."

"Do you know anything about her life out of the office?"

He thought for a moment. "Mmm. Not really."

I sighed. "Are the books being checked?"

He looked across the room at the Supreme Court opinions

for a while before he answered. "I decided to do that after I got the news this morning."

"Why?"

He seemed surprised at the question. "Well, when I made the decision I was just thinking that whoever is going to take over needs to be sure everything is in order. We're having a review done by the accountants. It should be getting under way later this morning."

It was an interesting step for someone who said he had no reason to think her death had anything to do with the firm, but I kept that to myself. "You've been busy," I said.

"I've been up since four. You can get a lot done in six hours if you don't have any distractions."

"What do you have in the way of documents at this point?"

"I'll give you what I have." He handed me a slim folder. It was an office file, with "Thomas H. Richardson" as the client and "Emily Voss" as the file name. Tom was nothing if not organized. I opened it and found myself looking at her picture. There's a Jewish superstition about pictures of the dead, and seeing the photo sent a tingle up my spine. She didn't look like a person who ought to be dead—she was smiling at the camera, and her head was turned a little to one side. Her hair was gray. I'd never seen her hair in anything but a bun, but in this picture it was down to her shoulders. From the background, it looked like she was sitting at a table in a sidewalk cafe. She was wearing slacks and a loose-fitting scoop-neck top that did a better job of minimizing her middle-age spread than the suits that she wore to the office. I corrected myself—that she *used* to wear.

I put down the picture. I'd known her only as the person who kept the books in order, not as someone who let her hair down and smiled in the sunshine. . . . It depressed me that we'd worked closely for years and yet I really knew very little about her. I realized that she was fifty—only six years older than me.

Next was her personnel file, in its own folder, which I put aside for the moment. Last was Tom's notes from his conversation with the medical examiner's office, written on a yellow legal pad. His handwriting was clear and precise, and it read as easily as a typed memo. I reviewed it carefully and looked up at him.

"Tom, you said she didn't drink heavily."

"No, she didn't."

"What makes you so sure?"

"She was here for every Christmas party for nearly thirty years, plus the employees' annual dinner. I never knew her to have more than two glasses of wine."

"Could she have been a weekend binger?"

"No." He was annoyed by my questions. "She was in the office most Saturdays and sometimes on Sundays, and I never had a hint she was hung over, not once. And I keep an eye out for that kind of thing, you know." I nodded; he had been the first to suspect that one of our associates was addicted to cocaine when none of the younger partners had a clue. He could be a surprisingly modern man when he wanted to be.

"What if she just didn't come in on the weekends she was loaded?"

"She was in a lot more weekends than she wasn't. And even when she was at home, sometimes I'd need to talk to her about finances. I never found her drunk, or even drinking."

"Sometimes alcoholics can fool the rest of us pretty well. They can act sober even when their blood alcohol is high."

"Answer me this—even if someone drunk could pull off an act, she wouldn't be able to do things that alcohol impairs, like complicated calculations, would she?"

"That's right."

"Even on the weekends she wasn't in she took work home, and it was always done by Monday. Always."

I thought about what he'd said for a minute, looking for flaws. Then I held out one of the yellow pages to him. "Tom, right here, you have written 'point three-three-seven.' You see where I mean?"

He leaned toward me and moved his head up and down,

hunting for the proper angle out of his trifocals. "Yes, I see it."

"What does that mean?"

"That was what they said her blood-alcohol level was."

"That's what I thought. Are you sure you got it down right? I mean, could it have been point oh-three-three-seven?"

"No, I'm sure of it. I made him repeat it for me. Does it mean anything?"

"How much did she weigh?"

"What? How would I know?"

"I'm guessing around a hundred and forty."

"I suppose. But what does that mean?"

"If she died before she ate the food that was on the stove then her stomach was probably empty."

"What are you talking about?"

"Someone of her weight, on an empty stomach, would have to drink the better part of a fifth of hard liquor to get that kind of a reading. In Pennsylvania, you're guilty of drunk driving if you're caught with point one percent blood alcohol—she was more than three times the legal limit. It's more than enough to make someone pass out who wasn't a heavy drinker."

"I'm not sure I'm following you."

"Maybe she drank that much herself—you know, you have a drink and a cold pill, and you forget what you've done, and you keep drinking till you've gone too far. People die that way from barbiturates and alcohol accidentally all the time. But maybe she didn't drink it; at least, not voluntarily."

"What are you saying?"

"Maybe, just maybe, someone forced her to drink it and set the fire after she passed out."

He gave no reaction. For a moment I thought he hadn't heard me or hadn't understood. Then I saw that he'd dropped his eyes and was staring at an empty space on his desk. A full five seconds went by before he raised his face. "That's horrible!" he said softly. "How could anyone want to do that to poor Emily?"

"I don't know that they did, Tom. It's just a possibility."

He shivered and pushed himself back from the desk. Suddenly he didn't seem to know what to do with his hands. "Emily being gone is bad enough, but this . . ." His hands made an aimless gesture and collapsed into his lap.

"It's worse than that."

"How could it be?"

"She wanted to see me about something to do with the firm—I don't know exactly what about, but I'm sure it wasn't a personal matter. If her phone call to me is tied in with her death, the killer could be someone in this firm."

Chapter Two

Tuesday 11:00 A.M.

Richardson leaned back in his chair and pressed his fingertips together in a position of prayer. It was his unconscious signal that he'd made a decision and was about to speak officially. "Dave, I'd like you to take this on as a case. I know I'm acting on behalf of the firm when I say that."

"You understand that this may not lead anywhere. No guarantees."

"I know," he said.

"And you realize that the police might be able to do more."

"It's a closed book to them, already."

"They might be willing to reopen it. They can't be in that much of a hurry," I said.

"They know what this blood-alcohol level means just as well as you do, don't they?"

"Yes."

"And they still think that it's an accident. Why should I spend my time arguing with them?"

"They have resources I don't."

"I know that. But you knew her. You're motivated. That more than makes up."

Tom was old school—the winning attitude could overcome any obstacle. Trying to argue with him only made him suspect you weren't the right person for the job. "Fifty dollars an hour, plus expenses," I said.

"Very reasonable."

"You mean, considering I was a hundred-and-seventy-five-dollar-an-hour lawyer? You bet."

"How about a retainer?"

"Come on, I know the firm's good for it."

"You shouldn't have to wait thirty days for your money. How about three hundred? I'll get it for you right now, and you can get started."

"How are you going to cut a check without Emily?"

"I'll get a funny-money check." We kept a stock of blank checks on yellow NCR paper that could be filled out by hand, without the need for the bookkeeper to use the check-writing machine. The older attorneys called them The Yellow Peril because of the problems they caused. Attorneys would fill them out and forget the amount, or even lose the whole check. But it was the only way to handle check writing if the bookkeeper wasn't around.

The offer of a job included the use of some office space. Tom showed me to a small unused office with an empty desk. I didn't recognize the office at first. Then I realized it had been created by dividing one of the larger offices into three smaller ones.

There were no windows, but there was a telephone. I decided to start with the deputy fire marshal who'd investigated the fire.

I was able to reach him right away. "Dempsey," he announced in a bored voice. He had me on a speakerphone, and all the noises of his office—typewriters, conversations, shouting, even a television—burst into my ear. "Mr. Dempsey, my name is Dave Garrett. It's hard to hear you with all the background. Could you pick up, please?"

"Nah, it's okay." He sounded like he was in the middle of eating something.

"I'd like to talk to you about the fire—"

"I do lots of fires, bud."

"Someone was killed in this one. Last night. An apartment fire—" I consulted Tom's notes "—on Spruce near Eleventh."

"Yeah, I remember."

"I'd like to talk to you about it. Can we meet?"

"You from the *Daily News*?"

"No, I'm a private investigator."

He ignored my answer. "You doing one of those stories on how unsafe the city is? Well, it ain't. Almost as safe as the suburbs. The only problem we got is, the niggers keep torching abandoned buildings. And if they gave us the money to fund the firefighting services right, we could put them out faster—"

"Mr. Dempsey, I'm not from the paper. I'm not doing a story on anything. I'm investigating the death of the woman on Spruce Street, that's all."

"The ME's ruled it accidental. I called it accidental. End of story."

"My client still has some concerns. I'd like to talk to you about them."

"How fucking nice for you. Buddy, you know how many fires I gotta investigate? Ones with whole families wiped out? With multimillion-dollar buildings gutted and every insurance adjustor in town screaming down my throat? What's one more or less alkey? We're all lucky she didn't take half a dozen people with her. The file is closed and it stays closed."

"She wasn't an alcoholic."

"Then how did she get that much booze in her?"

"I think someone forced it on her."

For once his voice showed interest. "Why would somebody do that?"

"I don't know."

"Well, who was it, then?"

"I don't know that, either."

"Pretty lame, bud. What else you got?"

"Nothing yet. You're the first call I've made."

"Well, let me give you some advice. Don't expect me to take you by the hand on city time."

I thought for a moment he was holding out for a bribe, but I was wrong. He simply hung up.

I didn't like the idea of running for help five minutes into the case, but it was the only smart move. I put the phone down and went back to Tom's office. "Find out something already?" he asked.

His face was so hopeful I had to fight the urge to lie to him. "You know anybody in the city fire marshal's office?"

He leaned back in his chair and thought. Richardson had been active in Democratic politics in the city for more than three decades, and a lot of his contacts had moved from one department to another over the years. "No, I don't think I do. I know plenty of chiefs."

"No, I need someone in the marshal's office."

"Getting a runaround?"

"That, I can handle. The assistant who handled the case just won't give me the time of day."

"Doesn't the fire marshal report to the mayor?"

"I wouldn't know."

"Well, whether he does or not, I've got some markers I can call. Where will you be?"

"The library."

"Courthouse?"

"No, yours, right here. There's plenty of other things to do while I'm waiting."

I left him on the phone and headed down the familiar corridor to the library, carrying the file with me. Like most Center City offices, space was at a premium, and one side of the corridor was lined with workstations and typists. I looked at each face as I passed, but none of them was familiar. Could the turnover be that high? I remembered what my supervising partner had told me when I was first hired: the average tenure of a legal secretary was less than three years. I'd been surprised, but looking back, he'd been right.

The firm's library was hardly more than a widening of the corridor, but there was a table in the middle, surrounded on all sides by the heavy mustard-yellow volumes that contained the decisions of the Pennsylvania courts. It was quiet and private there, and when I'd worked here I liked it better as a work space than my own office.

The table was occupied. And even though it was big enough for three or even four to work comfortably, the one user had spread her papers over the entire surface.

"Hi," I said. "Mind if I have a little room here?"

She looked up and brushed long blonde hair out of her face. "Do you work here?" she asked. Not suspicious, but not friendly, either. She had a wide, even face with pale skin and freckles. She looked like she would be pretty if she smiled, but she wasn't smiling now.

I could have given her the long version but I didn't have ten minutes. "Yes."

Without moving from her chair, she pulled in her papers and cleared a space for me. I wasn't sure how she fit in, which, I realized, made us about even. I didn't recognize her. The documents she was working on looked like bonds and mortgages, which made me think she was an attorney. She was somewhere on the shy side of thirty, which certainly made her old enough to be a lawyer. But the way she was dressed—big dangling earrings and a bright lemon-yellow blouse with a plunging neckline—seemed a little casual for a professional. As she moved her papers around I realized she wasn't wearing a bra, and even from what I could see, she had a figure that required one.

"My name's Garrett, Dave Garrett. I'm an investigator."

She looked at me across the table with interest. "Susan Min-nik." We shook hands. "What are you investigating?" Her voice was high and bouncy, like a teenager's. It didn't seem to fit with a well-built woman approaching thirty.

"I'm looking in to what happened to Emily."

She wrinkled her nose. "God, that was awful, wasn't it?"

"It's not the way I'd want to go."

Her voice dropped. "Do you suppose she . . . felt anything?"

"I doubt it. It must have happened when she was unconscious. If she'd been awake at all, she should have been able to get out."

"Well, that's one consolation. But still, it's awful, isn't it? I mean, just last week she was here, and now she's gone for good."

"Did you know her well?"

"Not really. I've only been with the firm a year and a half. She helped me out with some medical bill problems, but that was about it."

"Are you an attorney?"

"Uh-huh. Mostly real estate and commercial lending, and some foreclosure work."

"Who are you working under?"

"Really nobody. I worked for a two-person firm in Upper Darby for a couple of years, doing just real estate. Then the firm broke up and the partner I stayed with was brought on here. But he retired right afterward."

"Sounds like they were just buying up his practice."

"I suppose so. But it's lucky for me, 'cause I've got a job. And I keep right on working with a lot of the clients I had in Upper Darby."

"Does the firm still have an office there?"

She nodded. "I have office hours there two days a week, plus by appointment."

I turned my attention to the file, but I kept thinking about what she'd said. Things had changed a lot; I couldn't imagine my old firm making a decision to grow like that. It was the legal equivalent of a leveraged buyout—quick, simple, and full of problems down the road. Would the clients of the old firm stay? Would this associate work out? How do we handle hiring staff for a location where they'll be working without any real supervision? Tomorrow's problems. Ah, well. If it helps the bottom line today, that's all we need to know.

There was nothing in Emily's personnel file that came as much of a surprise. She'd worked for an accounting firm for a few years, and then came with us. She started as an assistant bookkeeper, and was promoted in 1965 to head bookkeeper. No job changes since, just raises. Never married, at least as far as I could tell from the file. The only relative mentioned was a sister in California, who was identified as the beneficiary of the small life insurance policy the firm provided as part of its benefits package. Tom was right about her attendance record; in over twenty-five years she'd never taken more than a handful of days off, except for an appendectomy in 1979. He was also apparently right about her willingness to work hard—she'd received a merit bonus every year since we'd instituted the program. Paper-clipped to her last performance evaluation was a small black-and-white photograph, showing her the way I remembered her—sitting at her desk, with a pleasant but businesslike expression, and her hair pulled back. I put the photograph in my pocket.

Except for the bills from her appendectomy, there were no medical expenses in her insurance file at all. No drug or alcohol rehab, no psychiatrists, no evidence of psychotherapy.

I rubbed my eyes. Investigations are largely a matter of finding dead ends, but it's never fun to find you've wasted time, especially when someone else is paying for it.

A phone rang, somewhere close. I looked around and saw it on the wall behind me. I looked at Susan. "Go ahead and answer it," she said.

"Library," I said.

"This is Denise out front. Is Mr. Garrett there?"

"Speaking."

"Oh, good. I've been looking for you everywhere. There's a gentleman who's been on hold for the longest time, waiting to talk to you."

"I'll take it here. What's his name?"

"It's a Mr. Dempsey."

"Put him on."

"Mr. Garrett?"

"Yes."

"Hi, this is Bob Dempsey over at the fire marshal's office. We spoke earlier this morning."

I counted to three, slowly. "I haven't forgotten."

There was a pause before he continued. "Yes. Well, uh, I just wanted you to know that we'd be happy to assist your investigation in any way we can, sir."

"Then meet me at the fire scene in an hour. Bring a copy of the ME report for me. And a key so we can look inside. And I want the investigating cop along, too."

"No problem, sir. See you then."

I disliked him even more.

Chapter Three

Tuesday, Noon

It was easy to spot Dempsey. He was the overweight one who was afraid of losing his job.

"Mr. Garrett, pleased to meet you." I ignored the offered hand. I hated people like Dempsey. He reminded me of Churchill's quote about the Germans—either at your throat or at your feet.

"Let's see the ME report."

"Sure. We didn't have a copy in our file, but I called the office and they faxed it down. These are just the rough notes —the actual report will take a couple of days."

I took it from him and started to skim through it. Well-nourished white female, appearing to be approximately the stated age. The body had been badly damaged by the fire, with most of the injury to the back and the backs of her legs and arms. The face and front were relatively intact. Aside from the fire damage, there were no marks of violence. The body had been brought in wearing a cotton dressing gown that was partially consumed by the fire. Panties, but no other underwear or socks. Examination of the mouth, larynx, and bronchial tubes revealed extensive deposits of soot, ash, and smoke residue.

The lungs showed the results of many years of smoking, plus changes secondary to exposure to superheated air. The stomach contained no solids, but a significant amount of fluid. An abdominal scar and no appendix. No other findings of significance.

The lab report indicated that the stomach contents were water, sugar, alcohol, and other unidentified substances. Blood gases showed very high concentrations of carbon monoxide and carbon dioxide. The blood showed very poor oxygenation, which was consistent with the observed levels of carbon monoxide and dioxide. The blood alcohol was 0.337 percent by weight. Cause of death: smoke inhalation.

I looked up and folded the papers away. "Mr. Garrett, I'd like you to meet Sergeant Anderson, the investigating officer." Dempsey moved to one side and I saw a slim man in his early thirties with a thin mustache. "Pleased to meet you, Sergeant. Glad you could make it."

"No problem, sir. You *are* licensed, right?" I extracted my identification from my wallet and handed it over. He looked at it without expression and handed it back. Even though he wasn't in uniform, I would have spotted him as a Philadelphia cop anywhere. Unless they're on the take, they dress like hell. Anderson had my confidence immediately—he was wearing the ugliest suit I'd ever seen. It was polyester, badly stitched, and two sizes too small. He was showing no less than three inches of cuff, and the jacket was drawn so tightly across his chest I could tell he was packing an automatic and not a revolver. And the color—I'd only seen that shade of brown once before, on something I'd left too long in the back of my refrigerator. "How can I help?" he asked.

"I'd like to see where the body was found."

While Anderson looked through a ring of keys, I had a chance to study the exterior. The house was brick, three stories, with five mailboxes fastened to the outside wall. It was in good shape—small brass carriage lights flanked the main door, and the windows all had window boxes. At this time of year they were all empty, but most of the buildings on the block had no places for flowers at all. The neighborhood was in transition, and it was hard to say where it was going to end up. Perhaps gentrified residential, like Society Hill; perhaps commercial, like Chestnut or Market; perhaps mixed-use sleaze, like parts of South Philadelphia. I saw a couple of storefront real estate offices specializing in apartment rentals, and put my money on sleaze.

The steps leading up to Emily's building were barred by a yellow POLICE LINE—DO NOT CROSS tape. Led by Anderson, we ducked underneath and went up to the door, which was half glass. Anderson opened the door and stood well back.

When I stepped into the foyer, I understood why. The air inside reeked of soot, smoke, and ash. We headed up the stairs. As we moved away from the light in the foyer Andersen turned on a powerful flashlight. Dempsey had one of his own, which he kept pointed at our feet. Wallpaper, blackened by the smoke, was falling down in large sheets and crunched underfoot. Everything was covered with soot.

The smell was worse when we reached the third floor. The door to her apartment was closed, but Dempsey just pushed on it and it yawned open. On the inside the door was dark—not charred, just blackened with smoke. We moved down a short corridor and entered what must have been her front room. I noted two small sofas and an easy chair, all soggy with water. I was glad it was above freezing; if the puddles on the floor had frozen, the place would have been a skating rink. I saw a black-ened transfer case on the easy chair, empty. Some soggy papers were scattered around the floor. I tried to pick up what looked like some ledger cards, but the ink had run and the pages were hopelessly stuck together. There was no way to know what she'd taken home except by checking for what was missing from the office.

The next room back was the kitchen—or what was left of it. I was no expert in fire investigations, but it was obvious that this room had suffered the worst damage. The walls were charred, and the damage was most severe directly above the stove. The plaster and lath ceiling was under our feet, in little chunks that crackled as we walked. I could see the remains of the ceiling joists above our heads. The floor above had been burned through in places, and I could see the undersides of pieces of furniture above me.

"The fire bring the ceiling down?" I asked.

"Some," Dempsey said. "Fire spreads upward, of course, so you can expect the ceiling to have a lot of flame and heat damage compared to the floor and walls. But a lot of this would have been the firefighters ripping the ceiling down to give the water a good pathway. These old ceilings and walls—a little spark gets back there, and if we go home without getting to it, it'll flare up again a few hours later and we're right back here again. Especially in a place with wood this old. Don't take much to get it going."

The floor was a mess, but it seemed solid enough. I moved closer to the stove. It was a standard, apartment-sized electric four-burner stove, or at least what was left of one. The Formica countertops on either side were melted into a black goo that reminded me of licorice. On the left side the cabinets were charred, but still recognizable. But to the right of the stove, all I could see was the fastenings that had held cabinets to the wall. There was nothing between the stove and the remains of the refrigerator, four feet away.

"Mr. Garrett, if you look right in front of you there, you'll see why we say this is the point of origin. Fire burns upward, and in an interior space, with no wind and no complicating factors, it'll burn in a V pattern. The bottom of the V is your point of origin. And I gotta tell you, this is a pretty easy one to read. You get a building that burns to the ground, how the fuck do you ever prove anything? You get a quick fire that's put out in a couple minutes, a ten-year-old kid can spot it. This one burned a while, but hell, you can see the V for yourself."

He was right. If you paid attention, the char marks on the

wall were deepest and blackest to the right of the stove, and they pointed downwards toward the right rear burner.

"Right here?"

"Yeah. Here, I can show it to you better." He opened his coat, drew out a small whisk broom, and brushed the wall. "I did this this morning, getting off the char, but I can get more off." He was right; after a little work the V was even more pronounced.

"So what was on the stove?"

"A big metal skillet. An old-fashioned cast-iron one. Not aluminum; that might have melted. Anyway, we took it back to the lab. We don't have a formal report yet, but I've seen the same thing a hundred times. Just from looking at it, I can tell you what it'll say: lotsa carbonized organic residues. Food and cooking oil. We found similar residue on the stove top for a radius of about ten inches around the burner. The rest of the top was clean except for smoke and soot."

"Could you identify the food?"

"It was some kind of meat; that's all we could tell. And a lotta cooking oil. I dunno; maybe the lab could do more tests if you want."

Anderson spoke to me. "Is there some reason to think that's important?"

"No, not really. I was just asking."

"Why?" he wanted to know.

"You ask enough questions, the answer to one of them could turn out to be important."

"Or you can wind up ten investigations behind."

Well, at least I knew where he stood. He thought I was wasting his time. "Was the deceased a vegetarian?" he asked.

I thought for a minute. "Not as of two years ago. That was my last contact with her. She ate meat and chicken at firm dinners."

He made some notes in a small notebook. "Did you know her well?"

"I used to work at the firm where she worked."

He made some more notes and nodded. He was through with me for the moment.

I looked at Dempsey. "Where was she found?"

"In the loft bedroom, right through there." He led the way through the back door of the kitchen into a windowless room that contained a washer and dryer. To the left was a small bathroom, and to the right, a set of stairs led upward. Like the front room, the area had only suffered from the smoke and water, not from the flames themselves.

Dempsey flicked his flashlight on again and went up the stairs. The walls were charred, but not as heavily as the kitchen ceiling. "Gotta be careful up here," he said. "The floor's been weakened."

The three of us stood on the landing at the top of the stairs and surveyed what was left of the bedroom. A heavy barbecue smell filled our nostrils, but no one mentioned it. The floor was eaten through in a number of places, and it sagged noticeably in the middle where it was pressed down by what remained of the bed.

"Was she in the bed?"

"I saw her before she was moved," Dempsey said. "She was in bed, all right."

I gestured around the room at the damage. "So how come she didn't wake up? This is a lot to sleep through, no matter how much you've had to drink."

He shook his head. "The smoke gets them first. Unless you've got an accelerant of some kind, people don't often die of burns. The bodies may be burned all to hell, but they're dead of asphyxiation before the flames get to them. Especially in a setup like this. Myself, I don't like the layout of this place. The kitchen is a really common place for fires to start, and where do the fires go but up? And what does the smoke from the fire do? Knocks out the people right upstairs. In the old days, if you had money, kitchens were separate buildings. Or built onto the rear of the house with nothing above. That was a long time ago.

Now, as long as there's two exits, the landlord can lay it out any way he pleases. From a design standpoint, it was an accident waiting to happen."

"I still have trouble seeing how this wouldn't have gotten her up."

"It didn't, take it from me. We would have found her in a closet if she'd been conscious at all. Hell, people die in mattress fires caused by their own smoking every day. And with lower BACs than this lady had."

I turned to Anderson. "You think she got the point three three seven on her own?"

"An empty bottle of gin was found in the bedroom, and a glass."

"Prints?"

"Negative. Both were distorted by the heat. Not a lot, but enough to screw up fingerprinting. If the bottle had been even a little more than half full, it could account for the blood alcohol."

"Did she drink gin?"

"She kept her liquor in a closet in the front hall on a shelf." He consulted his notebook. "We found one bottle each of Scotch, vodka, whiskey, two kinds of wine, and brandy. No gin. We think that she kept a bottle of gin there, and that was the one she drank last night."

I had to admit his reasoning was sound. I would be suspicious if there was gin upstairs *and* downstairs when there was only one bottle of everything else. "Point three three seven is a hell of a lot of booze."

"Depends how much she drank. There are people who are out driving right now with that in their systems, and they're doing just fine."

"She wasn't much of a drinker."

"I thought you didn't know her well."

I started feeling like a suspect instead of an investigator. "I've talked to her employer and he says she wasn't a drinker."

For the first time there was an expression in Anderson's

face, and it was disdain. "I don't think we need to pursue that one any further, do you?"

"I know what you're going to say—the boss is the last to know."

"Mr. Garrett, people hide things so well I can't begin to tell you. If the victim was known never to drink at all, that's one thing. But this, where the victim's an admitted user of alcohol, I wouldn't even buy a husband's testimony about the *amount* she drank. You want to know the case I was working on when I got called down here? Hooker, working South Street in the afternoons, giving twenty-dollar blow jobs in cars. Been doing it for years. This day, a customer doesn't want to pay, they argue, he pulls a knife and slashes her throat. We go to the woman's address, nice middle-class neighborhood in Chestnut Hill, her husband is there, he refuses to believe it. He says his wife told him she was working at the church thrift shop all this time."

It wasn't noon, and I was already dealing with my second person of the day with a closed mind. I looked around the room. "Any sign of forced entry?"

"The front apartment door was so badly damaged you couldn't tell anything. There's a rear door that leads to a fire escape, but it hasn't been used in years. The hinges were rusted shut. There were no windows where anyone could have gained access through the fire escape. As for the front door to the building, there were no marks. But it's a piece of shit lock; I'm not going to tell you that it's impossible for someone to work it without leaving a sign."

"Did you check anywhere else for prints, besides the bottles?"

He shook his head. "A fire scene is one of the worst places to look. Surfaces are covered with soot, or destroyed by fire, and the prints you can get usually aren't very readable. But we gave it a once-over. Some we can match with the victim, some we can't. But keep this in mind—we could only get prints off her left hand. The right was too badly damaged. As far as we know, she was never fingerprinted, so the ones that don't match don't tell us anything. And even if we had both hands, and we found prints that didn't match, so what? People have people over to their apartments—guests, cleaning ladies, delivery people, you know what I mean?"

I looked around the room again, but it gave me nothing back. "Sergeant, thanks very much for your time." I wrote the firm's number on one of my business cards and gave it to him. "Feel free to get on to your other cases. But if anything were to come up here, I'd appreciate it if you let me know."

"If you'd return the compliment, sure." I wasn't sure if he meant it in a friendly way or not, but there was no point in arguing with him. If he learned something he'd either help me, or not. And the odds of him learning something new in a case that was inactive, if not already closed, were pretty long. He turned and went down the stairs. Through the holes in the floor I saw him walk through the kitchen and out the front door.

"Anything else we can do for you, sir?" Dempsey wanted to know.

"Lend me your light. I want to look around for myself."

He handed me his flashlight reluctantly. "It's not safe to go moving around up here. The damage to the floor is worse than it looks. Before the fire ate those holes, it was eating at the joists and the undersides of the floorboards for a while. You could go right through where it looks solid."

"That's okay; I just want to check one thing."

Moving cautiously, I went to the only piece of furniture that was halfway intact, a bedside table. The single drawer came open with a strong pull, dumping the contents on the floor. I kneeled down and sorted through it. Some stamps. A pair of scissors. A dozen blank envelopes. A couple of photographs of Emily and a heavy-set woman with short blonde hair, who I assumed was her sister. A tube of Vaseline. Some magazine clippings on how to deal with menopause. Some warranty cards on appliances, all of them long expired. And, underneath it all, with the inevitable tiny symbolic lock, a black volume about the size of a thick paperback book entitled *Personal Diary*. For a moment I stood still, wondering how the police could have possibly overlooked it. Then I realized that in all likelihood they hadn't. It was an open and shut accidental death, just like any of the dozens that happened every month in Philadelphia—who needed to read the victim's diary?

There was no way of hiding it from Dempsey. I simply held it in one hand while I handed him back his flashlight. "I'm finished here. We can go now."

"But—you just can't take personal property from a fire scene. I mean, you're not—"

"Mr. Dempsey, we can go now."

We went.

Chapter Four

Tuesday, 1:00 P.M.

Richardson was out when I got back to the office. Since all the news I had was bad, I was just as happy to be able to avoid him for a while. I went to the office they'd given me, unwrapped a hoagie I'd bought on the street, and spread out my file in front of me.

The first thing I did was reread the medical examiner's preliminary report in light of what I'd seen at the fire scene. I went over it word by word, looking for holes, inconsistencies, omissions—and came up with nothing at all. The official version was accidental death, and even if they were wrong, their case was tight. Emily *had* been drunk, more than drunk enough to pass out in her bed. The fire *had* started in the kitchen and was caused by cooking grease. The smoke *had* moved upstairs and killed her. As far as what could be proved, that was the end of the story. There was no evidence that she'd been restrained, or injured by anything other than the fire. It was possible that someone had forced her to drink and then set the fire—but hell, anything was possible. If someone had done it, they'd been careful not to leave any clues.

I tried the sister in California. Myrtle Voss, Sacramento. The line was busy. Well, at least someone was at home.

I was going to try the diary next, but there was a knock at the door. "Come in."

"Hey, Dave!"

A tall, stooped man with a ruddy complexion and an easy smile came in. "Vince!" We shook hands and held the grip for a long moment. Vince DeAndrea had taught me almost everything I knew about trying cases.

"You old sonofabitch; good to see you again!"

"Take a load off your feet."

It looked like he needed to. When I'd last seen him he'd been losing weight, and now he was halfway to a skeleton. The more I looked, the less I liked what I saw. His nose and cheeks were crisscrossed with tiny red lines, and although he tried to control it, I saw that his hands were trembling. I couldn't smell anything on him, but if he was drinking something straight, there wouldn't be any odor. His hair was completely gray now, but still neatly trimmed. His blue eyes still twinkled in the light.

"Tom said he's brought you in to work on Emily's case."

"That's right. Nothing to show for it up to now, though."

"I want you to know, I voted that this be a firm expense. We think it's important, at least that you look into it. Tom and I were voted down, so fuck 'em. He and I are going to split it ourselves."

I was surprised that Richardson and DeAndrea couldn't get their way, and even more surprised to hear Vince accept defeat, even on a small matter, so easily. There must have been a lot of other defeats for him to take this one so casually.

"You still doing trial work?" I asked.

"Oh, sure. Got a trial tomorrow, as a matter of fact."

"I thought you were going to quit when you hit fifty."

"I thought so, too." He pulled out a cigarette and lit it, despite the fact there was no ashtray in the room. "But shit, you ought to see the kind of people they give me to take over my practice."

"So, they're kids. You got to train them."

"They're not like you were, Dave. When you came on board you'd only been out five years, but you had a couple of dozen Common Pleas jury trials under your belt, and a shitload of bench trials in municipal court."

"You can't blame them for not being experienced."

"No, but, shit, how do you get them experienced anymore? With the new drunk driving law, you'd have to be nuts to go to trial. It's so expensive to litigate anything, those collection cases and insurance subrogations don't go to trial anymore." He took a drag on his cigarette. "And besides, they don't have it in 'em anymore."

"How do you mean?"

"You and me, we tried cases 'cause we loved it. We cared about what happened. That old shit about the client's fate being in our hands, we bought it. The kids now, this is just a job. They show up at nine and leave at five, and if they didn't research the law, or didn't talk to the one other possible witness, or make the extra effort to get a shitty case settled, they don't care."

"You used to tell me you were going to start getting out when you were forty-five. That trial law was a young man's game."

He gestured impatiently with his cigarette. "So every year I say, this is it. That I'm going to start doing some business law, but it never happens." He rested his hand on the desk and I saw that the trembling was worse. He looked down and moved his hand to his lap.

I said nothing for a moment, letting him know that I'd seen his hand. When I spoke, I was as gentle as I could be. "Are you okay, Vince?"

"Never fucking better. Can't you tell?"

If he didn't want to talk, I couldn't force him. "So why business law?"

" 'Cause it's so fucking simple. Two guys wanna make a deal. Like, one guy is selling his business to the other, and he's gonna leave money in. Some kid a year out of law school draws up some hundred-page sales agreement that nobody reads and no one understands, let alone the kid who wrote it. Hell, even *he* didn't write it—he got it out of some form book. The two guys, they look at the thing, and they either sign it or they don't. Hell, I can look in a form book just as good as the kid, and my hourly rate is three times as high."

I wondered what a corporate lawyer would think of his analysis. "It might be a little more complicated than that."

"Bullshit it is. The only problem is if the two guys really don't want to make the deal. Then the lawyers find problems and the guy with cold feet has an excuse. But hell, you were a lawyer for twelve, thirteen years, right?"

"Right."

"Your agreement with Tom about this investigation, it's not in writing, is it?"

"No."

"Get a retainer?"

"He volunteered to give me one, but he hasn't given me the check yet. Either way, I figure he's good for it."

"But you're taking that on faith, right?"

"Yeah."

He nodded, satisfied with himself. "Ever think about having a form contract for your clients to sign?"

I shrugged. "When I got started I asked around; none of the solo investigators I talked to used them."

"And why?"

I had to smile. "They all said it was more trouble than it was worth. The good clients would pay on a handshake and the bad ones wouldn't pay unless you got it up front."

"I rest my case."

"Mind if we talk about Emily for a minute?"

"Since I'm paying for half of it, no. What's your thinking?"

"Nothing complicated. I'm just at the stage of eliminating possibilities. I'll start out with the assumption that her death wasn't accidental, just for the sake of argument. If she was murdered there are two possibilities. One is that it had nothing to do with the firm—a random killing, someone who killed for some personal motive, something like that. The other is that she was killed because of something to do with the firm. You know about her call to me last week?"

"Tom told me."

"That swings me toward thinking that if it was a murder, it was connected to the firm. And I've got another reason."

"What's that?"

"Because a random killer, or an amateur killing for personal reasons, wouldn't have been so careful. If it was a killing, it was a pro. And pros only do things when there's a lot of money involved."

"So how can I help?"

"Did you notice any changes in her routine lately? And by lately, I don't have any particular time frame in mind. Just anything different."

"Nothing at all. She was always like clockwork. She was so good about being in the office, there was talk about it when she left an hour early on Friday to go to the doctor's."

"Notice any change in her moods?"

"Emily didn't have moods. Not that I ever could tell."

"Did she ever talk to anyone about her personal life that you know of?"

"She didn't have one of those, either."

I thought about the picture with her hair down. "Come on, Vince. She was just businesslike during working hours. Other than Margaret, did she have any friends in the office?"

"Not that I ever saw. Emily'd been here so long—shit, she was the same way as me, when it came to work. None of the new people could do it as well as she could, there was no point in trying to teach them anything, it was better to just do it yourself."

"Did anyone here have a grudge against her?"

He shook his head. "To people your age and older, Dave, she was a fixture. You didn't think of complaining about her any more than you'd complain about the weather. The younger people never got close enough to her to build a grudge. She was just a stranger to them."

"I've looked at her personnel file. There's nothing in it of any help. Would you mind if I looked at the other files?"

"Staff, or attorneys, too?"

"Everybody. Associates and partners."

"Okay. Tom has the files in his office. I'll have them brought to you."

"Thanks. You said you had a case tomorrow?"

He shrugged. "Indecent Exposure. Defendant was seen wagging his weenie in a park in Germantown."

"Why's it going to trial? Sounds like it could be pleaded for a four-hundred-dollar fine, costs, and a year's probation."

"Third offense. The DA wants ninety days and the kid won't budge."

"Why are you doing it?"

"The kid's mother's on the city council, and she's up for a stiff primary fight in two months."

"Oh, shit."

"It's worse. Tom and her are buddies from way back. She's been responsible for steering a lot of conflicts work our way from the city. We owe her big."

"Good luck."

"If you're not doing anything, we pick a jury at nine. *Commonwealth* versus *Brookner*. Come and see the fun."

"Sorry, I have a lot of work to do. How about some breakfast instead?"

"Sure. Come by at seven and we'll go out."

"You're still at the same place?"

"Right."

"See you then."

He stood up. "Okay. And Dave?"

"Yeah?"

"God, it's good to see you again."

"Thanks."

I picked up the phone and dialed Sacramento again, but the line was still busy. Maybe it was off the hook? Then I picked up the diary.

Considering it had been exposed to a considerable amount of smoke and heat, it was in very good shape. I supposed that the dresser had protected it. The cover was warped and the edges of the pages were discolored brown, but that was the only damage. It was held shut with a flap and secured with a tiny padlock, but the point of a letter opener made short work of that.

I opened it to the middle and found it blank. I worked my way toward the front, not wanting to miss the most recent entries. I was within fifteen pages of the start before I found any writing.

I was familiar with two types of diaries: the day-to-day kind where people detail the weather and what they did; and the intermittent kind where people recount important events, or how they struggle with particular problems. The one in front of me didn't fall into either category. If the book hadn't called itself a diary, I don't know what word I would have come up with. Ramblings, maybe.

None of the entries were dated, but heavy double lines were drawn from time to time to indicate where one stopped and another began. Some of it seemed to be quotations, but there were no attributions. The last entry was by far the longest, and made the most sense:

Another quiet evening at home alone, and another, and another—to what end? Passed up, passed by passed over past perfect. No, present perfect. Not what I thought I needed, surprise, surprise—who does? I go, and arrive, and find why I went—he faces away from me, his tawny shoulders displayed against the backdrop of my bedchamber. Then he turns and my heart beats faster at the sight of his powerful chest. He comes toward me, his mouth cruel with desire, and my whole body opens for him. I am ready for anything he asks of me,

and yet there is no need even for him to ask, because I find
such joy in giving my most private parts, all of them, whatever
may be his pleasure, to him. Now I take his organ in my mouth
and it springs fully alive, pulsing, tangible proof of his desire
for me. He . . .

My eyes started skipping, and I read only enough to make
sure it was more of the same. I was as embarrassed as if I'd
walked in on her naked. Poor Emily, all alone, forced to copy
purple prose out of some bodice-ripper to keep herself company. And then it occurred to me how much nerve I had in
pitying her. After all, she was fifty and alone and a failure in
her intimate relationships—while I, on the other hand, was
forty-four and alone and a failure in my intimate relationships. . . .

I put the diary away, sorry that I'd ever seen the damned
thing. What did my mother used to tell me? Something about
prying into places you don't belong is its own punishment. What
had I been hoping to find? If it was a murder by someone she
knew well, and if there was any chance that she had any papers
that could implicate him, the killer would certainly have tossed
the apartment before he left. Anyone serious about looking for
incriminating papers would have searched the bedside table. I
had to face that the book had been there because the killer
didn't care if it was found or not. If there was a killer at all.

Before I had time to try Sacramento again, an unfamiliar
secretary knocked at the door, dropped off an armful of files,
and left. The personnel files for every member of the firm. I
decided to start with the junior associates and work my way up.

The least senior member of the firm was Michael Flora,
from Ocean City, New Jersey, twenty-six years old. He worked
in litigation and was assigned to Vince DeAndrea. Presumably
he was one of the kids Vince had been complaining about. NYU
and Villanova Law School. His transcripts showed good but not
outstanding marks. Well, the best trial lawyers weren't academ-
ics, anyway. He'd been with the firm for a year. His first per-

formance review, two months ago, was unfavorable. The review focussed on intangibles like poor motivation, lack of attention, bad attitude. It didn't sound like Michael would be long for the firm. I wondered how much of it was Flora and how much of it was DeAndrea; Vince could be a hard man to work for.

I found a copy of his résumé. Someone had written in the margin, probably during an interview, "Two older brothers— not married—both fam bus (constr?) father/uncles." What the hell did that mean? I dialed Tom's number on the interoffice line.

"Yes?"

"Tom, this is Dave. Have a second?"

"Go ahead."

"I'm looking at Mike Flora's résumé."

"Uh-huh."

"What can you tell me about his family background?"

"Well, Italian, of course. He's not married. He's the youngest. The other kids work in business with their father."

"What kind of business?"

"Funny you should ask. If I remember right, he said his father was a contractor. Yes, he did. I remember him saying that he could bring in representation of some labor unions. But when I asked him about it recently, he said his father was a caterer to casinos in Atlantic City."

"Do you know any lawyers in Ocean City? I'm looking for somebody pretty well established."

"I have a classmate from Penn who heads up a good-sized firm in Atlantic City. Not too far away. Steve Mailman."

"Could you do me a favor and place a call to him? Introduce me? I'd like to ask him about the Flora family."

"Certainly."

I put down the phone and picked up the second file. This one was Susan Minnik, the blonde I'd met in the library. The file was a mess, compared to Flora's, and then I remembered that she hadn't really been hired for herself, she'd come along when the firm had acquired her firm in Upper Darby. She was a Pittsburgh girl—U of Pitt and Duquesne Law School. Her transcripts showed mediocre grades. Her résumé, the one she'd submitted to the Upper Darby firm, was unremarkable. No mention of her class rank.

I was about to put the file aside when I saw a photocopy of a clipping from the *Pittsburgh Post-Gazette*. The indicated date was nearly four years ago.

ONE KILLED, ONE INJURED IN HOLIDAY CRASH

Lawyer injured, assistant dead in Oakmont pileup

A young Pittsburgh woman was killed and an attorney severely injured in a two-vehicle accident in Oakmont late this afternoon when the woman's car ran a stop sign into the path of a truck. Pronounced dead at the scene was Marjorie Axell, 23, of 1407 Avondale Road, a legal assistant with the firm of Spiegel & Bollinger in the city, whom police identified as the driver. Susan Minnik, 27, an attorney with the same firm, was riding as a passenger in the Axell vehicle. Ms. Minnik was taken to Allegheny General Hospital in critical condition with spinal injuries. The driver of the truck, Victor Koscluszko, of Erie, was not cited.

Ms. Axell is survived by her mother, Regina Axell, and three brothers, Charles, Thomas, and Raymond, all of Pittsburgh, plus a cousin, Keith Hopwood, of Uniontown. This marks

(Continued on page 8)

The second part of the article was missing, but there were photocopies of some photos that had apparently accompanied the story. Marjorie Axell, according to her photo, was a plain girl with short dark hair. The photograph of Susan was a candid shot showing a slightly thinner girl than the one I'd met that morning. Last, there was a photo of a demolished VW in front of a restaurant with a tow truck in the left half of the picture.

The phone rang.

"Yes?"

"Dave, this is Tom. I've got Steve Mailman on hold. Are you ready?"

"Put him on."

"Steve?" Tom said. "Are you there?"

"Right here."

"David?"

"I'm here, too."

"Well, now that the two of you have met, I'm going to get off the line. It's getting close to five and I have to make some calls. 'Bye, everyone." I heard a click as he left the line.

"Steve, I suppose Tom has told you about me."

"Your reputation has preceded you. I owe you condolences as well as greetings. What happened to you was a damned shame. I'm sure they wouldn't let something like that happen in New Jersey."

"Well, thank you."

"Tom said you were calling about the Flora family."

"That's right. There's been a death in the firm under circumstances that might be considered suspicious. I'm just checking leads at this point, and Flora is where I started."

"Hmm. So how can I help?"

"We have a new associate, Michael Flora, from your area, and I'd like to know anything you can tell me about the family background. Tom's recollection is a little vague."

"That's quite a tall order. Is it Mike junior?"

I checked his résumé. "Yes."

"Well, the Flora family is very well known around here. They're not what you would call a socially prominent family, but it seems that whenever you turn around, you run into a Flora. There are three older Floras, by that I mean men in their fifties. Michael senior is a plumbing and heating contractor. There's a rumor, and I have no personal basis for believing this, but I'll pass it along for what it's worth. The rumor is that if you want a building built, and no trouble with the unions, you hire Flora as the plumbing sub, even if he doesn't have the lowest bid. There is another brother, Joseph, who lives in East Orange and is with the Teamsters. The third brother, I can't remember his name, has some kind of an arrangement to supply all the flowers to the casinos in Atlantic City. *All* the casinos. No one else gets in. Between the three brothers there must be a dozen children in their twenties and thirties, and as far as I know nearly all of them are in one or another of the family businesses."

"I get the picture, Steve. Any suggestion of just how rough they get?"

"This is a small-beer operation, as far as I know. You underbid Mike on a job, you might get sugar in the gas tanks of your trucks, but you don't get your kneecaps broken and you don't wind up sleeping with the fishes."

"Of course, maybe the next generation is more aggressive."

"I couldn't speak to that. I don't know any of them personally."

"Including Mike, Junior?"

"I knew they had a kid going to law school, but I don't recall anything specific about him. If he came around here looking for a job I don't know about it."

"Any criminal convictions in the family?"

"Let me think a minute. I think there was something, but I can't remember. Want me to run it down at the courthouse?"

"If you could, please."

"No problem. It'll take me a day or two, though. I may need to check records in more than one county."

"The soonest you could get to it would be appreciated. It could be important."

I heard the rustling of papers. "Tomorrow's a mess. But I think I can promise Thursday, or if not then, Friday for sure."

I had a dead woman on my hands and he was talking about the end of the week. "Is there anybody else in the firm who might be able to run over there?"

"There's only one other lawyer here who knows how to

search the criminal indexes, and he's on vacation. It's going to have to be me."

"Thanks. I'll be waiting for your call."

I replaced the phone and looked around my tiny office. I was annoyed with myself, as usual. If it was really important, either I should press him hard to do it tomorrow, or drive to the county seat myself. I needed to be more forceful, just like my ex-wife always said. It's a funny thing about ex-wives. Like your parents—enough time goes by and you realize they were smarter than you thought at the time.

Chapter Five

Tuesday, 5:00 P.M.

I heard the unmistakable clatter of calculator keys and followed the sound to Emily's office. Ron Wolfe was sitting at her desk, the fingers of his right hand flying up and down the keypad. Every few seconds the hand stopped long enough for the calculator to grind out a few inches of tape. Except for his hand, he was perfectly still. Even in his shirtsleeves and with his tie loosened, he looked every inch an accountant.

I waited until the machine was spitting out paper. "Hi, Ron."

He turned, nodded slightly, and offered me his hand. "Dave." It was as powerful a display of emotion as I'd ever seen from him.

"How long you been at it?" I asked.

He leaned back in his chair and swiveled to face me. "Since about eleven. Tom was pretty insistent we get right on this. Even though it's tax season," he added pointedly.

"It wasn't Emily's idea."

"She would have preferred August for her short year. Everyone's on vacation then anyway."

"Short year?"

"For Federal estate tax purposes. The taxpayer's year of death is called his short year."

Leave it to the government to come up with a euphemism like that. Like in the war. People weren't killed or wounded—units just experienced casualties. So this was Emily's short year. Short month, short day, short life. Probably a good twenty-five years short. "I assume Tom told you it was okay to talk to me."

"He did. He filled me in on your suspicions, by the way." I couldn't tell whether he shared them or not.

"They're still just suspicions," I said. "What are you doing?"

"The firm's bank accounts both have statement dates in the middle of the month. So the statements for the period February fifteen through March fifteen arrived in the mail last week—"

I had a thought. "Can you tell when?"

"They didn't save the envelopes, but probably Tuesday or Wednesday."

"Could she have been killed because she found something in the statements? Or was about to?"

"No."

"You sound pretty certain."

"She'd been through both statements before she died. Both of them balanced."

"You're sure?"

"Absolutely. Every check is in order, every credit and debit is checked off."

"So the bookkeeper gets the statements, finds nothing wrong—because nothing *is* wrong—and is murdered immediately afterward to ensure her silence."

Ron blinked, but made no other response. Spinning out theories wasn't part of his job description.

"Have you finished?" I asked after a while.

"Hardly. I've got at least another day or two. Just getting into the books and checking the Mellon and First Pennsylvania statements took most of today."

"I'm trying to remember. Mellon is where they keep the client funds?"

"Right. And First Penn is the firm's own money."

"Which account would be bigger?"

He took off his glasses and rubbed his eyes before answering. He'd always disapproved of my casual approach to the financial side of the business, and this was his way of showing it. "Well, it would depend, wouldn't it? But generally, unless a very big fee came in, the trust account would be the larger one. That's where the money is from all your clients in retainers and trust funds. The First Penn account, most of the time, is only going to have enough in it to meet short-term expenses, unless you're showing a big profit."

"Is there such a profit?"

He hesitated before answering. "No."

"Any big checks come in recently?"

"Generally, the big checks would be if a big personal injury case was resolved, or if we held a real estate settlement, or if we took a lump-sum fee for an estate."

"So tell me what you've found."

"I checked last month's activity. Vince brought in an eighty-thousand-dollar fee, which is being held in trust now. There were several real estate settlements where the firm received more than a hundred thousand dollars apiece, but checks would have to be written out right away to cover the costs of satisfying the mortgages, of course, so those transactions wash out. No sizable estate fees recorded."

"So I can exclude Roger Palmer. He does the estate work."

Ron took off his glasses and wiped the lenses on his handkerchief. "Well, uh, I said none were *recorded*."

"Roger stays on the list. Any indication any funds are missing?"

"It's too soon to say, but there's nothing irregular so far. As far as I can tell, it's just that the receivables are up a little. Nothing suspicious about that."

"Any records missing?"

"Not so far. Why do you ask?"

"She was known to take work home. She was killed in a

fire. It could have been set to cover the murder. But the fire could also cover the theft or destruction of records."

"Like what?"

"We'll know when it turns out you can't find them."

"Oh."

I gave him a card with my home phone number and said good night.

The lights were on, but no one was in the corridors. I heard a noise I couldn't quite place, then realized it was a fax machine. I followed the sound into the library. The fax machine was set into a recess between two bookcases, churning out an enormous roll of waxy paper. I took a closer look; it had obviously been running for some time, because the current page coming in was 46, and there was no end in sight. I worked my way through to the front, which involved an odyssey through more than forty feet of fax paper, and found that the sender was only a couple of blocks away. The transmission had started more than half an hour before.

I heard a sound behind me. Not footsteps. A soft rumbling and a squeaking noise. I turned, and saw Susan Minnik coming toward me in a wheelchair. I remembered the newspaper clipping, that it mentioned spinal injuries. Permanent injuries, evidently.

If I hadn't seen the wheels I wouldn't have recognized it as a wheelchair. The wheels, spokes, and hubs were matte black, and if there were any handles to the rear, they were somehow folded out of sight. Instead of the bulky footrests I expected, there was nothing but a couple of thin black bars that paralleled her legs and curved in sharply to support her feet just in front of the heel of each shoe. That was another thing; somehow I expected to see clunky black orthopedic shoes. Instead she was wearing a pair of delicate black pumps with gold buckles. High heels made as much sense as flats if you're not going to be walking on them anyway.

I realized I was staring at her legs and had the presence of mind to look up. She knew what I'd been looking at, but her exact emotion was unreadable. How were you supposed to handle these situations? When I was a kid my mother warned me not to stare at people in wheelchairs. But I'd also heard that handicapped people didn't like being treated like they were invisible.

She saved me the trouble. "Is that from Morgan, Lewis?" she asked.

"Sure is."

"Bastards."

"I've heard them called that."

She wheeled past me, up to the machine, and scowled. "You know what kind of game they're playing?"

"No, I don't."

"I'm helping out one of the partners on a commercial loan. Morgan, Lewis has the bank. We represent the person borrowing the money, and the deal is supposed to close first thing Thursday morning. I don't pretend to understand everything that's going on—this is a learning experience for me. We sent them over our proposal three weeks ago. I've called them half a dozen times since then and all I get is a lot of excuses. They wouldn't even tell us if they had read our stuff. And now look at this."

"And if you call up to complain about it, they'll tell the bank that they gave you their loan documents for review *two whole days* before settlement, so what's your problem, right?"

"I suppose so. Mainly I'm just fried that I'm going to have to spend tonight looking this over and dictating a memo."

"That's interesting. I was just talking to one of the partners about how associates only work nine to five anymore."

"You can count me in for that, but if it's got to be done, what the hell, right?"

"That's a good enough attitude."

"Thank you."

We both watched the fax machine grinding away for a while. "I heard about you through the office grapevine," she said suddenly.

"What did you hear?"

Her eyes moved to my face. "That you used to be a partner here and that you had to leave."

"Does anybody know what happened?"

"Not my sources."

The circumstances tempted me to explain myself, once again. I was a one-man campaign manager for the most lost of all lost causes. If I'd lost my license for stealing from clients, my life would actually have been easier. When people asked, I'd just smile and say nothing.

"I assume that you'd like to hear."

"Only if you want to talk."

"My wife went to law school a few years behind me. Her father and a couple of her brothers were lawyers. She was the only girl. Somehow she got it into her head that she had to be a lawyer, too. She did well in school, but passing the bar exam meant having to deal with the pressures of practice, and she really didn't want to. Her dad had an office waiting for her in the family firm. Her solution, unconsciously, was to flunk the bar. She kept taking it and taking it. She was at war with herself, half of her wanting to pass, and half not. She took hypnotism and counseling. She even made a half-assed suicide attempt."

"Why didn't she just give up?"

"There was enough of her father's spirit in her that kept her coming back for more. At the time I admired her; now I think it was some kind of masochism. But anyway, after the suicide attempt she asked me to take the bar exam for her. I turned her down, of course, but she kept working on me. To make it short, I did it. She passed, but we were caught and both of us were disbarred."

"They were awfully hard on you."

"Everyone agrees, except the justices of the state supreme court, and they're the only ones that matter."

"And your wife?"

"Ex-wife. She left me and said I wasn't being sufficiently supportive."

She looked at my face, trying to decide if I was kidding, and saw that I wasn't.

I sat down on the edge of the table. "It looks like we have a few more minutes to kill before the fax is finished. Would you mind answering some questions for me?"

"I guess I left myself open for that, didn't I?"

"How well do you know Mike Flora?"

"Not real well. He started here almost a year after I did, and I came in with my old firm, so I didn't go through a lot of the new associate orientation with him."

"How about since then?"

"No. I'm out of the office a couple of days a week, seeing clients in the Upper Darby office. We don't see each other much."

"You're both single. Have you dated or socialized?"

Her look stopped me cold. It was the same look I'd seen when she saw me looking at her in her wheelchair. "I mean, it's not a crime. The firm isn't going to care what the two of you do on your own time—"

"Once, I think, we went out for a drink when he got his performance reviewed. It was a bad day for him. It was my idea, and that's the closest we've ever come to socializing. Mike's interested in a nice fat Italian girl who'll give him lots of babies and be able to run around after them. I'm sure it's never occurred to him to be interested in a crip."

I wondered if she was interested in him, regardless of whether it was reciprocated. "Is he close to his family?"

"Too close. He goes home every weekend and even during the week sometimes, for dinner."

"I was thinking more of the family business."

She took her time in answering. "What's this got to do with Emily?"

"Does that make a difference in how you answer?"

"I don't like your tone."

"I'm not crazy about yours, either. I've got a job to do."

"Okay, okay, you're right. What do you want to know?"

"What does he say about his family's business?"

She thought about how she was going to answer. "He drops these little hints that there's more to his family than it seems. Either his family is serious Mafia and he's really indiscreet, or they're just regular guys and he likes to create an impression."

"Why would he be out to impress? You said he wasn't interested in you romantically."

"Oh, not for my benefit. For his own. He's on his own, at least a little bit, in the big city. Maybe he needs to talk himself up."

"So what do you think?"

"I just don't know. I'm blue-collar Pittsburgh; what do I know about New Jersey Mafia?"

Whatever she knew, or suspected, she wasn't sharing it with me. It was time to try another topic. "Do you know whether Emily had any particular friends?"

"Friends? Well, no. She always ate alone in her office, or went out alone. Nobody really wanted to talk to her much unless they needed to. Mr. Richardson drove her home some nights, but that's about it."

Behind me, the fax machine suddenly stopped. "You'll have to excuse me now," she said. "It's going to be a long night."

I made a final circuit of the offices and saw a sliver of light at Jerry Huyett's partly opened door. Huyett was our corporate lawyer and the assistant managing partner. He was responsible for firing unsuitable employees, and we all had the impression that he enjoyed it more than he was willing to admit. I waited a long time, thinking he might be on the phone. But I didn't hear any voices, and when he finally said, "Come in," there was no sound of a phone being replaced.

He was thin, with carefully combed short dark hair. I was pleased to see that he was starting to thin on top. His suit jacket was on and his plain dark tie was neatly knotted. The eyes were large, but focussed on me without expression. Everything was neatly in its place except his humanity.

The desk was bare, except for a legal pad. A mass of documents and notes were piled on the floor next to his feet, at least a foot high, and neatly covered with some sheets of computer printout paper. The red light on his dictating machine was on, and the microphone was out of its cradle, lying on his credenza.

"Evening, Jerry."

"Dave. Long time no see." He didn't say, it hadn't been long enough. He didn't need to. "What do you need?"

"Well, first of all you might want to turn off your dictating machine. No point in bothering to record us, is there?"

He turned in his chair and replaced the microphone, but not so quickly that I didn't catch a sour expression on his face. The red light went out.

"I suppose you're going to ask me where I was last night," he said.

"No, I wasn't."

"Oh?"

"Assuming it was murder, nobody in this office personally killed Emily."

"What makes you say that?"

"Two reasons. Whoever did this, it was a muscle job. A smart one, but still, a lot of violence was called for. Either she was abducted on the street and forced to take her killers into the building—which I doubt, because she was probably too sick to go out on the street—or someone forced the main door, and the door to her place, too. Without making any noise either time. Then they overpowered her, so fast she couldn't make a sound, did whatever their business was in there, poured a bottle of booze into her, set everything up, and left her to burn in a fire. No, nobody here did it."

"You said you had two reasons."

"Anybody from here would know they'd be suspects if anyone decided to treat it as a homicide. They'd be careful to set up the best alibi they could."

"You're not making sense," he said.

"All I said was, none of you were personally there when she was killed. I didn't say you didn't arrange for it to happen."

He nodded slightly. "Well, at least I know where I stand with you."

"We always did, old friend. You've had it in for me ever since I was made a partner ahead of you."

"I was here first."

"And I'd been practicing three years longer. Look, give it a rest, will you? It's all history, and I've got a job to do. When did you last see her?"

"Thursday."

"Not Friday?"

"I was out of the office at a meeting."

"All day?"

"Mmm . . . in and out."

"Then tell me about Thursday."

"There's nothing to tell. I was just in her office to pick up an advance on my draw."

"Did she give it to you?"

"Certainly she did," he said.

"Why were you so short of cash?"

"That's none of your business." If it was possible for his voice to get any stiffer, it did.

"What makes you say that?"

"You know very well the books are in order."

"How do you know that?" I asked.

"I talked to Ron this morning."

"Bullshit you did. I just found out from him myself, and he didn't know till he checked the deposits. As a matter of fact he's not sure even now."

He looked down at his desk. "I had the books reviewed last month when Emily was on vacation."

"By Ron?"

"No. Another accountant."

"Why?"

He leaned back in his chair and regarded me coldly. "Let's just say I was concerned about the financial health of the firm."

"Does Tom know about this?"

"Sure, he does."

"Come on, Jerry, why did you do it?"

He looked out the window for a moment. "Emily had been here a long time. She was set in her ways. She'd been taking care of the books for so many years, I didn't know if any—bad habits were slipping in. When she went on vacation I decided it was a good time to have a little look without embarrassing her."

"And what did you find?"

"I underestimated her. Everything was in tip-top shape."

"Now tell me about the two associates. They're strangers to me."

"Mike Flora's no rocket scientist. I voted against hiring him. There's nothing I can personally use him for, but I suppose he's smart enough to do litigation."

It was a slap but I decided to let it pass. "Can't you give me anything more?"

"Why? Are you going to tell me that a new associate could have enough contact with the bookkeeper to want to have her killed? I don't know that they ever spoke except to say hello."

"Well, that answers my question. What about Sue Minnik?"

"I've worked with her a little. She was pretty raw when she started. She didn't get much training in her old firm; all she could do was settlements. But she works hard, and she's coming along."

"Anything else?"

"She and Emily seemed to get along well. Susan has medical bills that need to be worked out so the two of them had a fair amount of contact."

"Would you suspect either one, Flora or Minnik?"

He shook his head. "If it was murder, and if it was firm-related, it was a partner. Someone with access to the financial information. Someone who could do things with the accounts, that she could have found out about. The associates were on the outside, financially."

At last I'd gotten something candid and sensible out of him. I decided to quit while I was ahead. "Thanks. See you tomorrow."

Chapter Six

Tuesday, 8:00 P.M.

When I left the building it was dark and raining, with cold, gusty winds. It was close to freezing and I wanted to avoid the Schuylkill Expressway. Someone, probably an engineer educated at Villanova, had designed some sections of it with zero slope, which made for nasty ice patches. My old Civic had plenty of strong points, but good response on ice wasn't one of them. As I said to my friend with a BMW, my car featured one-wheel, positive-lock braking, and a passive restraint system that doubled as a steering wheel.

I went home on Lancaster Avenue. It was hours after the rush, and it took me less than thirty minutes to wend my way through the decaying neighborhoods of West Philadelphia, cross City Line, and hit Upper Merion Township. At that point I bogged down in a ten-mile-long traffic jam that I escaped only when I reached my turnoff in Radnor Township, just past the St. David's Industrial Park.

My apartment complex was on a winding suburban street lined with old trees. It sounds better than it actually looks. I suspected that they built the industrial park to hide the apartments. The street was full of potholes, the trees were bare, and the neighborhood gave off a general sense of having seen better days. Well, so had I.

I had an assigned space in the parking lot; it even had my apartment number painted on it in slightly blurred yellow paint, but I never used it. Why advertise whether you're home, and which car is yours? I either used someone else's space or parked on the street. Tonight the lot looked fairly full, so I kept driving. On a night like that, I felt a little guilty taking someone's space and putting them to an extra walk.

My exercise in consideration took me a good half a block from the complex, around the corner on a narrow side street with hardly any parked cars at all. I swung into the first legal parking place up from the corner and shut off the engine. Before I could get out an old Ford Galaxie went past and took the space directly in front of me. I looked at the distinctive taillights, square but with slightly rounded sides, and realized it was a '66. I'd owned a '66 Galaxie—it was my very first car, as a matter of fact. It handled like a truck, drank down gas so fast you could almost watch the gauge move, and had a back seat big enough for two people to get their clothes off at the same time. A great car. Mine had started off as a pale copper, but by the time I'd sold it the paint had faded to a muddy tan. The car ahead of me was a nondescript light brown. Could it possibly be my old car? I'd kept mine in great shape, as every boy does with his first car. Just maybe it was still on the road. I looked at the rear more closely, looking for a ding I'd put in the chrome strip that ran across the rear of the trunk. The ding was from the edge of a beer cooler, the weekend Janet and I went to Wildwood. It was hard to tell—the car was so filthy. Such a shame, I thought, to let a car like that rust away. A couple minutes in a car wash would add years to its life. . . .

And then I saw it. The license plate was clean. It came from some other car.

I felt my heart beating a little faster. A stolen car was none of my business, but this one had been behind me. Following me? I looked again. Two people in the car, neither of them moving. The engine was still running but the lights were out. I glanced around. There was no one on the street, and we weren't close to any particular house. What were they waiting for?

I don't know what I would have done, left to myself, but they made the first move. The two—both black men, I saw—got out of their respective sides of the car at the same time, and left their doors open behind them. Both of them looked at me and started toward me. The one on the passenger side had his hands in his pockets. The driver had a long coat with something underneath.

My first thought was to shove it into reverse and get the hell out of there, but I'd already shut off the engine. Laying on the horn wasn't going to help—there was no one else in sight. The driver opened his coat and pulled out a double-barreled sawed-off shotgun. I looked quickly over at the other man. He had stopped, with his hands still in his pockets, at the front of my car. Then I realized why—he didn't want to get in his partner's line of fire.

I stuck my right hand under my seat, fishing desperately for the handle of the .357 Magnum I kept there for situations like this. The man with the shotgun moved quickly, and my fumbling around on the floor seemed to take forever. I grabbed something round, but it was too small—only the control that moved the seat forward and back. The next thing I found was the scraper for my windshield. The man with the shotgun sidestepped toward the driver's door, trying to make it a point-blank shot through the side window. I moved my hand again and this time it closed on the handle of the gun, but it was too late. The shotgun was two feet from my face, the barrel glinting in the street lights. I saw him set himself to take the shock of the blast, level the gun at my head, and squeeze the trigger.

I shut my eyes, yanked on the seat back release with my left hand, and flung myself backward. I felt myself falling. As I did I saw a brilliant yellow-red flash through my closed eyes and felt a heavy thump, like I'd been hit across the chest with a two by four. I heard nothing at all, just a distant, heavy rumbling, like thunder far away.

Lying on my back, I opened my eyes. There was no sound, not even the sound of my own breathing, and for a moment I was certain I was dead. But I felt blood running down my face, and I could taste it in my mouth, and I smelled the acrid smell of gunpowder, so I decided I must still be alive, somehow.

The gunpowder smell reminded me of the gun in my right hand. There was no time for aiming, or even to look. I just brought it up to the level of my lap, pointed it to the left, and pulled the trigger. A yellow flash leaped out of the barrel, but there was no sound. My grip was loose, and the gun kicked right out of my hand and flew into the darkness somewhere on the passenger's side.

I sat there for several seconds, still stunned and deafened. Then I looked out the window—or rather, where the window had been—to see what had happened. The man with the shotgun was on his back, his torso covered with blood. The shotgun was still cradled in his arms. He wasn't moving, and I wasn't sure if he was still alive. I looked around for the second man and didn't see him. I sat there stupidly for a moment, wondering where he might have gone. Then the taillights of the Galaxie came on and it started to move.

I opened the door of my car and stepped out. As I got out, thousands of tiny pieces of glass cascaded off me. I saw my feet stepping on bits of glass, but I still couldn't hear anything. A wave of dizziness came over me and I leaned against the side of the car for support. The Galaxie pulled to the left and started to move down the street.

I looked for my gun, but it was somewhere in the shadows on the passenger side. I stumbled forward, and my feet ran into the man with the shotgun. Carefully, trying not to lose my balance, I bent down and picked it up. It came free from his hands without a struggle. It was the old-fashioned kind, with two separate triggers. Whoever had modified this shotgun hadn't just cut down the barrels, they'd cut down the stock to a pistol grip.

As I held it I dimly realized it was warm and sticky with his blood.

The rear end of the Galaxie was thirty feet away and the car was starting to gain momentum. I wasn't familiar with double-barreled shotguns and for all I knew both barrels had already been fired. I set my feet wide apart, braced my elbow on my hip, and pulled the first trigger.

Nothing happened.

The Galaxie was moving faster, and it was getting to the outer limits of a safe shot. Any farther and the pattern would be so dispersed that pellets would scatter over half the neighborhood. Christ, he was going to get away. Why hadn't I been more watchful? What kind of detective was I, anyway?

I pointed the shotgun at the rear window and pulled the second trigger. It went off with a roar so loud that even I heard it, at least distantly. The gun bucked hard and drove me back, almost causing me to fall over its owner.

The rear window of the Galaxie disintegrated in a silent explosion of thousands of tiny shards of glass, and both tail-lights went out. The car swung hard to the left, jumped the curb, and slammed into a tree. The driver's door flew open. He fell out onto the sidewalk on his face and lay still.

The only logical thing was to do nothing. I had no loaded gun, he almost certainly did, and if I just waited a couple of minutes, half the police in the Main Line would be there. But people do crazy things when their blood is up. If they do them in a war, we give them medals. I just deserved to be called nuts. I walked over to him, holding the empty shotgun at my side. I don't know why I bothered to carry it—if he could count to two, he'd know it was empty.

He was stirring when I reached him. I made it there about five seconds before he would have been fit to draw a gun. I put my shotgun to his temple and went through his pockets with my free hand. No identification, but I found something hard and angular in a belt holster and drew it out.

"Shit, buddy, you know what you've got here?" I said. "A

Glock. Double action. Nine millimeter. Holds—what is it, sixteen, seventeen rounds? This gun cost more than that whole car." My voice sounded far away, as if I was listening to someone else in the distance.

"Didn't cost nuttin', man." My ear was only a few inches from his face, but still I had trouble hearing him. He was young, in his early twenties, and dressed little better than a bum. His eyes moved around, sizing me up and looking for a way to make a break.

I pressed harder with the shotgun. "Enough pleasantries. Who are you and who sent you?"

"Eat shit and die, man."

"I can make this a two-for-two night, friend, real easy."

His eyes met mine and I saw no fear at all. "Then go ahead."

"You can die right now."

"I talk to you, I die later for sure."

"You're in a lot of trouble, friend. Conspiracy to attempt murder, auto theft. Got a concealed weapons permit? If you don't you've got a Firearms Act violation. Is the gun hot? That'd be a Receiving charge. Even if the gun is clean, we're talking a mandatory sentence enhancement because you used a firearm. You're looking at some hard time. Ten, fifteen years. But it can go easier on you. Talk to me."

"You're just a private cop. You can't make no deals, man."

"I can make it easy for you, though, if you cooperate right now."

Something flickered across his face. "What you talkin' 'bout?"

"This gun is the evidence of a Firearms Act charge. And if it's stolen, which I think it is, and they can tie the theft to you, that's a felony."

"So?"

"I can toss this down the storm sewer. Without the gun, you're just along for the ride with your buddy. They've probably still got you on conspiracy, but with no evidence you were going to help, your lawyer might be able to cut your time in half."

He moistened his lips but said nothing.

"Come on, buddy. The police are going to be all over us in a minute. This is the only chance you're going to get. Who wants me dead, and why?"

He put his head down and said nothing.

I put down the shotgun and backed off, keeping him covered with the handgun. Neither one of us said a word till the police came.

I was rushed by ambulance to Bryn Mawr Hospital, where half a dozen doctors, nurses, and medical technicians fussed over me. I was probably the closest thing they'd seen to a shooting victim in a long time. After ninety minutes of tests and examinations, they arrived at a diagnosis of some superficial facial cuts from flying glass, plus tinnitus.

"What's that mean, doctor?" I said, a little louder than usual. He was young enough to be my son.

He consulted the chart and looked at me earnestly. "Ringing in the ears."

"Thanks a lot."

A nervous young detective was waiting to interview me. It was my second interview, actually; I'd gone over the whole thing at the scene with the first two officers who responded. We sat in his cruiser in the hospital parking lot.

"The dead man," he said, reading from his notes and not looking at me, "is Taylor Washington, of Philadelphia. Did you know him?"

"He died, then?"

"Dead at the scene. Dead before he hit the ground, probably. What did you use on him?"

It makes me nervous when police ask me questions they know the answer to. "My three-fifty-seven."

"We'll be running some tests with it. We'll let you know when you can pick it up, provided you can show your registration. You using hollow-points? Wad-cutters? Semi-jacketeds?"

I shrugged. "Whatever's on sale."

"Oh. Well, the way I see it, your bullet hit something inside the door that flattened it as it went through. It hit him square on the breastbone so his body took the whole shock. No exit wound, so it stopped somewhere inside. My guess is they'll find it in his heart. Good shooting."

I didn't know if he was being ironic, and I didn't care. I said nothing, and eventually he went on. "Why were these guys out to rob you?"

"Robbery? Are you kidding?"

"We get a lot of robberies around here, sir. You told the other officers you think they had been following you."

"They must have been. I hadn't told anybody I was going home."

"And they very well may have followed you from Philadelphia?"

"They probably did."

"So where exactly did you start from?"

I decided to leave things a little vague. "Center City. I was coming from a law firm."

"And you left kind of late, just before eight?"

"Uh-huh."

"You left alone?"

"Right."

"I see it, they had the building staked out. They want to rob somebody they think will have something worth taking, so they want a professional person. You leave alone, fairly late in the evening, and they decide on you. They follow you out here, you oblige them by parking on a deserted street, and they go for it."

"Wait a minute. He came right up to me with a shotgun and fired it. There was no demand for money."

"I figure they were going to make one, but then they saw you make your own move. He decided to get off the first shot."

"Does my car look like it would attract robbers?"

"Did you know these men?"

"No."

"Well, then what would be their motive for a homicide?"

"Maybe if I knew a little about them I could help you."

He looked at his notes. "The deceased, Mr. Washington, had no current address. He was on probation, failed to keep appointments, so his probation officer violated him about eight months ago. A detainer was issued but he was never picked up. We have no information on his activities recently. I'm going to guess that if he was hiding out, he wasn't working a regular job."

"And that's why he'd try robbery, you think."

"Everybody's got to eat," he said.

"What was he on probation for?"

He checked his notes. Didn't this man have any memory? "Burglary, twelve counts. Did two years in Graterford."

"What else did he have?"

"Receiving Stolen Property, one count, Prohibited Offensive Weapon—a switchblade knife—one count, Violation of Controlled Substances Act—cocaine—one count. It was originally possession with intent to sell, plea-bargained down to mere possession. That one was six years ago. And there's a juvenile record, burglary, underage drinking, malicious mischief."

"Was he an addict?"

"Very possibly. But it's going to take a couple of days to check all the rehab programs. There's a lot of them. And he could have used one in Jersey, for that matter."

"I knew someone who was a professional burglar once. Always hit unoccupied homes. Made a pretty good living till he was finally caught. You know what he told me? 'If I wanted to meet people, I'd have been a mugger.' "

"So?"

"So it doesn't fit. This guy was a bad actor, but he wasn't into personal violence. When he needed money he did a burglary, stole some stuff, and fenced it. He didn't stick shotguns in people's faces."

"He carried a knife for fighting."

"Was that after Graterford?"

"Yeah."

"Every con carries a shiv. He probably felt naked without it."

"I didn't know you knew him so well."

"So I'm guessing," I admitted. "But there's no record he ever used it, is there?"

"No *record*, no."

"I hear you."

"Mr. Garrett, you know something I don't, and we'd appreciate your cooperation."

"Any way I can."

"We know you're a private detective. Were you working on a case in Philadelphia this evening?"

"That question doesn't have much to do with your robbery theory, does it?"

He smiled. "You noticed that. Well, I have to cover the possibilities."

"What do you mean by that?"

"Nothing for you to be alarmed about, Mr. Garrett. We have two sets of neighbors who saw enough of what happened to put you in the clear. The physical evidence matches your story. These guys were looking for trouble, one way or the other."

"I feel better knowing that."

"So what kind of case were you working on?"

"I'll tell you on a no-names basis."

"Okay, for now."

I told him the facts of Emily's death, plus the analyses of the fire marshal and the medical examiner. I left out the existence of the firm and gave the impression Emily's family had asked me to check into things.

"So you think it's a murder because of an unexplained high blood alcohol?"

"It's a possibility I haven't been able to exclude yet." I was getting tired of saying that.

"You get paid by the hour?"

"I told the client it might not go anywhere before he hired me."

"Well, I'm glad to hear you're getting paid anyway, because it sounds like a wild-goose chase to me."

"Unless this business tonight is connected with it."

"Was your victim on anything?"

"You mean drugs?"

"Uh-huh."

"Not as far as we can tell. Just the alcohol."

"Then how the hell would her death be connected to a couple of Philadelphia junkies?"

"I don't know, Detective. And if you're right about robbery as the motive, there's no connection. But you know something?"

"What's that?"

"I'm thinking out loud. The more things that happen, the more you have to keep saying 'if.' *If* her death was an accident there's no connection. *If* this was a robbery attempt there's no connection. It just might be easier to assume they *are* related."

He wasn't impressed. "Well, you get paid by the hour."

"You said a couple of junkies. Tell me about the second man."

"Johnson Bentley, no current address either. He took grazes from shot pellets, but there's no fractures, no penetrating wounds, just some scalp lacerations and maybe a slight concussion. Pretty lucky guy. The back of the seat took lots of pellets."

"He's lucky he was driving a car like that. Back then, the backs of the seats were sheet steel. Where's he now?"

"They're finishing up with him here now. Then we arraign him, get a bail set, and take him to the county jail."

"Can I talk to him?"

"Sorry. No victim–defendant confrontations."

"You're not afraid I'm going to go after him, are you?"

"Not me personally, no. But we have our policies, and this is how we do things."

"Would you at least give him one of my cards and ask him to call me?" I scribbled the firm's number on the back. He nodded and stuck it in his pocket. "Can you tell me a little about him, at least?"

The notebook came out again. "Twenty-two years old, prior juvenile record for grass and cocaine, several busts for each. An adult conviction three years ago for possession with intent to deliver. Cocaine. Did his three months and walked."

"No address, huh?"

"No, and I wouldn't give it to you if I had it. We got a clean case here and I don't want anybody messing it up, including you."

He drove me home and left me at my door, alone.

Chapter Seven

Tuesday, 11:00 P.M.

I knew Kate's number by heart by now, but for some reason I still needed to look up the area code for Miami.

I'd met Kate last month, when I was working on the Chadwick kidnapping in Lancaster. She was a cousin of the victim and happened to be visiting the family when everything blew up. I don't know if I could have solved the case without her. Kate was a real find—strong, smart, funny, and sensible. Of course, there was a problem, a hulking dark-haired contractor named Frank McMahan. Her husband. I liked to think that I never would have become involved if she'd told me she was married at the start. It was comforting to think that I might have acted so much more responsibly and honorably. It was also, almost certainly, nonsense.

As always, she answered on the first ring. "Hello?"

"Hi, it's Dave."

"Great! Am I glad to hear from you."

"It's only been a couple of days. Hope I didn't wake you."

"No, I was working and I was ready for a break."

"What are you doing?" I asked.

"For the last two hours I've been sitting at the kitchen table trying to figure out what I'm going to do for a living."

"What happened to the teaching job?"

I heard her sigh. "The state budget looks worse than ever. I've got papers spread out all over the table and the floor, trying to put together a résumé."

"For anybody in particular?"

She laughed. "For myself. So I can figure out what kind of a job to look for. I don't know if I want to be in teaching anymore."

"What are you wearing?"

"I'm a vision of loveliness. I'm wearing slippers, sweatpants, and one of my son's old sweatshirts from college."

"And what else are you wearing?"

"Mmm. Not tonight. I don't feel up to it."

"That's a switch for you." Kate had introduced me to phone sex not long after she returned to Miami. My phone bill was evidence of how enthusiastic a participant she usually was.

"Actually, I think I've had a touch of the flu the last two days. Nothing wants to really stay down. But besides that, I feel good." She paused. "There's problems in Frank's business, too."

"Meaning?"

"Things are looking shaky. He may have to close down."

"I thought he had lots of work."

"Mmm. It's more like problems with his investors. It's more than I want to get into now, okay?"

"You sound a little strung out."

"So do you," she said.

I thought about my words. "It's been a busy day."

"Let's hear it."

"If you have a while."

"Well, that's why you called, isn't it?"

I went through everything that had happened today, omitting nothing. She listened without once asking a question.

"So," she said when I was finished. "You're doing pretty well for someone who's had a brush with death." The bounce was gone from her voice.

"The brushes I don't mind so much. It's the one that gets you square in the back of the head that worries me."

"Is that how you want to deal with this?" she said sharply. "With humor?"

"I'm being very serious. I could write treatises on what it's like to be scared, waiting for something to happen. But when it happens and is all over in a couple seconds, and you're still alive, there's never time to be scared."

"Well, I'm glad you're all right. I think I'd miss you if something happened."

"I can't stand it when you're mushy."

"This is as mushy as I get. I assume there's no point in telling you I'm worried about you, or that you should quit this stupid case before you get hurt."

"That's right."

"You men."

"Let's just say, if I'd received what I thought was a serious death threat I might have walked away. Maybe. But now I'm too mad to be scared."

"What happens next, as far as the police?"

"Nothing, probably. Radnor Township thinks what happened was a robbery attempt. And since Philadelphia thinks Emily's death was an accident, I don't think they're going to care."

"But that's crazy. Someone tried to kill you."

"Well, from the bureaucratic standpoint, it's exactly what I would expect. Each event, taken in isolation, doesn't lead anywhere. From their point of view I'm just making extra work with my theories. The detective out here pretty much said that."

"I've been thinking," she said. "In everything you've done, you've made a couple of assumptions, and one of them has already proven wrong, in part."

"What are they?"

"The one is that the people that hired you really want you to get to the bottom of this. Maybe, just maybe, they want to have someone come in, nose around a little, just so they can point to you later and say that everything was done."

"You're saying that they're counting on me not to do a good job?"

"You shouldn't ignore the possibility that you're being manipulated."

"Not a very cheery thought, is it?"

"If that is the way they're thinking they've seriously underestimated you."

"What was the other assumption I've been making, that might be wrong?"

"That this bookkeeper is a victim."

"It's a hell of a way to commit suicide."

"No, no. Let's say it's homicide. But that doesn't mean she's totally innocent. Have you considered at all that she may have been stealing money?"

"I gave it some thought, but the audit shows no discrepancies."

"After only a day's review. It could take weeks to find it, if she was clever or if she deliberately kept some of the records in a mess. I help Frank with his books. Not every day, but I helped set up his system and I take over from time to time. If there are enough transactions going on, a good bookkeeper can get away with whatever she wants, at least for a while. There are dozens of ways to bury things you don't want seen."

"I suppose. I don't know much about bookkeeping."

"You could sound a little more enthusiastic about this. After all, it's important. Everything you're doing is based on those two assumptions, and if either one of them is wrong you're going to get way off the beam."

"I can't see Emily doing anything wrong."

"There could be all sorts of double lives you haven't suspected. Could she have had a nice discreet drug habit? Gambling? There are lots of ways to go through money. And you want to know something else?"

"Go on."

"I'm no expert, but I've done lots of entry-level bookkeeping in my time, and the way the systems work is like the federal government, checks and balances. No one does everything. Certain large checks have to be countersigned, unusual transactions have to be authorized, someone above you has to give their okays and approvals."

"That sounds right."

"So who would be above the bookkeeper? Does the firm have an office manager?"

"We did years ago. She left and went to a big firm in Reading."

"So who does the bookkeeper report to? Your friend Tom Richardson, right?"

"Uh-huh."

"If there was going to be a major theft of firm money, that took place over any significant period of time, he'd have to be in on it, wouldn't he?"

"And so would she."

"Exactly."

"You've given me a lot to think about. As usual."

"One thought more, then I have to go. Suppose someone, X, was after your bookkeeper. I don't care if it was personal or related to the firm. Let's just say that the person is smart, and careful. They want to go to a lot of trouble so the killing couldn't be traced anywhere, especially to them. So they hire someone to do it in a way that makes it look like an accident, and they hire people unlike themselves—so even in a worst-case scenario, even if the death is seen to be murder, and even if these black drug addicts are found out, it still won't be traced back to them."

"Congratulations. You've just narrowed it down to everyone who *isn't* black who *doesn't* take drugs."

For a moment the line was quiet. Then there was a short, soft huffing noise. "Well, you don't expect me to do *everything*, do you?"

Chapter Eight

Wednesday, 7:00 A.M.

Vince DeAndrea lived in a five-story apartment building on Washington Square. He liked to say that he could look out his living room window and see the accumulation of pigeon shit on the roof of Independence Hall.

I was at the front door of his building a little early, at ten till seven. No response to the buzzer, but after a few minutes a young husband and wife in almost identical business suits let me in as they went out.

I took the elevator to his floor. There was no response to my knock, but when I tried the door, unbelievably, it was open.

"Jesus, Vince, what the hell kind of security is this?"

I stepped inside and looked around the living room. Except for a plate of half-eaten food on the coffee table, everything was in order. "Vince! Time to get moving!"

A noise came from the bedroom and I knocked on the door. "Vince? You all right?" There was a muffled noise, similar to the first, but a little louder. I waited for a few seconds, then went in.

Vince was sprawled on the bed, fully dressed except for his shoes. He was even wearing his jacket and tie from the day before. It didn't take much of a look to see that he'd slept that way. He raised his head and looked in my direction, but his eyes didn't focus. I wondered if he recognized me.

"Goddamn, Vince, you been in the sauce again?"

He smiled and made a slow, airy gesture with one arm. " 'S all right, Dave . . . all right."

"The heck it is! In two hours you're trying a case. Come on, let me get you into a shower."

He didn't resist as I helped him out of his clothes, but if I thought that a cold shower would bring him around, I was wrong. It was a good thing he was in the shower, though, because he threw up whatever he'd eaten the night before. I turned off the water and let him air dry while I made some instant coffee, so strong that it was barely drinkable. By the time I got the coffee into him and had him dressed again, it was well after eight.

We sat across from each other at the kitchen table while he drank a second cup of coffee. He paid a lot of attention to the cup and not much to me.

"Vince, you're in no shape to try a case."

He looked in my general direction and waved his hand again. "I'm jus' defending. No witnesses 'cept my weenie wagger. Besides, Mike can do it if we need him. Good idea to bust his cherry anyway."

Having backup made me feel better, but I'd seen brand-new lawyers do a lot of damage in a courtroom. "Let me have your secretary call and get it continued."

"No way, man. Judge'll say, okay, he's sick. Are there other lawyers in his firm? What about that kid who's been sitting second chair with you? He ain't dead, is he? No? Great, send him over."

The only thing to do when you find yourself in the middle of a stupid conversation is shut up, which is what I did. I got him to drink a third cup of coffee and told him it was time to get down to the courthouse. On the taxi ride he became more alert, if not exactly more sober, but his hair went in every direction, his eyes wandered, and despite a gargle of mouthwash he smelled like a liquor store after an earthquake. I wondered if he could convince the judge he had the flu.

By the time we cleared the array of guards, inspections, and metal detectors, it was five till nine. The client, a short, frail youth in his early twenties, was pacing back and forth in front of the courtroom, his hands in his jeans. His grimy, bearded face brightened when he saw us. "Mr. DeAndrea! Good morning, sir." He smiled broadly. For him, all his problems were over—after all, his lawyer was there. Vince smiled back, and I could tell from his expression that he wasn't quite sure who he was looking at. Before he had a chance to ask the client who he was, or call him by the wrong name, I hustled Vince into the courtroom.

It was a typical Common Pleas courtroom—lots of battered wooden furniture that had originally been blond, now dark brown with years of sweat and grime. A disorderly pile of video equipment, blackboards, and easels filled the area behind the court reporter's seat. I looked around and saw a few retirees in the spectator's seats, the DA and the cop at their table, and a couple of bailiffs. No one else. "Vince, where's Flora?"

"Isn't he here?" He seemed only mildly curious.

"What does he look like?" I asked.

"Medium height and build, short, black curly hair."

I looked around the courtroom and then quickly checked the hall. "No, Vince, I don't see anyone like that."

He shrugged philosophically. "Well, what can you do?"

I didn't trust Vince to stand unaided, so I headed him toward his chair at the defense table. "No, no," he mumbled. "Over there, near the jury."

"You're *defending* today, Vince," I explained gently. "This is a criminal case, remember? The DA has the burden of proof." He shrugged and allowed me to help him get to a chair. There were three chairs at counsel table, and for the moment I sat beside him, in the middle chair. The client took the seat to my right, and I had a better look at him. Then I leaned over to

Vince and whispered in his ear. "Jesus Christ, what is going on here? This guy looks like shit. He needs a haircut and a shave, he's dressed like he's ready to do heavy construction. He's even got dirt under his fingernails. Didn't anybody tell him to clean up his act?"

"He's dressed as well as half the jury'll be. 'Sides, a suit and tie on a guy like this? Nobody's gonna buy it."

I looked around the room. The assistant district attorney, an earnest young woman with close-cropped dark hair, dressed in a severe blue suit, was whispering to a policeman at counsel table. No makeup or jewelry. She didn't look more than twenty-seven, but she was wearing reading glasses. I wondered if they were fakes, to help her look like more of an authority figure. Her complexion was pasty, even by late-winter Pennsylvania standards. The cop was a big blond jock with a round, unlined face. Younger than the DA, with probably not too much court-room experience of his own.

A tall, pretty court reporter came in through the rear door and took her seat next to the witness stand. I was unhappy to see that the judge's bench blocked my view of her legs. "Vince," I whispered. "The court reporter's in place. That means the judge'll be out any second. You're in no shape to try this, and your assistant is missing. Talk to the DA about a continuance. At least till tomorrow."

He turned to say something to me, but at that moment the bailiff stood up. "Oyez, oyez, oyez. The Court of Common Pleas of Philadelphia County is now in session, the Honorable Jerome Kijewski presiding. All persons having business before this court, come forward and you will be heard. God save the Commonwealth of Pennsylvania and this honorable court."

We all stood; even Vince was on his feet. The judge took his seat and nodded briefly at us. He was a heavy-set man, nearly bald, with a pale complexion and large blue eyes. His hands, protruding from the generous sleeves of his robe, were tiny, and I wondered what he had weighed in college. He surveyed the room with an expression of carefully calculated boredom. Somewhere, I thought, there was a school where new judges were taught that it was injudicious to act too interested.

"Counsel ready to proceed?"

The district attorney stood up, and I realized she was visibly pregnant. At least six months, maybe seven. Christ, just what we needed, a pregnant DA in a sex offense case. I bet for these few months the DA's office was parking her in front of sex crimes jurors like a magic charm. A cynical thought crossed my mind—just maybe she had a pillow stuck under her dress. I wondered what the maximum sentence was for Indecent Exposure. "The Commonwealth is ready to proceed, Your Honor."

Vince got to his feet. His movements were smooth, but I saw that his fingertips were white from steadying himself on the table top. "Defense is ready, judge."

Kijewski's eyes narrowed as he focussed on me. "Counsel, who is that?"

I stood up, ready to explain myself, but Vince took care of it for me. "Your Honor, this is my partner, David Garrett. He'll be assisting me today."

"What happened to your regular assistant?"

Vince shrugged eloquently. "Kids."

Satisfied, the judge nodded at me. "Very well. You all may be seated. You want to pick any alternate jurors?"

"Commonwealth does not, Your Honor."

"None for defense."

The judge turned to the bailiff. "All right, then. Have them bring down twenty veniremen." He looked at both counsel. "All right with you?"

Vince spoke up. "Judge, if I might, I'd suggest twenty-four. We might get some challenges for cause, and who wants to go through *voir dire* twice for the twelfth juror?"

The client tapped me on my shoulder and I sat down. His breath was worse than Vince's, and I could see at least one missing tooth. "Yes?"

"What's going on here?"

"Picking a jury."

"What's this about numbers? Is the fix in?"

"No," I whispered. "Each side has four challenges. They're called preemptory challenges, because you don't have to give a reason. We need a twelve-person jury. Twelve plus four plus four is twenty. So we'd need to have a minimum of twenty prospective jurors to pick from."

"So what if this woman's sister is in the pool?"

"That would be a different kind of challenge. That's a challenge for cause, and those are unlimited. They don't happen very often. Actually, that's what they're discussing—whether to bring down some extra prospective jurors in case some of the first twenty are challenged for cause."

"If they just took twenty, and some got throwed out, would I get a mistrial?" His eyes gleamed at the thought.

"No. They'd have to bring down a few more people and go through the whole jury selection process again, just to get the last one or two people."

"What if, maybe, one of the jurors didn't come back from lunch?"

I didn't like the way he said it. "Then you'd get a mistrial, but they'd just get a new jury and start all over."

"Don't I get no double jeopardy?" He sounded indignant.

"No."

Vince and the DA were at sidebar with the judge. I took the opportunity to go into the hall and look for a public phone. None was to be found, but I cajoled a middle-aged secretary with a physique like an elephant into letting me borrow her phone. I called the firm. "This is Dave Garrett for Mr. Flora, please."

"I'm sorry, he's signed out to court all day."

"I'm at the courthouse now, with Mr. DeAndrea, and he's not here."

She didn't seem surprised. "Well, if he shows up here, shall I send him down?"

"Please."

Just as I got back to the courtroom, Vince and the DA were returning to their seats. He was unsteady on his feet, and he sat down harder than he should have. "We're goin' with twenty-four," he said to me.

"Vince, you gave the judge the impression I was an attorney."

"So let the DA sweat a little, that we're double-teaming her."

"Feel okay?"

"My stomach is all fucked up from all that coffee you made me drink, you son of a bitch. And I gotta piss."

"Are you in shape for this, Vince?"

"Sure I am. Christ, half the cases I ever tried, I threw up right before they started."

I'd only thrown up twice before a trial, but I couldn't count the number of times I'd felt like it was going to happen. Trial lawyers, if they were drunk or unguarded enough, could speak from personal experience about every possible way that tension could express itself—insomnia, migraines, vertigo, nail-biting, impotence, diarrhea, back and neck pain. No symptom a soldier might have before combat could be a stranger to a trial lawyer. It was rumored that one of the most prominent and successful trial attorneys in the city regularly wet his bed the night before a major trial. Despite it all, we pulled ourselves together in the morning, put on our suits, and got through it. Even more remarkable, we came back for more. The people close enough to see the damage thought we were nuts, and we probably were. Maybe Flora wasn't so dumb after all.

"Vince, are you going to put the client on the stand?"

"Sure. His story is bullshit and the jury isn't going to buy it, but what are you going to do? You're not going to win without the jury hearing his side of it."

"Any character witnesses?"

"The DA would get a chance to cross-examine them on his priors. And anyway, his character sucks."

A side door opened and the bailiff led in a motley collection of twenty-four men and women. Except for three kids who looked eighteen to twenty, most of them were in their fifties, sixties, even seventies. Four blacks, two Hispanics, the rest white. About evenly divided between men and women. Vince was right—most of them weren't dressed as well as the defendant. I saw ripped jeans, sweatshirts, untied tennis shoes, and women with their hair in curlers. What was that line on the Statue of Liberty? Something about the wretched refuse of the teeming shores? I wondered where we could send ours, besides putting them on jury duty.

The bailiff recited the names and jury numbers of each of the veniremen, and as he did so Vince and I studied the jury information sheet. It gave us the name, address, and occupation of each member of the entire jury pool, which was several hundred names. Since we only had twenty-four of them here, we had to do a fast job of shuffling through the pages to keep up. Over and over again, for "Occupation" I saw either "Retired," "Homemaker," "Custodian," or, simply, "None." Looking them over, about half of them didn't look bright enough to make change. I knew the odds that close to half a dozen of them were functionally illiterate. In other words, it was a typical big-city jury, the kind that regularly decides questions of life and death, whether nationally distributed products are unsafe, if brain surgeons have correctly followed surgical and diagnostic protocols, and whether split-second decisions made by tired people on rainy nights ten years before showed a reasonable exercise of due care. It was the American system of justice.

The judge made a short welcoming speech, explaining how the trial would proceed, introducing the attorneys—including me—and thanking the panel for doing its part in making our system work. The judge didn't look stupid. Did they tell him in judge school he had to *thank* them? What a crock. Everyone knew that people only appeared for jury duty because of a court order, and that practically none of them would be there if they had any way out. That was half the problem with the jury system; if you had an important enough job, or connections, or were smart enough to lie the right way, you got out. So the actual jurors were the leftover ones. The more I thought about the American trial system, the happier I was to be out of it.

The district attorney stood and addressed the panel, and I heard a murmur as they noticed she was pregnant. I had a sense they disapproved. They were probably a little uncomfortable with the idea of a woman authority figure anyway—a pregnant authority figure sent mixed messages. I tried to see it from their viewpoint. Were they supposed to be solicitous or respectful? What was a pregnant woman doing out of the house? Shouldn't she be at home? Didn't she care about her baby? If she had a husband, why did she have to work? I looked at her hand and she wasn't wearing a wedding ring. That meant nothing, of course; lots of women couldn't wear their rings during the advanced stages of their pregnancies. But just maybe, I thought, she was a single parent. I wondered what the jurors would do with *that* possibility. They didn't look like a crew that was ready for it.

I leaned over to Vince and mentioned my speculations to him. "Maybe." He shrugged. "And maybe they're just wondering how such an ugly woman ever got laid. Don't think so much. It screws up your case."

She sat down and the judge nodded at Vince.

"Members of the panel, as you know, my name is Vince DeAndrea, and today I have the privilege of representing the defendant in this action." I tried hard not to frown. It was for the DA to dehumanize the defendant by calling him that. The defense lawyer's job was always to call the defendant by his name. There was only one explanation—Vince had forgotten the client's name. He looked at the panel, then at the judge, and smiled. "Your Honor, we have nothing to hide. Nothing to fear. These all seem to be fine people and I see no reason why they shouldn't be seated. We move to seat the first twelve as our jurors."

He sat down, and the judge and the district attorney exchanged grim looks. Waiving preemptories was done frequently enough in misdemeanor trials—it had a certain grandstand appeal—but never in sex offense cases. Too many people have their minds made up where sexual conduct is involved, one way or the other, and *voir dire* was your only chance to weed out the ones whose minds were made up the wrong way. Vince himself had taught me a maxim of trial law: Give me the most prejudiced jury in the world, as long as I'm sure it's prejudiced my way.

The judge looked at the DA. "Counsel?"

She made her first mistake; she thought about it too long. It was a pure roll of the dice, not the kind of problem that logic could solve. Either she felt lucky with that first twelve or she didn't. Sitting and thinking about it just made her appear indecisive. "Yes, Your Honor," she finally said. "That will be all right, I guess."

The judge nodded to the bailiff, who ushered the first twelve into the jury box and administered the oath. The rest of the panel was led away. The trial was on.

The district attorney made her opening statement. I hadn't expected much, but it was awful. She stood at the counsel table, thirty feet from the nearest juror, and read it off a yellow pad. She spoke for twenty minutes and didn't look up once. Essentially, she read a summary of what the testimony would be. In a week-long trial with twenty witnesses and thirty exhibits, it would have made sense. Describing the testimony in advance in a two-witness case just robbed it of any surprise value. Well, maybe things weren't so bad after all.

Eventually she ran out of yellow sheets, paused for a moment, and sat down. The opening statement of the Commonwealth was over.

"Mr. DeAndrea?" asked the judge. His boredom looked genuine now.

"Vince," I whispered. "Are you sure you're ready?"

"Ready as I'll ever be."

He smiled at the judge and started to stand up. I was ready for him this time, and we got him on his feet fairly smoothly. He stood there for a moment. Whether it was for dramatic effect or just to get his balance, I couldn't tell. It succeeded in getting the jury's attention, though, which was more than the DA ever

had. He moved around the table until he was standing in front
of it. His movements seemed natural and unhurried, but I noticed he kept his hip pressed hard against the edge of the table
for balance.

"Your Honor, counsel, members of the jury. My name, as
you know, is Vince DeAndrea, and I represent the defense. This
is my chance to speak to you before the evidence is heard, and
to tell you what the case is about.

"Now, in a way, every criminal case is about the same thing.
They're all about whether the Commonwealth can produce evidence of guilt beyond a reasonable doubt. That's true enough,
but it's not very helpful in a specific case.

"What *our* case is about is mistake . . ." He went on for
about twenty minutes, without notes and without a pause. At
some time during his speech he made eye contact with every
juror. Several of them smiled and nodded.

He sat down, a little more smoothly this time. "Good job,
Vince," I told him. "Nice and tight."

"How many times did I mention reasonable doubt?"

"At least three, maybe four."

He looked at me without any change of expression. "Shit,
that's not enough. Dumb fuckers'll forget it. I usually put it in
six times."

"Want me to call again for Mike?"

"What the fuck use would he be if he was here? He's missed
voir dire and opening."

"What do you keep this guy around for, then?"

"Hell if I know. They started him in Corporate and Huyett
found he was too dumb to do paperwork, so they gave him to
me."

"You must have been pissed."

He shrugged again. "Ah, you don't need brains to try cases.
You just need guts."

At the prompting of the judge the DA called her first witness, the woman who'd called the police. I was hoping either
for a teenage girl or a dried-up old maid, someone whom the

jury might not trust as a reliable witness in a sex case. What we got was an attractive brunette in her middle thirties. As she took the stand I saw she was wearing what Lisa, my old girlfriend, would have called fuck-me high heels. And Lisa should have known.

The DA took fifteen minutes plodding through the preliminary questions and got to the point. "Ma'am, can you tell us what transpired on July eleventh last year at about four-forty in the afternoon?" It was leading, at least technically, but only a sucker would have objected. I didn't need to worry; Vince wasn't exactly straining at the leash. I wasn't even sure he was still awake.

"Yes. I live in a row house on Priscilla Street, across from the community park. I happened to look out the front window, I was looking for my babysitter to bring Karen home, when I saw that man across the street. He was sitting on a bench in the park."

"What drew your attention to this man?"

She didn't miss a beat. "He had unzipped his shorts and taken out his penis. He was playing with it with one hand."

"Is there any doubt in your mind about what you saw?"

"I know what a penis looks like." And no one in the room doubted her for a second.

"And what did you do?"

"I called the police. The officer sitting there next to you responded. He came up and made the arrest."

"Did you see that happen yourself?"

"I saw the officer's car arrive, but then the babysitter came. The next time I saw him was when the officer brought him to my door."

She ran through everything else that was on the checklist the DA's office had, including, of course, the inevitable identification of the perpetrator as the person sitting next to the defense lawyer. Just once I'd like to be a witness and identify the bailiff, the DA, or juror number twelve.

The judge turned to Vince. "Your witness, counsel."

He looked up slowly, like a fighter rising after taking a count of eight. The caffeine had run its course and the alcohol was taking over again. Or maybe it was sheer fatigue overwhelming all the chemicals in his system. I wondered how he was going to make it through the rest of the trial.

"Ma'am, how long have you lived at that address?" he asked.

"Nine years, since I got married." This woman was good. Without being asked, she'd managed to tell the jury she was a wife and mother.

"How far back is your living room window from the curb?"

"How far? I don't know. I never measured it."

"Give us your best guess, please."

"Oh, thirty or forty feet." Vince looked at me and I knew what he was thinking. Unless there was something very funny about this row house, it probably was only half as far from the curb as she estimated. If she habitually exaggerated distances, we had a shot.

"All right then, and how wide is Eighth?"

"Oh, probably fifty to sixty feet."

It was as narrow as most of Philadelphia's residential streets, no more than twenty-five feet. "Does the park start right at the far curb?"

"No." She knew she was being set up but she didn't see how. "There's a sidewalk and a fence, and then the park starts beyond that."

"How much distance is involved on the far side? Before the park starts, I mean."

She was starting to get nervous. She didn't like the way Vince seemed to be enjoying her answers. "I don't know."

"Perhaps the same distance as your house to the curb on your side?"

"Uh—I guess so."

"So, another thirty to forty feet. Now, you saw the defendant on a bench, correct?"

"Yes, I'm sure of that."

"And how far is the bench into the park?"

"A hundred yards," she said firmly.

Vince stood still for a moment, giving the answer time to sink in, and excused the witness. There was no redirect. The district attorney nodded at the judge and called the name of her next witness, the arresting officer.

Both sides made short work of the arresting officer. His memory of the incident was indifferent, and anyway, he never claimed to have witnessed the client actually expose himself. The Commonwealth rested. Then, as promised, Vince called the client, who admitted being present but denied exposing himself. He did better than I would have thought—evidently Vince had prepped him in a more sober moment—and the jury listened to him carefully. Not just politely—they really wanted to hear what he had to say. The DA's cross barely laid a glove on him.

When Vince was done with his redirect he looked down at the desk. Without rising, he said, "Your Honor, the defense rests." His voice was barely audible, and I could see he was fading fast.

"Anything further from the Commonwealth?"

"No, Your Honor."

The judge looked at his watch. "I want to keep this one moving. Either of you have any points for charge? All right, then. Let's take a ten-minute recess. Then let's have the closings, no more than fifteen minutes a side, and I'll charge the jury before lunch. If they don't have a verdict by twelve-thirty the bailiff will take them to lunch. The court stands in recess till ten-forty-five."

Everyone filed out, including the client, until Vince and I were alone. His breathing was labored and the sweat was standing out on his forehead. His hands were shaking so badly the jury would have seen it if they were in the box.

"You look like hell. Is gray your regular color?"

"Dave, I need a big favor."

"Sure. I'll try Flora again."

"That's not what I mean."

I stiffened. "Don't even think about it."

"Come on, you can finish up for me. All you have to do is pitch them a closing, sit through the judge's charge, and wait for the verdict."

"Are you nuts? Taking over in the middle?"

"It's such a simple case, and you've been here for the whole thing."

"That's not the point. I'm not a lawyer. It would be completely illegal."

"And who's to know?"

"I know."

"Don't give me that shit. You should have been trying this from the beginning, not me." He smiled. "And besides, what kind of trouble could you get in? What are they going to take away now?"

I looked around the room. The idea of getting up in court one more time . . . "Vince, this is nuts."

"Dave, I gotta get out of here. And if I just split, they'll declare a mistrial and even that ugly cunt will do a better job next time around. This is the kid's best chance, right now."

"I'll do it on one condition."

"What's that?"

"You get yourself into a thirty-day *inpatient* alcohol rehab program by next Monday. Say yes right now or I walk out of here."

He looked at me for a long time and then down at his hands, as if they were the problem. "It's that bad, isn't it?"

"Yeah, Vince, it is."

"I should have quit trying cases already."

"It's easy to hang on too long."

He leaned back in his chair. "Remember Ted Williams?"

"He's a little before my time."

"He was ready to retire. One day he hits a home run. He rounds the bases real slow, shaking hands with the coaches, taking in the applause, then he goes into the dugout, takes a shower, and goes home, just like that. Now that's knowing when to quit." He closed his eyes and smiled with pleasure at the recollection. I wondered if Vince might have seen the game. Then he looked up at me. "You drive a hard bargain, Dave."

"Because I'm your friend. I want you to live long enough to get fat shoving little pieces of paper around, not beating your head against the wall like this."

He sighed. "Okay, you got a deal. But one condition of my own."

"What's that?"

"Get me the name of that court reporter."

"All right. Now go home, Vince, and get some sleep."

I helped him to his feet and took him as far as the elevator. By then I could see the DA going back into the courtroom. I followed her inside.

I looked around the courtroom. Except for the judge, everyone was in their assigned places—the court clerk, the reporter, the bailiff, the jurors, the DA, and the police officer. My client was huddled in his chair, holding a plastic cup of water like he was trying to warm himself. He looked sad and alone, and he was right to feel that way. With the single exception of me, every person in the room was either indifferent to what happened to him or was actively trying to put him in jail.

I'd barely settled myself into Vince's chair when the bailiff announced the judge again. We all stood. "What happened to Mr. DeAndrea?" he asked.

"He's been taken ill, Your Honor," I said. "If the court please, I'm prepared to proceed for the defense."

"You're ready to close?"

"Yes, Your Honor."

"Need a couple more minutes? We're not in that much of a hurry."

"I'm ready."

"Proceed, counsel."

I stood slowly, my hands empty, and walked around the

counsel table. "Your Honor, counsel, members of the jury." I picked a spot about ten feet in front of the center of the jury box, planted my feet, and began to speak.

I was short, simple, and direct. I didn't use a word that would have been unfamiliar to an intelligent fifth grader. The heart of my closing was easy; Vince had already set it up for me.

It only worked because of Vince's cross-examination. Not what he'd asked—what he didn't ask. A lesser man would have asked the witness about the total distance from the witness to the defendant, but that would have allowed her to weasel out, or at least alerted the DA to the need to rehabilitate her. Now, testimony was closed and it was too late.

"Members of the jury, you'll recall the uncontradicted testimony, from the prosecution's own witness, about how far away she was. Remember the details? She said it was thirty to forty feet to the street, that the street was fifty feet wide, and that it was another thirty to forty feet on the other side of the road till the park started. And the defendant was one hundred yards into the park. If you take a moment, you'll see that the prosecution is asking you to believe that this woman saw my client's penis two football fields away."

I mentally counted to five, allowing the jury to absorb the distance in a measure they were familiar with. When I went on I mentioned the theme of reasonable doubt four different times; once when explaining the law, once when reviewing the facts, again when I talked about common sense, and last in my final remarks.

"Members of the jury, I'm about to sit down. But before I do, I want to leave you with one last thought. All the things to think about, all the law and the rules, boil down to one thing. If you're not convinced beyond a reasonable doubt by the evidence you've heard this morning that my client is guilty, then your legal duty is to find him not guilty. Thank you."

I turned and walked slowly back to my seat, conscious that there wouldn't be any other chances like this, that when I sat down, it would be for the last time. I tried not to let it poison the moment.

I sat and listened politely while the DA gave her closing, which consisted of a review of every bit of testimony, plus a reading of the relevant statutes. It was every bit as boring as it sounds. Then the judge instructed the jury on the law. For nearly forty-five minutes he read the carefully chosen words of the state supreme court's Pennsylvania Standard Jury Instructions. He told them about the burden of proof, the presumption of innocence, the standard by which to evaluate the testimony of witnesses, and the rules regarding how to reconcile conflicts in testimony. He read them the elements of the crime charged and explained each element to them. He explained the special rules concerning the testimony of the defendant.

As all juries do, they listened politely without understanding a single word, and went back to the deliberation room to vote their prejudices.

The client, of course, was nearly hysterical. Why didn't we call his mother as a character witness? Why didn't Mr. DeAndrea ask the woman if she was sure it was him she'd seen? Why didn't we bring in five people who looked like him and see if she could have picked the right one? Was it too late for a plea bargain? He'd cop to anything if it meant staying out of jail—did I know what they'd do to him if he went inside? At times like that I wished I'd persisted in my dreams of going to medical school. Patients didn't ask why you used a certain size retractor, or how come you didn't irrigate with one thousand cc's of saline instead of only five hundred. Or maybe they did —with all the medical shows on television, maybe doctors had to put up with that shit now, too.

It didn't take long. After less than twenty minutes they were back in the box. Not guilty.

As the jurors filed out, anxious to get out on the streets and find something to eat, I looked over at the client. It was there, the same look I'd seen dozens of times. A little relief, no satisfaction, and certainly no gratitude. What had we done for him?

The cops had just been harassing him all along, he'd never done nothin', and of course the jury had let him go. He could have taken care of it himself, of course, but his mother had insisted we get involved and run up a big bill for doing nothing.

Normally I shake hands with opposing counsel once a trial is over, win or lose, but not today. I didn't think she'd caught my name, and I didn't want to give her a second chance.

Outside it was starting to rain. I looked around for an umbrella vendor, but there wasn't one in sight. Goddamn city; in New York there would have been four on every block. I cupped my hand over my wristwatch and checked the time. Nearly one o'clock.

As a lawyer, when I'd finished a case, I made it a point to take the rest of the day off, to go home and have a long soak in a hot tub. I was just as wrung out as I'd ever been, maybe more, but I headed east on Market through the rain, back toward my old firm. After all, the day was half over and I hadn't done any work yet.

Chapter Nine

Wednesday, 1:00 P.M.

A nine-block walk in the rain wasn't much of a substitute for a hot tub, but in its own way it helped. By the time I reached the office the trial was old business and I was a private eye again. Being cold and wet suited my mood, too.

I stopped at the reception desk. "Is Mr. Flora here?"

"Yes, sir. He's in his office."

"What time did he come in?"

"A little after ten, I think."

"Did he say why he didn't join Mr. DeAndrea at trial this morning?"

"Not to me."

Flora wasn't in his office, or the library, or the coffee room. I knocked on Tom's door, intending to complain about him.

"Come in."

Tom was behind his desk and a sallow-faced young man with dark hair was sitting in one of the leather chairs in front. He was hunched over, like a gambler trying to keep his cards close to his chest. "Morning, Dave," he said. "I'd like you to meet our junior associate, Mike Flora."

The younger man extended his hand but didn't bother to

stand up. "Call me Mike. Everybody does." It sounded like an order.

I remained standing and ignored his hand. "Where were you this morning?"

Flora dropped his hand. "Well, I was busy."

"There's no such thing as being too busy for a trial."

"Well, Vince was there, wasn't he?"

Tom broke in. "What's going on here, Dave?"

"Your prize junior associate didn't show up for the trial today involving the councilwoman's son. Vince couldn't finish. We called and we couldn't find your associate here. I left a message for him, and he never came down. I wound up having to close and take the verdict myself."

"Oh, Lord," Tom said. "Oh, Lord. Mike, is this true?"

He shrugged, not nearly as well as Vince did. His gesture carried a hint of defiance, even menace. "I've carried his briefcase to a dozen trials and never did nothin' more than pull papers outta the files, y'know? I figure, today was my chance to make my pitch to you about Rosalie."

Tom looked up at me. "Mike has a sister who's a highly qualified bookkeeper. We interviewed her this morning. She understands our type of check-writing system, and she's available to start immediately."

I was thinking it was quite a coincidence, but I wasn't going to say that in front of Flora. "Can I speak to you privately, Tom?"

Flora considered the request. "Well, guess our business is done for right now. Get back to me on this, right?"

"Certainly."

He left without shutting the door behind him. I shut it myself and fell into the chair he hadn't used.

"Dave, I apologize for him," Tom said.

"This conversation gets more stupid every second."

"The hell with him. How's Vince? Was it bad this time?"

"There've been others?"

"I don't know if it was going on when you were still here or not, Dave. I think as long as he could split the workload with you, he was all right."

"Has he had any help?"

"I made him go to a counselor a few months ago, but he didn't go back. How was it today?"

"He must have gone on a toot last night. He was still half drunk at seven this morning, and I don't think he slept much. He got himself most of the way through the trial, but then he folded."

"We've tried to get him out of trying cases, but there's no one else who can do it."

"If you're going to let him go on the way he is, you'd better keep a line open to the malpractice carrier."

His tone became sharper. "That's easy for you to say. Do you have any idea how few really good trial lawyers are left in this town? Unless you're a prodigy you don't really know the job till you're thirty-five, and unless there's something mighty special about you, by the time you're fifty you're past your prime."

"I know, Tom."

He took off his glasses and rubbed the bridge of his nose. "He's going to kill himself."

"I made him promise to do a thirty-day alcohol rehab program. Inpatient."

He looked up, surprised and pleased. "Good. That's very good. Now—"

"Tom, let me ask you something. Just how bad, in terms of what he's actually done, are his episodes?"

He spread his hands, palms upward, and shook his head. "None of us has all the details. I don't even know if *he* has all the details himself. But I think he's what they call—what was the word you used yesterday—a binger. He'll be fine for a couple of months, and then drink himself unconscious. Sometimes just on a Saturday night and sometimes before a trial or an important deposition."

"What does he do when he's loaded?"

"I'm sure we don't know about all of the episodes. I try to keep a close eye on it, monitoring the medical bills, you know. Twice in the last year he hurt himself—there were bills from hospital emergency rooms. And once there was an auto accident—he was driving, ran into a parked car and fled the scene. I can't be sure, but I'm pretty certain he was drunk then, too."

"Does he remember afterward?"

He shook his head. "That's the part that concerns me the most."

"The emergency room bills. What were they about?"

"Cuts and bruises. Apparently he got involved in fights."

"That doesn't sound like Vince."

"Not when he's sober. But isn't that one of the symptoms of alcoholism? That a different personality emerges when you've been drinking?"

"I think so. It certainly means he's fighting to keep things under control when he's sober. And when he's drunk, he loses. Tell me, who sees the medical bills first?"

"You know very well. Emily does. I mean, did. Why are you asking all this?"

"It's pure speculation."

"Let's hear it anyway."

"We have a death of the person responsible for processing the insurance forms. For all we know there could be something very embarrassing to Vince on some of those forms. If her death was a homicide, it was committed with alcohol. We have a partner who abuses alcohol who has blackouts. During his blackouts he becomes violent."

"You're not serious."

"I have no proof, but it's a perfectly serious speculation. Name one fact, taken by itself, that isn't accurate."

"Dave, come on. Vince knew Emily for twenty years."

"If you're murdered, you're far more likely to be killed by someone you know well than by anyone else."

"But Vince is your client, too, you know."

I thought about what Kate had said about their motives in hiring me. "Are you telling me to back off?"

"That's not what I meant."

"Then what did you mean?"

He looked down at the desk and frowned. "I mean, nothing. Take your investigation as far as you need to."

"I'd like to get on to another subject."

"I won't object."

"This wonder boy of yours."

He sighed. "Dave, things have changed in the practice of law."

"Not that much in two years."

"They've been changing for a long time. As managing partner I've been watching it. You had the luxury of not having to pay attention."

"To what?"

"Fifteen, twenty years ago, you looked for the brightest people you could find. You didn't expect them to come in with any skills, just be ready and able to learn. They spent two, three, perhaps as long as four years in training before they started being really profitable. Now it's changed. There's so much competition, and salaries are so high, associates have to be profitable almost right away. They have to train on the run. And we need to bring in associates who can bring in business, if we can."

"So that's it."

"Mike isn't our most promising associate, but he more than pays for himself already. We're even thinking of opening a satellite office in New Jersey to help handle his referrals."

"What kind of work?"

"Unions, small businesses, some individuals. He's the first lawyer in his extended family, and he can steer a lot of people our way."

"Quite an arrogant little fuck, isn't he?"

Tom considered his response. "He's not as conscious of his place in the firm as I'd like."

"You'd have fired me in a second if I'd ever acted like he does."

"You didn't bring in any business, Dave. Money talks."

I heard Kate's voice in my head. She was telling me that Richardson seemed to know a lot more about Flora's background today than he'd known yesterday. I decided to let it rest for the moment. "Do you have an idea where he was when Emily was killed?" I didn't care what the answer was; my anger was talking.

"Oh, come on, Dave. I think you're letting your feelings about him color your judgment."

"It's a problem I have. But in my experience, really likeable people don't turn out to be murderers. And besides, his not showing up where he was supposed to cost me half a day's time. Maybe time for someone to destroy or fabricate evidence. Time to talk to people and get stories straight. His not showing up could be more than sloppiness."

He threw up his hands. "Dave, if I'm not going to steer you away from Vince, I can hardly tell you to respect Flora. Do what you have to do."

"Talk to you later, Tom." It was a bad end to our meeting, but I didn't want to wait for a better one.

I went back to the reception area and checked the sign-out sheet. Vince was as good as his word. He was listed as "out" with no date or time for return. His secretary said he'd cancelled all appointments and court appearances for the next thirty days. He'd left a message for me, that he would be in to see me as soon as he could. I remembered I hadn't gotten the name of the good-looking court reporter for him. Well, if he was up to it, he could get it for himself in thirty days.

My next stop was Emily's office, where the firm's accountant was pounding away at the calculator again. Except that the tie hanging loose around his collar was a different color, I wouldn't have been able to tell that he'd gone home.

"What do you have for me today, Ron?"

His hand stopped, but the rest of his body didn't change posture. "I've got something, but I don't know what."

"Let's hear it."

"Well, it doesn't really make any sense."

"Let me be the judge of that."

He put both hands in his lap. "Remember when I said the bank statements had been reconciled and everything was in shape?"

"Sure I do."

One hand went up and rubbed his chin. "Everything I said was true, as of the statement dates. But something . . . irregular happened last week, after the statements came in."

"Is money missing?"

"No, not that. The cash on hand balances."

"So what's the problem?"

"Well, it's quite a coincidence that it balances."

"Isn't that what it's supposed to do? What are you talking about?"

"Take a look at these."

He handed me the pink carbon copies of three Mellon Bank deposit slips. Each one was made out for a slightly different amount, each one a little less than ten thousand dollars. The amounts were in type, not handwritten. The total was a little less than thirty thousand dollars.

"Mellon is where our trust account is, right?"

"Right. And notice that these are counter deposit slips that had been made out to our account. They didn't come from our office."

"Where did the money come from?"

"That was my question, so I called them. And they told me they had nine more, besides these, that they'd just put in the mail to us, varying amounts, each one for less than ten thousand. The total of the nine I haven't seen yet is ninety thousand, seven hundred and fifty-three dollars. The total of all twelve checks is one hundred nineteen thousand, six hundred eighty-one dollars. Zero cents."

"Let me guess," I said. "The deposits were cash, not checks."

"That's right. How did you know that?"

"From doing RICO work. All cash transactions over ten thousand have to be disclosed to the Treasury Department. Somebody wanted to give us a hundred and twenty thousand without letting anyone know."

He looked at the tape again. "Of course, even counting those deposits, we're not ahead a penny. We're exactly where we should be."

"Which means that at some point someone took the money out, and now they're replacing it."

"Exactly. It's just that I can't tell how it got out. All I can tell is that it was put back."

"Can the bank trace anything?" I asked.

He shook his head. "The deposits were all made in various night depositories. And the cash was used, not new."

"When were the deposits made?" I asked.

"Sometime between close of business Monday afternoon and nine A.M. Tuesday."

"I'll go better than that. I'll say the money went in right after Emily's death was announced." I tapped the slips with my finger and studied the typing. "Whoever made these deposits killed her."

"Well . . ."

"Don't you see? This case is starting to hang together. The killer had taken money from the firm, a lot of it, and he wanted to replace it before he was discovered. He figured out how to put the money back without anyone being able to trace it to them."

"He sure did that," Wolfe said.

"But Emily was an obstacle, somehow. Think this through with me, okay?"

"Sure."

"Let's start with the least likely possibility, that this was a falling out among thieves. Could Emily have been part of an embezzlement?"

"No. We audit the records every year. We did a full audit in January, just two months ago, and everything was in order. We haven't checked every scrap of paper, but I can say with assurance that nothing irregular was going on as of two months ago."

I thought about what Huyett had told me about his own audit. Whatever was going on, it didn't seem to involve any dishonesty on Emily's part. "That gives me an idea, thinking about this in terms of time. If I were to steal a big chunk of change, how long till it would be discovered?"

"It depends on what account you used, and how much was involved."

"Go on."

"The firm's own account, the only time there's any large amounts in there is right before payroll is written. If you took any substantial amount, at least some of the paychecks would be dishonored when they were presented for payment."

"Forget that one. What about the trust account, at Mellon?"

"The partnership has a three-hundred-thousand line of credit on that one. If you drew out enough, the check would be dishonored when it was presented. But you could write a check for a hundred and twenty thousand, and it would be honored unless you happened to do it the same day you did multiple real estate settlements, or paid out in an estate or personal injury case that was big enough."

"And if the check didn't bounce right away, how long till Emily found out?"

"Well, depending on the bank's policy, they might send an acknowledgment for such a big transaction. In any event, it would show up in the next bank statement. So depending on your timing, it would take anywhere from two days to about thirty-three days till you were found out."

"I don't get it," I admitted. "Why steal money you're going to turn around and replace almost right away?"

"Maybe he needed the money just for a short time."

Now it was my turn to rub my chin. "I'm having trouble picturing it."

"Me, too. Somebody who could replace it so quickly should have been able to raise the money some other way."

"Listen, Ron. We know what bank account the money was taken from. And we know it was taken since the last bank statement. Can you find out which file it came from?"

"I'd need to check every ledger card."

"How long will it take?"

"The rest of the day, at least."

"Good." I smiled and patted him on the shoulder. "Get right on it." I got out of there before he could argue with me.

I went down the hall toward my office and smelled cigar smoke. When I'd been with the firm I'd lobbied for a no-smoking policy. I'd had a nasty struggle with Roger Palmer, the labor lawyer, who loved his cigars regardless of what anybody else thought. I poked my head into his office and there he was, wrapped in a thick cocoon of stinking blue smoke. Labor lawyers, in my experience, are—well, labor lawyers.

"Hi, Roger."

"Dave." He nodded. No greeting, no handshake, just the nod. Anything more would have been out of character.

I stayed in the hall, trying to keep out of the worst of the smoke. "How are you doing?"

"Shitty, but not as shitty as the firm." He put down the papers in his hands and gestured at the masses of documents piled in every corner of his office. Normally Roger kept a neat desk, and I was shocked at the mess. He was pale, with unkempt black hair that accentuated the circles under his eyes. He looked about the same, except for an expanding roll of fat around his middle. He waited for a response but didn't get one. "Which I'm sure you're discovering for yourself, anyway."

"You seem to be having your ups and downs, Rog."

"Met the skinny little wop?"

"Yeah." I left it to my tone to convey my impressions.

"Most of what he brings in is labor. Construction unions, teachers' unions, Teamsters, you name it. I run arbitrations and bargaining sessions around the clock. You think the firm gives me any help? No. There's enough work here to keep three people busy."

"So how come no help?"

"Flora's too stupid to do it himself. Shit, if he could do it himself he would never have needed us to begin with. And they won't give me an associate. Not in the budget, Tom says."

"Is that what Emily thought?"

"I don't know." He leaned back and put his hands behind his neck. "So go ahead, shoot."

"So where were you last weekend, and Monday night?"

He leaned back in his chair and smiled around his cigar. "I like a nice straight-up asshole question. Is your subtlety the product of your years as a trial lawyer, or did they teach you this in detective school?"

"Subtlety was always wasted on you, Roger."

"I was here all day Saturday, till five. All day Sunday, till three or four. And all day Monday. I stayed till eight or so Monday night."

"And then went where?"

"Away from the office."

"Can your wife verify you went home?"

"I was home by eleven. She can verify that."

"And in between?"

"Business."

"Where?"

"The Hershey Philadelphia."

It was a fairly new, upscale hotel on Broad Street at Locust. I thought of it less as a business hotel than as a place for yuppies to exchange social diseases. "If I were to look at your day book there, would I see your appointment?"

"No, it's a private matter." His cigar took an aggressive angle. "And none of your fucking business."

"Too bad you don't have an alibi."

"Yeah. Too fucking bad. Now you want anything else or can I get some work done?"

"Talk to me a little."

"About what?"

"About the firm. You said it was shitty."

He took the cigar out of his mouth and put it down. "We've got a collection of some of the best brains in Philadelphia, we analyze and review our options carefully, and we consistently make the stupidest damn choices imaginable."

"I'm listening."

"When we found out you were leaving, remember we brought in that junior partner from Dechert, Price and Rhoades?"

"Sure. Seemed like a nice guy."

"He stayed six months. Just long enough to get in good with your institutional clients. Then he left and set up on his own and took them with him. Then we buy up this supposedly profitable firm in Upper Darby. Two-man operation. Well established. Expansion, hold our market share, blah-blah-blah. The two partners quit as soon as the ink is dry, leaving us with their debt and a gimp associate whose medical bills have to be seen to be believed."

"She seems okay to me."

"Hey, she can do the work, sure, but the deal cost us big. And Vince is into the sauce, you know."

"So I've heard," I said carefully.

"Well, you must still be his asshole buddy or you're pretty goddamn stupid, because most people can figure it out just sitting in the reception room. He's costing us business, and Tom doesn't want to face facts."

"I haven't heard any complaints about Jerry Huyett yet."

"He's got his own problems. The corporate work is pretty slow. His department had to let their associate go. Now he has to use the gimp when he needs help, and she doesn't know shit about corporate law. You know he's a partner now?"

"So I heard."

"Anything else?" He picked up his cigar and began producing thick blue clouds. It was his way of asking me to leave, and I took him up on it.

I went looking for Flora. He was in his office, surrounded by mountains of files and documents, looking unhappy. His expression didn't improve when he saw me.

"How you doin'?" he asked, without much enthusiasm.

"You sound a little sour, Mike."

He waved his arm in a wide, expansive gesture. "Just look at all this shit. Not just my own work, but Vince's, too. Every time I turn around they put another half dozen files on my desk. This is really bullshit, man."

"I thought you were working with Vince already."

"When I had the time. I'm busy with a lotta other things, you know. I don't have time for this shit. What do they want from me?"

"I expect that they think you'll practice law."

"We all got things to do."

"Mine is to ask some questions. Where were you on Friday?"

"Mmm. In and out."

"What does that mean?"

"I was here some, and other places some."

"You see Emily that day?"

He shrugged. "I can't remember. Maybe I did."

"Come on. If you saw her that day it was the last time you saw her alive. Most people remember things like that."

"Sorry." He didn't sound it a bit.

"Ever been to her building?"

"Not that I remember."

"You don't seem to remember much, do you?"

"I remember what I need to. The rest I let go."

"Were you in Thursday?"

"Yeah, I'm sure of it. We talked about my getting my paycheck a little early. I had some bills I wanted to take care of."

"She do it?"

"Turned me down."

"You argue about it?"

"Nah. It was small-time stuff."

"What do you think happened to her?"

"Accident. I think she was more of a boozer than you guys knew."

"You seem to know a lot about what goes on around here."

He smiled in a way I didn't like. "I make it my business to know things."

"Like?"

"Since we're on the subject, like how Vince can't hold his liquor for shit."

"What makes you say that?"

"Everybody in the office knows. We've all seen him drag in his ass at noon, looking like hell. Happens once a month."

"Ever seen him violent?"

"No, but he told me a couple months back that he woke up with a big cut all across his knuckles, and his clothes all mussed and torn, and he couldn't remember who or what he'd hit."

"Ever see him drunk yourself?"

"Oh, sure. Last night."

It took a second to sink in. "The night before his trial?"

"Yeah. We got together at four in the afternoon to go over some stuff. He seemed tense, you know? So I said, let's grab a couple of quick ones. It got him relaxed. We had a good time. I left him about nine and went home."

I stood up slowly. Then I reached across the desk, grabbed him by his lapels, and pulled him out of his seat. I kept pulling until I'd dragged him clean across his desk and our faces were inches apart.

"You goddamn son of a bitch! There's not a thing lower in the world than someone who'll feed booze to an alcoholic, and you shoved it into his face! What the hell kind of an animal are you?"

His eyes were wide. He opened his mouth, but the lips didn't move. It just stayed open. I could smell the sour smell of fear on his clothes. "Hey, I . . ."

"Don't say a thing. There's nothing you could say that isn't going to make me want to throw you out the goddamn window. Poor Vince. He never had a chance with you around."

I flung him back, hard. He fell heavily into his chair and it rolled backward into the wall. I stormed out and slammed the door behind me.

Chapter Ten

Wednesday, 4:00 P.M.

It was high time, I decided, to do some investigating outside the building for a while. Not because I had any particular plan—I just knew if I stayed inside I'd wind up doing something to Flora I'd regret later.

The rain was still coming down in sheets when I left the building, but I bought a cheap umbrella from a vendor in the lobby and decided to walk. The streets were surprisingly crowded for a weekday, considering the weather, and I made slow progress until I turned onto Sansom, a narrow street hardly more than an alley, and headed west. A cold wind gusted off the Delaware and threatened to turn my umbrella inside out. The rain swept in underneath, and I wished I'd bought a decent waterproof hat instead.

There was only one place to go, and my feet took me there without much conscious input from me. Emily's block was primarily residential, and at that time of day it was nearly deserted. It had nothing to do with the weather. Even on the sunniest weekday in May, the street would be empty during business hours, except for people on their way somewhere else. It was a neighborhood of the working middle class couples who lived well as long as both of them worked full-time. If they hit it big they could afford Society Hill or Chestnut Hill or Chadds Ford. If they got divorced or one of them lost their job, it was back to Conshohocken or the far Northeast or wherever they'd come from.

I walked both sides of the street on Emily's block. The yellow police line tapes were down from her building, I noticed. Instead I saw a construction sign and a rusting red Dumpster. A couple of men in hard hats were setting up sawhorses to block the sidewalk, but no one else was in sight.

Next to the Dumpster was a stack of yellow hard hats. I folded my umbrella and put one on. In my suit I couldn't pass as a workman, but at least I looked like someone who might have some legitimate business. Like most investigators, I made it a habit to pick up as many business cards as I could. I tried to remember whether I had any architects' or engineers' cards with me.

I walked up to the front steps and took a careful look around. No one bothered me. The staircase was only five steps, but they were deep, and the lowest step projected into the street more than six feet from the front of the building. To the left was only sidewalk where the stairs met the building, but on the right was a railing and a set of stairs going down to a daylight apartment in the basement. I looked around. The carriage lights on the building had tiny bulbs—they were for ornament, not security. The nearest streetlight was across the street, almost halfway down the block. At night the stairs going down would be in shadow.

I walked partway down the basement stairs and looked around. A person hiding there after dark would be invisible except for the headlights of traffic passing by, and even those would be mostly blocked by parked cars. But someone on the stairs would have had a good view of both sides of the street of the western half of the block. If you knew which way someone would approach, you couldn't have picked a better spot for an ambush.

I studied the retail stores. A travel agency. A flower store. A drug store. A Vietnamese restaurant. And an all-night deli. I put back the hard hat and tried the drug store.

It was a typical Center City drug store, meaning that what was displayed, in order of prominence, was the owner's security precautions, his inventory of miscellaneous gegaws, and, way in the back, the prescription counter where he stood guard. While I waited to get his attention I studied the signs. I learned that the cash register had less than fifty dollars in it, that it was on a time lock that the employees couldn't open, that no controlled substances were kept on the premises, that the safe for drugs was unlocked, that the property was patrolled by a security service with guard dogs, and that the building was protected by an alarm system that rang at the local police station. If the name of the establishment was displayed anywhere, I missed it.

The owner was a balding man somewhere in his fifties. He smiled at me through a glass divider that looked thick enough to be bulletproof, but I saw that he kept his hands underneath the counter. If I turned out to be a robber, I wondered if he'd just press an alarm or whether I'd be looking down the barrel of a gun. There was something around the corners of his eyes that made me think of a large caliber automatic, loaded with dum dum rounds, lovingly carved.

"Can I help you, sir?"

"I hope so. I'm a private detective. You know about the woman who died in the fire Monday night, across the street?"

He nodded. "Nice lady. Damn shame."

"Did you know her?"

"She was a regular customer here for years. Never said much, but never gave me any trouble, either."

"When did you last see her?"

"Give me a second and I'll tell you exactly." He turned away and consulted a computer in the rear. "She had a prescription for Tetracycline filled here at six-thirty Friday evening. And she bought some over the counter cold medications, too. A decongestant and some gargle, if I remember right."

"Was she here herself?"

"Oh, yeah. I fill almost all the prescriptions myself. Especially for old customers."

"She say anything?"

"Not too much. She complained about being sick, and we talked about the late winter colds going around. She looked pretty beat."

"Was she alone?"

"Uh-huh."

"Anything strike you as unusual?"

"Well, just that, as sick as she was, she still had a briefcase of work with her. But for her that wasn't unusual. She had work with her more often than not."

"Thanks for your time."

"Don't mention it." He smiled slightly at me and then his eyes shifted to the left, toward the next customer. His hands were under the counter again. As I turned away I noticed that the front of the counter was made of freshly painted plywood, so thin that it bulged away from the merchandise racks on either side. It took me a moment to think why a merchant in a high-crime area would want such a flimsy divider, and then I thought of his hands under the counter. I considered the fresh paint again and nodded to myself. The owner wasn't a believer in giving a sucker an even break.

Emily was unknown at the Vietnamese restaurant, so I tried the deli. A strapping Greek woman in a white uniform presided over a long case of meats and cheeses. The smells made me hungry and I asked her to make me a gyro.

"Have you worked here long?" I asked while she cut the lamb.

"Five this morning," she said with a heavy accent. "Big work."

"No, I mean how many months, years?"

"Ten, fifteen hour."

I showed her Emily's picture. "Do you know this person?"

She wiped her hands on her apron, looked at it carefully, and handed it back. "No help need."

It was time to let the language of Shakespeare take a beating. I pointed to the photo. "You see before?"

"She no like work here. Too fancy."

"You know?"

She nodded. "Come in every week. Maybe my cousin get her job?"

"No need job. When you see last?"

She paused, and for a moment I thought that she didn't understand. "Eight-forty Saturday night," she said definitely.

"How you know?"

She pointed at herself and then at the wall clock behind me. "I go home nine. I see."

"What she buy?"

She held up her fingers and counted off. "Feta cheese, one pound. Greek salad, small. Chicken soup, one quart." She smiled at her ability to remember.

"Any meat?"

The smile disappeared. "Mit?"

I pointed at each of the meat items. She shook her head no each time.

"She alone?"

She nodded sadly. "No man."

"No. When she here Saturday night?"

"Just her."

I ate the gyro at a table in the front window and watched the street. Emily's building was out of sight, to my left. If I was going to pull this off, how would I do it? The simplest thing would be a break-in, but it was too risky. Forcing the outside door would attract attention, either right away or later, when the damage was discovered. Strange people on the stairs, unaccompanied by a tenant, might be noticed. Assuming you made it to her door without a problem, breaking into her apartment would be noisy and time consuming. And even if you made it inside without a problem, she might still raise enough of a struggle to attract attention.

No, there was a better way. You stake out the place, wait for her to leave, and grab her on the way back. The basement stairs provided the perfect place. You go in with her own keys, take her up the stairs with a gun in her back, and get her inside her own apartment. Then you tie her up and gag her. All you need is a little patience. Of course, it helps if she goes out at night, and there's always the chance she won't leave the apartment at all, but they could always break in as a fallback plan.

The rain had stopped, but it didn't make my walk back to the office any less depressing. Images of Emily being stopped on the street, taken inside, a prisoner in her own apartment. Images that led nowhere; they weren't clues or evidence, just bad dreams that might have come true. And whether I caught the killers or not, there was nothing that would do poor Emily any good.

Chapter Eleven

Wednesday, 6:00 P.M.

When I got back to the office I was surprised to find that the front door was locked. That meant no one was expecting a late client. When I'd been with the firm it was a rare weeknight when at least one of us wasn't seeing people outside of regular hours. If not clients, then witnesses. In Philadelphia you were lucky to get witnesses to cooperate on any terms; and if they said they'd be willing to talk, but not if they lost work, then you saw them on the evenings, on weekends, at their homes, whatever it took.

Inside, nearly all the lights were out. Another surprise, and one that made me more unhappy. When I'd been a partner— well, hell, there was no point in even thinking about it. If everyone wanted to go home at four, not work Fridays, and take the summers off, it wasn't my concern anymore.

The only light was way at the end of the corridor, in associate territory. When I'd been here, it had been Jack Sherwood's office. Before we found out about his cocaine habit, that is, and how he'd been juggling his bills and pocketing fees to support it.

I should have known just from the door; it was obviously

new, and extra wide. Susan was at her desk with a pile of contracts spread out around her. Not just on the desk; on the credenza behind her and on the floor on both sides. She was wearing a conservative white blouse today, buttoned to the neck, but so sheer that the embroidery on her underwear showed through.

"Just a minute. Can't stop now," she said without looking up. She had one finger on what looked to be the fiftieth page of some kind of bond instrument. With her other hand she was reading from a small dark green book. Purdon's. The annotated statutes of Pennsylvania.

I looked around. It was dark outside, but I knew the view, the backs of three brick office buildings and a couple of parking lots. When I'd first come with the firm, this had been my office. I'd made partner after a couple years and moved to a bigger office with a view of the river, but there was something special for me about this room.

I wasn't sure how long she'd had the office, but by any standard it was damned spare. No pictures on the walls, no family photographs. The only thing on the walls was a generic abstract print in a chrome frame, the kind that hotels put in public areas. Like most art that seeks not to offend, it succeeds in not being noticed at all. Her desk was set almost in the middle of the room, and I realized that she needed a lot of room to maneuver her chair in and out.

She put down Purdon's and looked up. "Oh, David. Nice to see you again." And it sounded like she meant it.

"What are you working on?"

"Term loan agreements. I have to make sure that the language in the forms we use complies with Article Nine and the new BCL."

"Don't use language like that around me, young lady."

"Sorry. Well, you know Article Nine—secured transactions—"

"I learned enough to pass the bar and immediately forgot it."

"—and BCL is the new corporations statute. Business Corporations Law."

"When I was practicing I was glad there were people like you. Otherwise I would have needed to do things like that."

"It's not really so bad. It's precise. There's always an answer to your question. And you don't have to go to court."

"Speaking of that, where are you going now?"

"Probably just home. I'm tired."

"Want to get a bite to eat? I owe you for taking up your time last night."

"Oh. I don't know if I should. I really ought to take some work home."

"I'm not thinking of anything fancy, just a sandwich and a beer, and I'll drop you off."

There was an awkward pause. When she spoke again, her voice was strained. "Well, a lot of places give me access problems."

Her answer took me by surprise. It hadn't occurred to me that she would hesitate for anything more than the usual male-female reasons. "You must know places that are all right."

"Okay. You've got a deal."

The deal turned out to involve more than I could have imagined. First we had to take the freight elevator to a subbasement that had a ramp. She was in a nonmotorized chair, and I had to push it up the ramp. I was sweating by the time I reached the street. It was raining again, a hard, cold, driving rain, just this side of sleet, and there was nothing to do but get wet. We went two blocks that way until we reached my parking lot. I'd never realized how terrible the Philadelphia sidewalks are. The bigger cracks caused the chair to stick fast until both of us gave a coordinated heave. The smaller ones shook my hands and must have rattled her fillings loose. The tree roots threatened to pitch her out of the chair completely. Fortunately she was good at leaning her upper body to compensate. "What would happen if you fell out?" I asked.

"It happens all the time if you're halfway active. Just a couple of weeks ago I took a spill in the trolley tracks on Fourth. There's a whole technique of how you get back into the chair and get it upright again, unassisted."

"Sounds hard."

"They don't let you out of rehab without it."

When we reached the parking lot Susan had to wait in the rain because the sheltered area under the overhang wasn't accessible. Then I helped her get from the chair into my car—transferring, she called it. That part went smoothly, but learning to fold her chair in the rain was an experience I could have avoided. The chair was too big to fit in the back of my Honda, even folded, so we had to drive with the tailgate up. The wind blew rain and exhaust fumes into the back of the car.

The restaurant she picked was a downscale Italian place I knew from my days with the firm, on Nineteenth near Chestnut. "So far so good," she said. "Our next problem is going to be where to park."

"We can look for one of those handicapped spaces."

"If they're not already taken. I wish they'd give up on them."

"Why do you say that?"

"It's more trouble than it's worth. Half the time they're taken by somebody with flat feet or a mild heart condition who has a doctor who can write the right kind of letter. And the able-bodieds resent us for using them, even if we have a real problem. You know, I've had people yell at me, even when they see the chair."

"You're kidding."

"They tell me to stay at home and leave the space for someone who really needs it."

I shook my head. "Every time I think I've heard of the biggest asshole in the world, somebody has a topper."

She pointed. "There's a loading zone space across the street. It's after six; nobody will care."

Getting her out of the car and up to the level of the wheelchair on the sidewalk was a chore. I know she wanted to do it completely by herself, but finally she gave in and allowed me to lift her.

I'd forgotten that the restaurant had two steps at the front door. We used the service entrance, skirting between crates of soggy garbage, past the kitchen, and then down a dark corridor so narrow that I repeatedly scraped the knuckles on both hands.

I set Susan at a table and went to the bathroom to wash the dirt out of my abrasions. When I came back she was drying her hair as best she could with a large cloth napkin.

"Don't bother," I said. "You look fine."

"For a drowned rat." But she was smiling.

I ordered a bottle of chianti and we studied the menu. It hadn't changed, as far I could tell. If we strayed very far from spaghetti with meat sauce we could be in trouble.

"So how did a girl from Pittsburgh get to Philadelphia? Did you go to rehab around here?"

She shook her head. "No, there was a place near Altoona they said was the best."

"Was it?" I asked.

"I'd hate to see the worst." She studied the chianti in her glass and then bolted it down. "You know what my mom had bought me for Christmas that year? New ski boots."

"I've got to tell you, I can't imagine what it must have been like."

"The hospital wasn't bad. It was just like a bad dream that you keep expecting you'll get out of. But the rehab—you're not anything special there, it's all routine to them. Hell, they couldn't understand how I could feel sorry for myself."

"Oh?"

"Hey, there's a whole . . . I don't know what you'd call it, among spinal patients, depending on where you're hurt. My injury is T-11—that's pretty far down, almost to the small of my back, so I can still do a lot of things. I can feel almost down to my waist. You get hurt at C-6, up in the neck, the arm function is really impaired. Much higher and you're a quadripalegic. The C-5 and C-4s, they look at us like we've just got colds or something."

"I figured all of you would have something in common."

"Hah. In my unit of ten beds, I was the only woman. And most of the guys were your basic animals who'd gotten on a Harley after drinking a fifth of Jack Daniel's one too many times. They were mad at everybody and they figured nobody could do anything to them that was any worse. The minute they could get around in chairs they were out trying to get into trouble. They scared the heck out of me. Finally the rehab people gave me a private room."

"That was considerate."

"Yeah. After two of those jerks tried to attack me in the day room. The rehab was just scared of being sued."

"It doesn't sound much like the movies."

She held out her glass for a refill. "The worst part was the way the staff treated you. 'Hey, it's no big deal, you're alive, and heck, you're only a T-11. What are you complaining about?' "

"I guess that's part of the therapy. That attitude."

She looked at the dark red wine in her glass. "Yeah. Can we talk about something else?"

"We were talking about how you got to Philadelphia from Pittsburgh."

"I didn't start out for this. I wanted a small town, really. But the firm in Upper Darby made me a good offer, and I found myself liking it."

"How long have you lived in Center City?"

"Just a year. I tried commuting in, but it didn't work out. Everything takes longer when you're disabled, and I couldn't afford the time."

"You still have to go out to Upper Darby a couple of times a week?"

"I don't mind. People think of it as a dump. Well, some of it is, but there are still some good sections. Some old Italian and Polish and Greek neighborhoods where the same families have lived in the same houses for two and three generations. It reminds me a little of Pittsburgh. I like dealing with the people."

"Were you there on Friday?"

"You never quit, do you?"

"Just a question."

"Yes," she said, with formality in her voice. "I was in our Upper Darby office all morning and part of the afternoon. I got back downtown around two."

"Was Emily still there?"

"Uh-huh."

"Flora?"

"I—don't remember."

Our dinners arrived, and while the plates were being set out, I thought of how to phrase my next question. "You seem to go out of your way to protect him."

"What am I protecting him from?" She saw the startled look on my face. "I mean, what are you doing here?"

"Well, investigating what happened to Emily."

"Anything else?"

"I've found it enough of a job to keep me busy so far."

"That's what police are for."

"Not always. Why are you asking?"

She played with the ends of her hair. "I don't know that I should trust you with this."

"You're not going to know unless you try."

"Keep this quiet, okay?"

"All right."

"Mike and I think you're here to get the dirt on us."

"It doesn't require a private detective to get dirt on Mike. That's not what I'm here for."

"Are you sure about that?"

"Look, I remember being an associate. There can be a lot

of us-against-them. But I'll tell you what I've heard, straight up. They like you, you're a hard worker, and they feel you'll develop just fine with some more experience."

"What about Mike?"

"I haven't even bothered to ask about him, that way. But they spend a lot of time defending him to me." I chose my words carefully. "They like having him inside the firm and not as a competitor."

She drained her glass and held it out to me. "Mike was out all day Friday. Business in New Jersey, he said. He called in once, in the late afternoon."

"He called for you?" I asked.

"Yeah."

"What did he want?"

"Just checking in, seeing if he'd been missed."

"Had he ever done that before?"

"If I can trust you, yes, a lot. He spends a lot of time out of the office, and most of it's just personal business, or goofing off. I've told him he's going to get into trouble if he's not careful."

"Where was he Friday?"

"Well, I assume New Jersey, but he really didn't say."

"Had Emily left by then?" I asked.

"I don't know. Really."

"But he could have checked that out by asking the receptionist," I pointed out.

"Why would he care if she went home early? She didn't spy on him."

"I wasn't suggesting *she* cared about *his* movements. Maybe he cared about hers."

She looked down at her plate. "Maybe. But she wasn't killed till late Monday. What difference does it make where she was Friday?"

"Well, maybe it doesn't. But if I knew exactly why she was killed, I bet I could answer that."

I asked her if she wanted coffee, but when she checked her watch she said she had to go.

The last leg of our journey was a breeze compared to what had gone before. The rain had stopped, and she lived only a few blocks away. We even found a parking space on her block.

"David, could you see me inside, please? I'm expecting someone."

It had never occurred to me to let a young woman go up to her door alone in the middle of the night in Philadelphia, even if she had two good legs. "Sure."

I wheeled her over the brick sidewalk, jarring both of us, until we reached her door. I took her up a long concrete ramp on the alley side. She fished out her keys, opened the door, and I took her inside.

The apartment was dark, and I put on some lights for her while she played back her messages off an answering machine in the kitchen. I stood near the door and waited patiently for her to finish so I could say good night. It was warm with my coat on, but the minute I took it off it would be time to put it back on again.

The living room was pleasant enough, with a high ceiling and a white carpet, but it was a cold, disquieting space. Partly it was the carpet—it was a thin, industrial grade, hard as a rock, with no pile at all. For a moment I wondered why anyone would have so uncomfortable a carpet. Then I realized how a wheelchair would sink in if the carpet had any pile. The room was bare of any furniture except for a sofa in the center and a built-in desk, with no chair, in one corner. I wandered over to her desk. It was wide and deep; even though it was half covered with computer equipment, there was plenty of space left over. Her programs were piled high on both sides and I glanced at the titles: *WordWriter PC, Symphony, Sincalc, Desktop Publisher, Drafix*, and a dozen other titles I didn't recognize.

The sofa faced a fireplace. Over the mantel was a large framed color photograph of a blonde teenage girl skiing down an impossibly steep slope. The sun was bright, and she was kicking up sparkled plumes of snow. I sat down on the sofa and waited.

She wheeled over to me and checked her watch again. "David, I have a problem."

"Something I can help with?"

"This is kind of personal. It's not the kind of thing for everybody. I hardly know you, and I won't think ill of you if you say no."

"Try me."

"My attendant hasn't shown up, and there's no message from her on the machine. I think something must have come up."

"Do you need me to get something for you?"

"It's—uh—more than that. I need some personal care at bedtime. I know it's an imposition, but—"

"If I don't do it, who will?"

"Well, nobody. They're not going to be able to find a substitute at this time of night."

"Then let's get going. What do I do?"

"Thanks. The first thing is—I have to go to the bathroom. I had half a bottle of wine and some water and I'm pretty sure I need to go."

"You don't know?"

"You only know for sure when it's too late, believe me."

She wheeled herself into the bathroom, backed up to the commode, and locked the wheels. "I'm going to raise myself up on the transfer rails. I need you to pull off everything below my waist."

She grasped the side rails, one with each hand, and smoothly lifted herself until she was well clear of the chair. I untied her shoes and slipped them off. Then I took off her skirt, half slip, and something that looked like diapers for adults. The diapers were held on with side tabs, and it took me a minute to find them. I doubted that I had the upper-body strength to hold the position she was in for more than a few seconds, but she waited patiently for me to finish without any show of effort.

"Am I dry?"

"Yes. Except for a couple of drops."

"Then we're just in time. That's my three-minute warning. Pull up my shirttail when I sit down; I'd hate to go all over that."

She sat herself down lightly on the toilet seat; it occurred to me that she had to do everything with her lower body carefully, since she could hurt herself and not know it. I'd never thought before that pain had a real use.

I heard the sound of splashing from the commode. "Lord, it's loud," I said.

"And it'll go on for a while. When you only pee a few times a day you pee a lot." She blushed. "You probably won't believe this but I'm basically really shy. If someone had told me five years ago I'd let a man see me on the toilet I wouldn't have believed it. Before the accident, I used to lock the bathroom door even with just my three brothers in the house."

"Would you like to be left alone?"

"No, I need some more help, if you're game."

"I used to help my mother when she was sick. Go on."

"Put my things on the wheelchair and get it out of here."

I had some trouble with the chair until I realized that the wheels were still locked. She watched me with amusement while I wrestled it out of the bathroom and back into the living room.

"I assume you need your bed turned down?"

"If you could, please."

Her bedroom had the same odd disproportions as the rest of the apartment—the doors too wide, the dressers and mirrors at waist level, and the bed itself not more than eighteen inches off the floor. As I turned down the covers I saw a triangular metal handgrip suspended from the ceiling by a sturdy chain. To help her transfer on and off the bed, I guessed.

When I returned to the bathroom she had just taken off her blouse. Underneath she was wearing a lacy white camisole. "You want me to run a bath for you?"

"People like me take showers. If you think about it, there's a hell of a lot of transfer problems getting in and out of a tub."

"I guess I hadn't considered. So do you want to take a shower?"

She didn't answer right away, and then she looked at me sharply. "Why are you doing this?"

"Well, because you asked."

"Because you feel sorry for me?"

"Don't give me that, Susan."

"Don't give you what?"

"You want me to tell you I don't feel sorry for you. Well, I do. I know that's probably not the politically correct thing to say anymore. I suppose I ought to ignore it or treat it like some interesting quirk, like having red hair or being left-handed. You've got a lot of guts and I admire how far you've come, but I can't look at you and not think how much this fucks up your life."

I took hold of both her hands. "Susan, look at me. I'm not going to kid you. When I look at you I see a bright, pretty girl with her life ahead of her and only half a body to live it with. And I'm sorry it happened to you. Is that so bad?"

"So you'd wish it on somebody else?"

"I wouldn't wish it on anybody."

"But accidents happen, right? So if it's not me, then who?"

"You're not making sense. There's no quota. It didn't have to happen to anyone."

She looked down at our hands together, without speaking. I had no sense of what she was thinking. "Well, I appreciate your honesty. Ready to help with that shower?"

"If you still want me to."

"Yeah. More than ever." She looked up. "I'm sorry for being such a jerk. I'm a little nervous."

"Don't worry about a thing."

"In the corner, behind the door, is a collapsible chair with a blue plastic seat with a hole in the bottom. Bring it over so I can transfer to it."

I unfolded it and wheeled it over to the commode. She pulled herself up on the rails and began the slow process of turning herself around to get into the chair.

"Want me to help?"

"No, I like to do myself what I can."

"This thing seems pretty flimsy compared to your other chairs."

"It is. You don't take this one out on gravel roads. All it's meant for is showers and—well, never mind."

She sat down in the blue chair and I wheeled her to the edge of the shower stall, which was separated from the rest of the room by a pair of large sliding glass doors that ran from the floor nearly to the ceiling. It looked like a conventional shower, except that it was much larger, the controls were lower, and the shower head was mounted at the end of a long, jointed metal hose.

"Wait a minute, Dave. Aren't you forgetting something?"

"Shall I turn the water on first?"

She sighed. "Well, yes, but you've still got your clothes on and I'm still partly dressed. Help me off with this thing." She pointed to her camisole. "With no sleeves, it's hard to get a grip. Take it from the bottom so you don't stretch it out." She leaned forward and raised her arms for me. I put my hands on her waist and took hold of the hem. It was sheer cotton, with delicate lace embroidery at the top and bottom.

"Be careful with it."

"Sure. It's very pretty." I pulled it to the level of her breasts, then worked it up her back to her shoulder blades.

"Quite a contrast to my diapers, isn't it?"

"I was thinking that but I wasn't going to say it."

"So much for your honesty."

"I'm honest. Just using some discretion." I lifted it in front and pulled it free.

"Now get your clothes off. If you're going to help, you're going to get as wet as me."

I went into her bedroom and took off my clothes. I looked

around for a chair to lay them on, then smiled at myself. Of course there wouldn't be a chair. I put them on the floor and went back to the bathroom. She was facing away from me, toward the shower. When I stepped in front of her and turned on the water, I felt a pinch. "Nice ass, except for the scars," she said.

"Wait till you see the front. I used to dispose of Viet Cong land mines by stepping on them."

"Wow. How often did you do that?"

"Just once."

Getting her over the door railings was easy, after my practice with the heavy chair outside. The water ran down her head, and, as she'd promised, splashed all over me, too. "Here," she said, handing me the shower head, "do me all over. And yourself, too."

I watched the water run down her face, down her breasts, and accumulate in a little puddle in her lap. The water was running hot, and soon her skin took on a healthy pink tinge.

"Where's the shampoo?" I asked.

"Behind you, on the floor." I squeezed some into my palm and began working it into her scalp. She put her head back and closed her eyes. "Oh, that feels good."

At last I turned off the water, found some towels, and dried us both off. When I was done I wrapped one of the towels around my middle.

"What are you wearing that for?" She had a towel wrapped around her hair.

"I guess I'm just an old-fashioned guy."

"Well, take me into the bedroom and help me transfer."

I was right about the handhold; she had me position her chair underneath it, then she lifted herself up with both hands and lowered herself onto the bed.

"Anything else?"

"Yes. There should be a bottle of white wine in the refrigerator. Bring it over, and a couple of wine glasses."

It was more than just white wine. I didn't know much about

wines, but I recognized a good Moselle when I saw one.

"Here you go, and uncorked, too. Anything else?"

"Light those candles over there and turn out the lights."

"Any matches?"

"By the candles."

"Aren't you worried about fire? How you'd get out?"

"Not from the candles. Besides, they're in holders."

"Then what about the fireplace in the other room?"

"It's fake. Gas logs. I'd love a real one, but it's too dangerous."

"The picture over the mantel, who is that?"

"Me. The winter before the accident."

"Oh."

The candles lit easily and began to fill the room with a gentle spicy smell. I turned out the light and watched the patterns of candlelight on the ceiling.

"Anything else?"

She stretched lazily with the upper half of her body. "No, that's it." She threw aside the towel that had been covering her head and lay back on the pillow.

"Then I can go?"

For just an instant she was too surprised to say anything, then she laughed and threw a pillow at me.

Afterward, I played with the ends of her hair. "I have a small confession to make," I said.

"I'm listening."

"Don't be insulted, but when I first met you I wasn't sure you were a lawyer."

"What made you think that?"

"The way you dressed. Big earrings, braless, and that screaming yellow blouse."

"You can see why I don't wear a bra, how much trouble it would be."

"I didn't then." I leaned back on the pillow.

She looked at the ceiling as she spoke. "Um, as long as

we're on the subject of the office, there's something I should tell you."

"Go ahead."

"It's something I didn't feel comfortable telling you the other day when you asked."

"Uh-huh."

"But first I need to know, you're really working on Emily's case, right? You're not here about anything else?"

"I thought we'd covered that already."

"Is what I say confidential? I mean, you can use it, but I don't want it used against me that I helped."

"I'll do my best."

"All right, then. In the last three or four months there have been a lot of closed-door meetings between Mr. Palmer and Mr. Huyett. Neither Mr. DeAndrea or Mr. Richardson are ever there. The meetings are sometimes pretty long, and they always have their calls held."

"You have any idea what the meetings are about?"

"I'm not stupid."

"No, but maybe I am. Help me."

"Something to do with the partnership. Either they want the older partners out, or at least they want to replace Mr. Richardson as managing partner. Or maybe they want to merge with another firm and they think the oldest people will fight it. Something like that."

"Are you sure about any of this?"

"No, but I don't think they're planning the next firm picnic."

I hoped she was wrong. Had things in my firm come to this? Maybe I'd gotten out when the getting was good. "Well, thanks for letting me know. I appreciate it."

"Is what we said private?"

"Oh, no problem. I don't even need to say that I heard it from a particular person—just that it's my sense of things."

"Thanks." She put her cheek against my shoulder and I felt her body relaxing.

I thought about what she'd said, and the fact she hadn't shared what she knew with DeAndrea or Richardson. There was no reason to resent her for wanting to stay clear of the storm. She wasn't a partner, just an employee, and a fairly recent one at that. The men at the top of the firm had no particular claim to her loyalty. I felt very alone.

She touched the scars on my belly. "Tell me about the war."

"What about it?"

"Is this what you think about the most? When you got hurt?"

"Hell, that land mine was my ticket home. Once I realized I wasn't going to die I felt great."

"Didn't it hurt?"

"It hurt like crazy but I didn't mind. It's hard to explain. There was just so much relief in getting out of combat it was hard to think about anything else."

"So what do you think about?"

"I used to have dreams about a patrol I was on, but they've stopped now."

She was persistent. "There have to be other things that you can't get out of your mind. I know I have them—about how I used to move, and play sports, and dance."

I took a while to answer. She was right—dozens of memories floated just below the surface, waiting for their chance. "Well, there was the replacement who was burned."

"What was his name?"

"I never knew. I was just a PFC then, and he was in another squad. He'd only arrived the day before. He was carrying flares when a mortar round landed nearby and set them off. He was burned all over. At the casualty clearing station he didn't make triage—they said he was going to die anyway, so they just shot him full of dope and gave him a quiet room. I was in there checking on a friend when he saw me and recognized me as being from his company. The corpsman asked me if I'd sit with him.

"His mind was perfectly clear, and he knew what was going to happen. At first he talked about himself—he was only nineteen, so it was mainly about his family. Then, when he started to slip, he asked me to talk. I told him about myself, I talked about baseball and football, the whores in Da Nang, anything I could think of except the war. I was with him for six hours straight. Then I told him I had to get some chow, that I'd be right back. He—asked me not to go, that he wouldn't take much longer, he even begged me to stay. I went anyway. When I got back he was dead."

"You must have been with other dying men. Why does he stick with you?"

"Because I was supposed to be there for him and he died alone."

"You spent all that time with him."

I tried again. "But I wasn't there at the end, when he needed me most. It doesn't count."

"I've got news for you. We all die alone. And live alone, too." For a while neither of us said anything. Then she leaned close to me. "I've got a confession of my own," she whispered.

"What's that?"

"I wasn't expecting an attendant. There isn't one."

"You could have done everything yourself."

"It was a way to break the ice."

"So you are a little old-fashioned, after all."

"How do you mean?"

"Well, the nineties woman is just supposed to flat-out proposition the man if she's interested."

"Does that happen to you much?"

"Never," I said. "But a lot of people talk like it's supposed to."

There was a pause before she spoke again. "You know, I was practically a virgin before my accident."

"You want to tell me something?"

She looked down at herself in a way that made me think that she didn't think of the lower half of her body as belonging to her anymore. It was someone else's, and she didn't like the other person very much. "When I look back I feel like a jerk.

I used to guard it like it was the crown jewels, and now it just sits there and I'm no damned good to anybody."

"Susan, that's not true. I've got no complaints about what we did. None at all."

"I'm twenty-seven years old and the only part of sex I'll ever be able to enjoy is the things I used to do in the back of a car when I was fifteen."

"You do them damn well. A lot better than when you were fifteen, I'm sure."

She wasn't listening. "Why to I have to *adapt* and *make the best of it*? I want to know what the hell I ever did that was so bad to deserve this." She turned away from me and started to cry. I put my hand on her shoulder but she shook me away. Her back arched away from me, and I realized she was trying to pull herself into the fetal position but couldn't.

It took a long time for her crying to stop, but when it did, it was sudden. She wiped her eyes on the sheet and turned to me, perfectly composed.

"Thank you for a lovely evening, David, but if you don't mind I prefer to sleep alone."

"This is a bad note to leave on."

"It's not you, it's me."

"Still . . ."

She took a breath. "There's nothing that you can say or do that's going to change anything. You might as well go. Please."

I dressed. When I was ready to go I leaned over to kiss her good night. But she was already asleep, or at least pretending.

Chapter Twelve

Wednesday, 11:00 P.M.

It was a depressing drive home. Vince was going into a rehab program, Emily, who'd called me for help, had died before I could meet with her, and Susan was . . . I wasn't sure what she was. All that was certain was my own inability to make a difference for the people who needed help.

I poured myself a short bourbon and walked around my apartment. I knew that if I didn't find myself some company the bourbon would turn into two or three or four, so I called Kate.

"How are you doing tonight?" I asked.

"That damned flu has got me down again. But I'm feeling better now. You don't sound too good, though."

"I'm okay. I just wanted to talk."

"Don't make me drag it out of you, David. Something's wrong."

"You get a lot out of a dozen words."

"That's changing the subject. Are you having the dream about the war again?"

"No, not since last month."

"It's not work, so what is it?"

"What makes you think it's not work?"

"You don't let your cases bother you that much. And even if it was work, you wouldn't dance around about it."

I had to laugh. "Remember that quote I gave you from Lawrence Durrell, 'Laugh until it hurts, and hurt until you laugh'?"

"I liked that."

"Well, okay. Sure you want to hear it?"

"Yes."

"I'm depressed because I spent a wonderful evening in bed with a pretty blonde who's almost young enough to be your daughter."

"Nice breasts?" Kate was the skinniest woman I'd ever been with. Except for a slight curve to her ass, she was nothing but straight lines.

"Yes, as a matter of fact."

"Poor baby."

"I'm getting too old for this sort of thing."

"I refuse to believe you couldn't function."

"I functioned just fine. It's just that I didn't respect myself afterward."

It was her turn to laugh. "Taking advantage of a young girl?"

"Hardly. She's closer to thirty than twenty, and she's been through more hard knocks than either one of us. It was Susan Minnik, the girl who's paralyzed."

"Oh. Then what was the problem?"

"I was alone. When I was in bed with her."

I heard an intake of breath. "Why are you telling me this?"

"Because when I was with you I wasn't alone. As a matter of fact, I don't feel alone right now."

"I'm glad to hear that. Even if you did call to tell me you were sleeping with another woman."

"Well, I assume you're sleeping with your husband."

"Oh, do you?"

"Don't be cute. Does he know about us?"

"No, but he knew the point of my vacation was to give me

some time alone to do what I wanted. He knew it might happen."

"I hope I'm not messing anything up."

"We have our problems now and we had our problems before I met you."

"I'm not sure you're answering my question."

"I'm not sure I am, either."

"I miss you."

The line was quiet for a while after that. Finally, she said, "I'm not going to give myself the luxury of wallowing in it."

"That's not the word I would have picked."

"When you've been married for twenty-five years and have two grown children, there's no other word to describe your fantasies about another man. . . . It's an indulgence."

"Your mother would have called it a sin, right?"

"And Grandmother would have called it a mortal sin. But I'm glad you called anyway."

"You know what I was just thinking about?"

"What's that?"

"Our last day together."

"It's nice to fantasize. It helps make real life bearable."

"Is that what I am?"

"Not when we were together. But now, well, what else can you be?"

"Are you sure you're not Jewish instead of Irish?"

"Quite sure."

"Well, you always answer a question with a question."

"Only when the answers are important. And I'd just as soon not talk about it anymore, if you don't mind."

"Okay," I said.

"Well, I don't have much choice, do I? All I've got is one end of this telephone, and you've got this woman who performs all these interesting sexual practices."

"Not as well as you."

"More enthusiastically, at least. This girl has almost twenty years on me."

"You're jealous."

"And ashamed of it. I'm married, we live a thousand miles apart, we had one long weekend together, there's no prospect I'll ever see you again—and I'm stupid enough to put energy into worrying about the other women in your life." She laughed. The sound was funny and not funny at the same time. "It's so ridiculous I can't think of a strong enough word to describe it."

"You know, I feel better getting a raft of shit from you than I would if I'd stayed for an encore with Susan."

"My God," she said slowly. "You said the only thing that could have made me feel better about this. Even though it's a lie."

"I wasn't kidding."

"It couldn't have been that bad."

"It was fine. But it was cold. I only met this girl yesterday."

"Do you think she took you to bed because of the case? To gain your confidence?"

"If she did, she sure went about it in a funny way. It wasn't a performance for my benefit. There were a lot of raw emotions hanging out, about how she feels about being paralyzed, and she didn't try to hide them. And besides, she didn't need to do that. She'd already given me some inside information on the firm."

"Tell me about it."

"I don't know what to think of it yet. But you know how the firm is set up—two partners in their late fifties, two in their early forties, and a couple of associates?"

"Yes?"

"The two junior partners have been having a lot of closed-door meetings. The two senior partners are never invited."

"What does it mean?"

"It could be anything from a breakup to a surprise birthday party. But maybe Emily stumbled into something she shouldn't have known."

"Come on, Dave. People don't commit murder over something like that."

"Somebody committed murder, at least I think they did. And I haven't found anything to suggest there could have been a reason not connected with her job."

"You're reduced to using double negatives to defend your logic," she pointed out.

"Well, it's all I've got."

Somehow, I was feeling better by the time we hung up.

Chapter Thirteen

Wednesday, Midnight

There was one more call to be made before I could call it a night. It was another long-distance call, but this time the line crackled and buzzed in between rings.

"Hello?" It was a woman, with a husky voice.

"Myrtle Voss, please."

"That's me."

"My name is Dave Garrett. I'm calling from Philadelphia, about your sister."

"Are you the man who lost his job?"

In the last two years I'd learned to answer to just about anything. "Yes, that's me."

"Emily told me all about it, God rest her soul." Her voice was quick and confused, not quite stopping between words.

"Your sister is the reason I'm calling. I'm very sorry to have to trouble you at a time like this."

"Well, I've just been on the phone all day and there's so much to do, you know."

"If your sister talked about me she might have told you I'm a private investigator now. I've been hired to look into what happened."

"I see. I'll help you in any way I can."

"Thank you. Was—"

"Is the gas company trying to get out of it?"

"The gas company?"

"You have to watch them like a hawk, you know. Gas is much more dangerous than they let you know, believe me."

"Her death wasn't a gas explosion, ma'am."

"Well, that's what they want you to think, but I'm sure a bright young man like you can get to the bottom of it."

I began to realize why Emily had put a continent between herself and her sister. "Well, while we're looking into that I have a few questions. Were you and your sister close?"

"Well, until about five years ago, close as close could be."

"What happened then?"

That was a mistake, and my punishment was a seemingly endless story about how Myrtle had become interested in a mildly nutty but harmless cult built around yoga, vegetarianism, and frequent contributions to a post office box flashed at the bottom of a TV screen. The kind of thing you'd get if you put Shirley MacLaine, Richard Simmons, and L. Ron Hubbard into a blender and hit PUREE. Emily had objected strongly, especially to Myrtle's financial contributions. I had the distinct feeling she was trying to convert me, or at least hit me up for fifty bucks. Finally I was able to break in. "Did the two of you break contact over this?"

"Oh, no; she still visited me once a year."

"Did you visit back here?"

"Oh, goodness, no—it's too crowded and dirty; and besides, the declination to magnetic north is so different. From where I was raised, I mean."

"I couldn't agree more. When did you see her last?"

"She came out every year at Thanksgiving and stayed till the fifth of December. Every year."

"Is there any other family?"

"No, there was just us girls after Daddy died, and that was fifteen years ago."

"Was she ever married?"

"No. She didn't have time for that. Too busy with her career."

"Was there anyone she spoke of back here? I mean, someone who was personally important to her?"

"Oh, she had a boyfriend, but she never said much about him."

"Just one?"

"I think so. She'd mention she'd been some fancy place for dinner, or on a weekend somewhere, and you could tell she hadn't been alone."

"No name?"

"No. I was curious, but she never would say."

I decided to let it drop. "Did she talk about anyone other than the firm? Either people she liked or disliked? Enemies?"

"No, nothing like that."

"I knew your sister for years, and I never heard her talk about anything but work. I liked her, but I don't think I ever knew her well."

"I blame that on Daddy. We girls were both raised that way."

"How do you mean?"

"He was always after us, especially after Mommy died, that someday we'd be rich and people would be after us for our money. He tried to scare us off of people, if you ask me."

"What do you mean about being rich?"

"Daddy had this lemon grove. Developers wanted it. He said no, he liked farming. He was a man of the soil, in tune with the harmonies—"

"But finally he sold?"

"He had to. Taxes got way too high."

"I wouldn't normally ask a question like this, but just how much did Emily have when she died?"

The line was quiet, and I thought she might be shocked at the question, or maybe that she'd just put the phone down. I was about to say something when she spoke again. "Well,

Daddy invested real good for both of us, kept his hands on it
till he died. We got equal shares then. If she didn't lost none,
she had about two million, I figure."

It was my turn to be silent. "She could have lived off the
interest," I said. "How come she worked?"

"Well, we didn't get our money till Daddy died and the trust
ran out. That was only eight years ago. We talked about it, but
she was too used to working, I guess."

"Do you know who she left it to?"

"We did wills when Daddy died, leaving everything to each
other."

"Could she have done a new will?"

She sharpened up fast. "You have to notify people that it's
changed?"

"No."

"Well, she could of, I suppose." Then her voice trailed off.
She didn't like thinking about it. For that matter, neither did I.
Two million dollars was a lot of money.

Chapter Fourteen

Thursday, 8:00 A.M.

When I got to my temporary office, Tom Richardson was there, waiting for me in the chair in front of the desk. He looked more tired than ever.

"You've been a hard man to find, Dave."

"So have you."

"This business with Emily . . . it's meant a lot of extra work. I'm sorry I haven't been more available."

"Have you hired Flora's cousin?"

"I brought it up with Jerry but we couldn't come to a decision. Her salary request is pretty high. How's the case coming?"

"Some progress. Nothing definite."

"Well, fill me in on what you've found."

"I've been over the fire scene. The police and the fire marshal are ready to let the thing slide as an accident. Your call got them to be polite, but it didn't change their thinking."

"Oh?"

"Tom, there's no evidence that they're not right. Everything fits, at least as far as the physical evidence."

"Except Emily wasn't that sort of person."

"Well, I've been coming up with some surprises in that department."

"Oh?"

"Nothing really central to the case. Just personal things."

"Go on."

I didn't know whether to go on or not. Emily was dead, but her fantasies were still her own business.

"I'm sure it has no relevance, Tom."

"No, I want to hear it. I'm the client, after all."

I hesitated, then I opened the desk drawer and tossed the diary across to him. The broken flap hung open and made a tinny metal-on-metal screech as it slid across the desktop.

He made no move to pick it up. He just sat there, looking at it. "David, the catch is broken. Have you read it?"

"Sure."

I was watching his face, but I missed it. Somewhere in the time I was looking his face went from his usual orange-pink to dead white. It happened so quickly that there was never a moment of transition. He slid back down in the chair and just sat there.

"Oh, my God," I said. "I had no idea."

He cleared his throat, but it was a while before he said anything. "Since Katherine died, five years ago. Up till then our relations were always completely . . . correct."

And for five years he'd been Mister Tawny Shoulders. "Who else knew?"

"No one at all. We both thought it would be better that way. She was afraid she would lose respect with the rest of the staff."

"If they'd known, I think she would have been liked a hell of a lot more."

"But not respected," he said stiffly. "That was important to her."

"The picture you showed me? The sidewalk café?"

"I took it. We were in Paris two years ago." He dropped his voice. "I trust this matter goes no further."

"You're asking a lot."

"What are you talking about?"

"First, you're assuming I'm going to continue with the case at all."

"Why shouldn't you?"

"What do you do when you find out your client has lied to you?"

"I never lied. I simply didn't disclose some personal things."

"Bullshit. I asked you what you knew about her personal life and you said, very little. Come on, you saw each other all the time, didn't you?"

"Oh, ah . . . yes, we did."

"And I bet you saw her *after* the last time you already told me about; I bet you saw her Friday evening or Saturday. Or maybe even Monday."

"I went by Friday evening to look in on her. I didn't spend the night at her place often. When we wanted to be together all night, it was at my place in Narberth."

"So what happened?"

"She'd been to the doctor and he told her she had the flu. He said to take it easy and sleep it off. We had a glass of wine and I left. That would have been about seven, seven-thirty."

"How was she doing?"

"Except for being sick there were no problems. She was in good spirits, generally. I warned her in no uncertain terms to follow the doctor's advice and not come in the office on Saturday. She said that would be all right, because she'd brought her work home anyway. She had a single glass of wine with me and put the bottle back in the refrigerator. I don't think she even finished hers."

"You know how stupid it is for a client to lie to his lawyer?"

"Does this mean you'll be staying on?"

"I haven't decided. But I can't promise to forget about what I know."

"It can't do anyone any good now."

"Are you so sure? If it was an accident, I'm wasting my time anyway. But if there is a murder underneath somewhere, how can you say that it doesn't figure in? Maybe it doesn't, maybe it does."

"David, how could it possibly?"

"How do I know? When you're dealing in possibilities it's hard to exclude anything." I paused, trying to think how to phrase my words. "Maybe she had another lover. Or maybe someone knew about the two of you and was jealous."

"Another lover? Besides me?"

"How can I be sure there wasn't one? Especially when I can't get the truth."

He bit his lip, but his voice stayed even. "Very well. Do what you have to do."

"Now think carefully; even if you don't think they really knew, who could have known? Or suspected?"

"We worked too hard at being discreet. I used to joke with her that it was worse than being seventeen. We seldom went out to dinner, and when we did, we'd go over to Cherry Hill or over to upper Bucks."

"Ever see anyone you knew?"

"Never."

"Did your children know? See her at Christmas or anything?"

"They're all grown with lives of their own. The holidays I spent with them, I didn't spend with her. When we were going to spend a holiday together, we'd go to New York or down to the islands. Nothing ever in the city."

"How about the other tenants in her building?"

"Once in a while I'd see someone while I was coming in or out, but I was never introduced to any of them. We both wanted it that way."

"Did you ever talk about getting married?"

He took his time about answering. When he did his voice was a little wistful. "No, I don't think either of us wanted anything like that. We played our little games about it, of course. We're both from the old school, that a gentleman should marry the lady unless there was some impediment, but no, it never came to that."

"Why not?"

"I've given that some thought." He paused. "More, in the last couple of days. You know what I think it was? People can forget a great deal in bed. But after thirty years, when we found ourselves there, we could never forget who was the boss and who was the employee."

"I want to know why you hired me, Tom, and not someone else. Was it personal or professional?"

"Well, it's like things were with Emily. A little of both."

I sighed, thinking of what Kate had said. I liked Tom, I respected him, I felt for him, but I didn't entirely trust him anymore. At least not in this; at least not until I knew for sure who the killer was. "I think you've been straight with me. I'm going to stay on the case, but you have to let me do it my way."

"All right. Thank you."

"And there's something else I've uncovered. Or maybe not."

"Go on."

"How has Jerry Huyett worked out as a partner?"

"Excellent. Very hardworking, brings in more than his share of the clients, helps with a lot of the management duties. I've never formalized it, but he's the assistant managing partner."

"I've heard that he's been calling a lot of meetings with Palmer. But not you or Vince."

"To discuss what?"

"I don't know, but the meetings have been long."

"Oh?" he said vaguely.

I let it hang there for a long while, hoping he would say something more. "And evidently it's true that you've never been invited," I added at last.

"Well, there are lots of meetings around here. I don't expect to be involved in all of them."

I just sat there, letting him go. "And anyway," he continued, holding a conversation with himself, "that's why I gave him some responsibility, so he'd do things on his own."

"Tom—"

His voice turned sharp. "What do you want me to do?"

"Don't give me that, Tom. I'm just the messenger. If there's something going on behind your back, you can make it your business, or not."

"You never liked Jerry, did you?"

I put up my hands in a gesture of helplessness. "Whatever you want. It all may be about nothing. Anyway, it's not my firm anymore."

He said nothing, and I was happy to let it drop. He mumbled some good-byes and headed down the hall.

I tossed the diary back into the desk drawer and locked it away, doubly sorry I'd ever seen it. When was something going to happen in this case that would bring me something besides aggravation?

I took out a yellow legal pad and a pencil. My ex-wife once told me that lawyers couldn't think without a yellow pad, and she was right. I wrote down what little I had.

PARTNERS

1. <u>Tom Richardson</u>—having affair with E. No motive, if truthful about affair. Was she asking for marriage? No alibi. Jealousy killing? If so, who?

2. <u>Vince DeAndrea</u>—blackout alcoholic prone to violence. Motive in keeping her from getting med info? What could be so bad? That's the point, isn't it? Maybe it was so bad it would put his career on the line. No alibi.

3. <u>Roger Palmer</u>—no alibi, no motive. Hostile to everyone in firm except Huyett. Planning to split off with him? Did E get wind? So what? Not a good enough reason.

4. <u>Jerry Huyett</u>—not fully interviewed as yet. Alibi un-

known. Is he leading move to break up firm/put out senior partners? If so, is E's death coincidence?

ASSOCIATES

5. <u>Susan Minnik</u>—as associate, has little access to financial information. Has alibi, but means nothing; she couldn't have handled killing herself anyway. Has a good deal for herself with firm re getting med bills paid.

6. <u>Mike Flora</u>—possible NJ mob connections, possibly low level. Taking advantage of E's death to move own people in. Alibi unknown. Motive? Seems firm is bending over backward for him already. Is firm helping him *hide* something, too?

I looked carefully at my list when it was done. After two days' work I had a total of six names, no good alibis, and thirteen question marks. Not only wasn't I nearing the end, it wasn't even much of a start.

Chapter Fifteen

Thursday, 9:00 A.M.

Ron Wolfe opened my door, stuck his head inside, and knocked on the wall. He was smiling broadly. Actually, it was closer to a smirk, but after all, he was an accountant. "I've got something for you."

"That's the first good news of the day and I'm sore in need."

He sat down. "Don't get too excited. I said I had something, not everything."

I leaned back in my chair. "Do I look like I'm picky?"

"I found out how they got the money out of the firm. It was a one-write check. As far as I can tell, it was written and presented on Friday."

"By one-write, you mean the funny money checks."

"Right. It's a logical way to do it, too. Anything else requires Emily's signature and the use of the check-writing machine."

"Do you have the check?"

"No, it's at Mellon. It was presented after the last statement period. But they're sending over a photocopy by messenger before noon."

"Good job, Ron. Who's the payee?"

His smile started to fade. "That's the problem. Or one of

the problems. I'm sure it's some kind of dummy. The check—which, by the way, is written for exactly the amount of the total of the cash deposits, a hundred nineteen and change—was payable to something called Good Start Investments. Good Start deposited it in Frankford Savings and Loan on Friday."

"Good Start?" I asked.

"Never heard of them," he said. "I'll get on it as quick as I can."

"What about the S & L?"

"It's legitimate. An old-fashioned neighborhood operation, just local branches."

"You say it was deposited on Friday. What's the date on it?"

"Friday, but that doesn't mean it was made out then."

"What file is the check drawn on?"

"No file at all; just on the firm's account."

"I didn't think you could do that."

"From the firm's point of view, you shouldn't, but the bank doesn't care. All the bank wants to know is if it's covered, either by funds in the firm's account or by the line of credit. The firm needs to know what file is involved so it'll know where to debit it. But whoever cut the check didn't care about that."

"Not that I think that it's going to help too much, but who signed it?" I asked.

His smile faded away completely. "Mellon Operations didn't know. We'll find out when it gets here."

"When I worked here, the blank funny money checks were kept in Emily's office."

"They still are. On top of the filing cabinets behind her desk."

"They still have a signout system?"

"Yes. You write down the number of the check you're taking on a yellow note pad. At least you're supposed to. Only partners have authority to sign the checks."

"I think I know why she was killed," I said. "Emily saw

somebody take a funny money check Friday morning. Or Thursday."

"But she called you on Friday," he pointed out. "She wouldn't have done that just because of a blank check, not knowing anything else. Mellon didn't know anything until the next Tuesday, after she was already dead, when it was presented by Frankford."

"What could have made Emily suspicious just because the check was missing, before it was filled out?" I was talking to myself as much as to Ron.

"I don't know. Lawyers take out those checks all the time. That's what they're for."

"It was either something about the person who took it or something about the way they took it," I said.

"What does that mean?"

"Just thinking out loud, Ron. This is going to have to gel a while. But listen, you're doing great work so far. Let me know as soon as the check gets here. In the meantime, go over the list of who took funny money checks in the last month, and the amounts, if you can get them. Look for any kind of pattern." He nodded as if he knew what I meant. I wished *I* knew. I patted him on the shoulder as I went out the door.

Susan was in her office. She looked up when I came in, and put down her pencil when I shut the door behind me.

"Good morning, Susan."

She swallowed. "David."

"I need a favor, if you've got a little time."

"Can we . . . talk about something first?" Her voice was so small I had to strain to hear her.

"Okay."

"About last night?"

It wasn't at the top of my agenda, but it was obviously at the top of hers. "Yes?"

"I just wanted to say I'm sorry."

"There's nothing to be sorry for."

She picked up her pencil and stared at it. "I was a jerk. I played yo-yo with you. I thought I wanted a nice little uncomplicated thing and then I blubbered all over the place."

"You don't need to say this."

"I want to say this once and close the door on this. It's not something I want to talk about much. I had no right to burden you that way. It's not your problem." She paused. "I don't think I'm as grown up as I think I am."

"It doesn't need to come up again. Friends, okay?"

She smiled. "Friends."

"Now I need your help. Things are starting to break and there's more than I can keep up with."

Her eyes narrowed. "What kinds of things are breaking?"

"Not the firm. Emily's case."

"I was afraid I was in trouble for what I said last night."

"No, you're not." I almost told her that Richardson was barely interested in her news, but I didn't. "Can you help me out?"

"What can I do?"

"Call the Register of Wills; see if Emily's will has been filed for probate."

She showed some irritation. "You know how busy I am?"

"I figured you'd be doing it by phone, anyway."

She looked at her appointment book. "I don't have anything today until my one o'clock settlement." She closed the file on her desk and pushed it aside. "Okay, I'll get right on it."

"Thanks a lot."

I went to Flora's office next, but he was out and his light was off. His secretary sat at a cramped workstation just outside his door. She looked up from her typing. "Lookin' for Mike?"

"That's right."

"He's out till eleven-thirty."

"You know where?"

She consulted his appointment book. "No. Want to leave a message?"

"Thanks, no." I tried Huyett's office next, and got the same response—out till eleven-thirty, no location given.

I didn't have any business with Palmer, but I decided to check anyway.

"No, sorry," his secretary said. "He just left."

"How recently?"

"Not more than two minutes ago. You may still be able to catch him in the lobby."

"Where's he headed?"

"He didn't say; just that he'd be back before lunch."

"Did he say 'eleven-thirty'?"

"Yes, he did."

Whatever was going on, it was worth a look. I grabbed my coat and went down the back stairs, two at a time. They ended in a fire exit that brought me out in an alley on one side of the building. I shut the door quietly behind me, threaded my way through the Dumpsters and construction debris to the street, and peeked around the corner.

Palmer was crossing the street, his back to me. He had a transfer case in his right hand, and from the way he carried it, I guessed that it was heavy. The others were nowhere in sight.

He reached the far curb, turned right, and stopped at the next corner. He shook hands with a tall man with sandy hair. They were nearly half a block from my hiding place, and I swore at myself for forgetting my binoculars. The other man had a briefcase of his own and was wearing a trenchcoat, but that was about all I could tell. He could have been anywhere from thirty to fifty. Whoever he was, I didn't recognize him.

They started walking away. I was too far away to be sure, but they seemed to be talking. If they were, so much the better—if they were distracted, it was less likely that they'd see me. I stepped out from the building and turned right, staying across the street from them and half a block behind.

They made a left onto Market and headed west, toward City Hall. I crossed the street to their side and dropped back to three-quarters of a block behind. From a technical point of view, this was The Original Amateur Hour of surveillances. It was pure crazy to follow a person who knew you by sight in broad daylight unless you had some form of disguise. If the target was just going for a walk you were wasting your time. If he was doing something he had a reason to feel nervous about, he just might look around. And if he did, there you were, right in front of God and everybody.

Thinking about it made me decide to look around myself. I stopped and pretended to check my reflection in a store window. The early morning rush was over, and pedestrian traffic was light. The only people behind me were two teenage girls looking in store windows, a Korean couple setting up a sidewalk stand, and a young black man wearing a red beret. I started walking again.

The two men stopped at the Eleventh Street SEPTA station. I'd closed some of the distance between us, and if Palmer looked back, I was in plain sight. I ducked into the recessed entranceway of a discount electronics store and waited. Judging from the volume of the music blaring out of the loudspeakers, the store owner wasn't concerned about the Philadelphia noise ordinance. It was good to know that my hearing was recovering, but just then I could have used a little deafness.

Fortunately, I didn't have long to wait. A dozen commuters straggled up the stairs from the subway. In the middle of the group was a young, short woman, well dressed, carrying a briefcase that seemed at least half as big as herself. She shook hands with Palmer and the blond man and the three of them continued west on Market. I let them get the better part of a block ahead. But when I was ready to step out, I decided to take a look around first.

Directly across the street from me, the black man in the beret was buying a hot dog from a sidewalk vendor. He was closer to me now, and I took the time for a good look. Twenty-five to thirty, with a wiry, athletic build. Jeans in good condition. Some kind of fancy white tennis shoes. I supposed you didn't call them tennis shoes if you didn't play tennis and spent a hundred and fifty dollars on them, but I didn't know what else to call them. Dark sweatshirt with a windbreaker over it, unzipped. I didn't like the unzipped part.

I moved out briskly, keeping my distance from Palmer and the others. The sidewalk became busier as we approached City Hall, and I had to close up to keep them in clear sight. Fortunately the blond man was tall enough to see over the heads of all but the tallest pedestrians. I paused once, at a light, to stoop over and pretend to tie my shoe. The man in the red beret was still behind me.

We reached the great concrete wedding cake that was City Hall but they didn't go inside. Instead they veered left, cutting past Wanamaker's, and turned south onto Broad Street. The sidewalks were crowded now, and I had to get within a hundred feet to keep them in sight.

In the middle of the next block they turned left and disappeared into the lobby of one of the large office buildings that line South Broad. I walked slowly by the door and saw the three of them standing together, waiting by the bank of elevators. The lobby was large and fairly crowded, but going inside was too great a risk. I stood by the side of the door and watched for the man in the red beret out of the corner of my eye. He was about half a block up the street, standing in front of a news kiosk without buying anything. His jacket was zipped up now, all the way to his collar. I had a pretty good suspicion of what a passerby would see if his jacket swung open. My palms began to tingle and I thought of my .357, securely locked in the evidence room of the Radnor Township Police Department.

When I looked inside the lobby again, the three of them were gone. I went inside anyway, knowing it was hopeless. The six elevators serviced twenty-two floors, and there was no way of knowing where they'd gone. I contented myself with looking over the building directory, which indicated that half the space was occupied by various law firms.

I went out, made a left, and walked all the way down to

Spruce. It was a long way round to go back to the firm, but I wanted to get rid of Red Beret and I needed a quiet alley. After I turned onto Spruce and headed east I waited to make sure he was still behind me. He was. He'd unzipped his jacket again, but other than that he didn't seem to be on his guard. More important, he still seemed to be alone.

I passed by Emily's building on Spruce just west of Eleventh. The contractors were busy, and the street was narrowed to one lane by Dumpsters, utility trucks, and other construction vehicles. In a couple of months people would forget the whole thing had ever happened. Seeing the changes going on made me feel irrelevant. If I wasn't being followed I might have even allowed myself the luxury of feeling depressed about it.

Between Eleventh and Tenth I turned off into a maze of alleys separating tiny three-story eighteenth-century red brick houses. Quince Street, the sign said. It was barely wider than the sidewalks on either side, and except for a few storm windows, the twentieth century hadn't intruded at all. No garbage. No parked cars. I loved that part of the city, but there was no time to look at window treatments or historic plaques. I was focused on finding as narrow an alley as I could.

The spot I found wasn't perfect. It was an unnamed alley that branched off of Quince to the left. It was a dead end, and a little wider than I would have liked. But it was narrow enough, the position of the sun was right, and it was private. And it had one other amenity I liked—a small metal trash can with a locked lid. I hefted it; I guessed it weighed about twenty pounds. I held it against my chest, moved to the corner of the building where the alley met Quince, and waited.

People who say they can't live in a big city because of the noise have never lived on a Philadelphia alley. The traffic noise could still be heard, but it sounded far in the distance, not the few yards away it really was. I could hear my own breathing and the rasp of the back of my jacket against the brick wall. And then I heard something else. Footsteps, very soft, very measured, coming down the alley on the cobblestones.

The sun was to his right and a little behind him, and just before he reached my corner, his shadow appeared first. His left hand was at his side, but his right was up, and there was something in it. Bulky, not long. It could have been a sap or a knife, but not the way he was holding it. A gun.

His shadow moved up to the corner and edged past it. Almost time. Despite the chill, my hands were slick against the trash can. I took a tighter grip and worked on controlling my breathing.

He was twenty years younger than me and he had a gun. But he wasn't sure I was there, and he wasn't on edge as I was. I took a deep breath, jumped out in front of him, and heaved the trash can into his face as hard as I could. I had a glimpse of a startled face, eyes wide, before the can slammed into him and knocked him down.

He was fast, and tough. He'd barely gone down before he was up on one elbow, trying to raise his gun. I kicked for his gun hand and connected; it went clattering across the stones. Then I threw myself on top of him and slammed the back of his head onto the cobblestones as hard as I could. He was tensing his neck, and I couldn't exert enough force to knock him out. I leaned back and gave him my best shot to his right jaw. The blow knocked his head back so hard that I heard the thud of his skull smashing into the cobblestones. He hit hard; even I winced. Now the fight was out of him. When I got up he just lay there with his arms stretched out to the sides.

I picked up his gun—a Browning Hi-Power 9mm automatic—put on the safety, and went over to him. He was on his side now, trying to roll into a ball, both hands holding his head.

"I'd like to talk to you a minute, if you don't mind." No response. "I was wondering why you were trying to kill me." I counted to five, but he gave no sign that he'd heard me.

I pressed the muzzle against the side of his head. "Well, I'll give you the benefit of the doubt. Maybe you were just funning. In that case, the gun won't have a shell in the chamber. Let's pull the trigger and see, shall we?"

His head turned toward me but he said nothing.

I dropped the safety and raised the hammer. "Last chance, friend. I'd really prefer not to do this, but you're not giving me much choice."

"No, man, don' do it." The voice was thick, but at least I had his attention.

"Then tell me who sent you and why."

"They'd kill me, man."

"What do you think your chances are with me?"

"I—"

All I needed was a couple of minutes with him, but I never had them. Behind me I heard the sound of a door being opened. I glanced over my shoulder. An old woman in a flower-patterned housedress and apron stood in the doorway, holding a broom with both hands and waving it in our direction. "What's going on here?"

My body was between her and the gun. I shoved the pistol into a pocket of my trenchcoat and dropped my hands casually to my sides. I spoke without turning my face to her—no point in helping her make an identification. "Nothing, ma'am. This gentleman here just fell over this ashcan and cut himself a little. But he's feeling better now, aren't you?"

She wasn't buying it. "Well, I'm calling the police!" The door slammed and I heard the lock turn. The historic district was one of the best-patrolled parts of the city. Everyone, but especially the city fathers, wanted the tourists to keep coming. I figured I had three minutes to clear the area, maybe less.

I leaned close to Red Beret. "You're in luck, little buddy. I'm leaving. I don't have half a day to screw around with the police on this. Get yourself out of here as best you can. I ever see you again, you may not be so lucky."

He made a noise. I took it to mean that it sounded like a fine arrangement to him.

Chapter Sixteen

Thursday, 11:00 A.M.

When I walked in the receptionist handed me a pink message slip.

"Steve Mailman?" I asked. "Sure this is for me?"

"He asked for you. He said he had some information."

It was a New Jersey number, and as I dialed it, I remembered. Tom's friend in Atlantic City. "Steve, it's Dave Garrett. Thanks for getting back to me."

"Sure thing. Hold on while I get my notes." He put down his phone, and for a minute I just heard office noises. "Okay, here we go. Mike Flora Senior, his father, is clean except for a simple assault fifteen years ago. He got a minimum sentence, which probably means there was no criminal record anywhere else."

"Or maybe the fix was in."

"Or maybe the fix was in. Yeah. Anyway, the uncle in the florist business had theft charges filed against him. Apparently he dealt with a competitor by stealing his delivery vans, three of them. But it was dismissed pretrial."

"When was that?"

"Four years ago. Got some stuff on Mike Junior, though. It interested me, so I called in a favor from the local police."

"I'm all ears."

"He has a fairly extensive juvenile record for minor stuff. A couple of truancies, a possession of a small amount of pot, a joyriding. As an adult he picked up an underage drinking and a bad check charge. Oh, and a retail theft, too."

"How recent?"

"The last thing was three years ago, the bad check."

"Could there be anything else, like in another county?"

"That's why I checked with the police, besides wanting a little peek at his juvenile record. No, the local police don't have any indication he's been in trouble anywhere else."

"Steve, thanks a million. Send your bill to my attention."

"Professional courtesy."

"Thanks."

"Good luck."

I hung up and looked at the blank wall of my office. So Flora was a sneak and liked to cut corners. So what? He sounded more like a chiseler than a killer. But there was the bad check business . . . was Emily on to something? The kind of thing to kill over?

I took the Browning out of my pocket and made sure once again that the safety was on. I made a mental note to throw it down a storm sewer at the first opportunity. It was a shame to trash it, but it was almost certainly stolen. Possession of the gun, plus a policeman with an attitude, could buy me a bogus Receiving charge. Worse, the gun might have been used in a shooting. I didn't even want to think about the varieties of trouble that might lead to.

I was in the restroom using the urinal when I heard the door open. The smoky reek of Palmer's cigar reached me before he did.

"How y'doin', Dave?"

"Pretty good, Roger. How's labor law these days?"

"Still sucks."

He checked the cubicle, saw it was empty, and moved over to the urinal next to me. He finished before I did and threw his cigar butt into the drain.

"You know," I said, "that's a pretty disgusting habit."

"Yeah. Makes 'em soggy and hard to light."

We moved over to the double sink. He turned on the water for his sink but didn't wash his hands.

He addressed my reflection in the mirror. For the first time I could remember, his voice was soft, just above a whisper. "Dave, I got to warn you. Leave this thing alone."

I looked at his reflection. "Who's telling me this?" I asked softly.

"I am. Nobody sent me."

I looked down at the water running in his sink. "Are the offices bugged?"

He shrugged. "You can never be too careful."

"That's no answer."

"We . . . they might be."

"Who?"

"I don't even know that they are."

"Come on, Roger."

He snorted. "It could be Richardson bugging Huyett, or Huyett bugging Richardson, or somebody else bugging us all. FBI, SEC, IRS, who knows?"

"You know for a fact we're being bugged," I said.

"I found a little microphone on the bottom of my calculator last week."

"What did you do about it?" I asked.

"I learned to keep my mouth shut when I was in my office. And everywhere else inside the building, too."

"You tell anybody about it?"

"Nope."

"This is crazy," I said.

"One way or the other, it won't be going on much longer."

"What do you mean?"

"That's not what I came in here to talk to you about, Dave.

I'm just telling you, let well enough alone. You're not making any friends."

"I wasn't brought in here to make friends."

He was losing patience with me. "I'll be a little more direct. You're making enemies. You ever think of trying to get your license back, you'd better not have anybody pissed off at you."

"Meaning what?"

He was exasperated now, enough to make him indiscreet. "Huyett's got a lot of suck with the Disciplinary Board. He's chief hearings officer for the Philadelphia region."

"So that's how it is."

"I'm telling you, it's not worth it. Nothing's going to change what happened, and all you're going to do is piss people off."

"It's the story of my life, at least lately."

His eyes became hard. He turned from the mirror and looked at me directly. "You're pushing hard, Dave."

"I can afford to, I've got nothing to lose. I don't have a partnership, I don't have any money, I don't have a wife or a family, all I've got is my cases. I see them through."

"You think Vince and Tom are such hot shit? They haven't told you half of what's going on."

"Like?"

"Like check Emily's will."

He stomped out of the restroom without bothering to turn off the water.

I resisted my initial impulse to rush out after him, and then my second impulse, which was to run and tell Richardson. Instead, I went to a pay phone across the street and dialed an unlisted number. It was a Philadelphia exchange, but it rings a phone in the rear of a garage in Camden without leaving a record of the call anywhere. The person I was calling was handy with electronics.

"Giuseppe's Pizza." The voice was a baritone drawl of purest Alabama.

"Dave Garrett."

"One, two, three?"

"Three, two, one." A small ritual to satisfy Shelby's need for security. If I was being compelled to call, or if someone was listening, all I had to do was screw up the numbers to put him on alert. As if he was ever *off* alert any minute he wasn't sleeping. I'd met Shelby ten years before, when I was still doing criminal work. He was the best electronics man in the area for either surveillance or security, depending on your needs. I got him off with probation even though it was his second fall for burglary, and he hadn't forgotten.

"What can I do for you?"

"Shelby, if you're going to pass yourself off as a pizza place, you could at least make a stab at an Italian accent."

He laughed. "In this part of Camden, all the restaurants is owned by brothers."

"Got a job for you, if you can get on it right away."

"I'm listenin'."

"I'm working for a law firm in Philadelphia. Seventh and Walnut area. There's at least one bug, probably more."

"Government?"

"Maybe."

"Just rooms, or phones, too?"

"The only one I know about is a room bug, but I called you from an outside line anyway."

"What you calling me for? You forget everything I taught you already?"

"I want the first team on this. Even if I find all the bugs, you can tell me things I wouldn't see."

"Your people can pay the freight?"

"No problem, but I need it done right away." I gave him the name of the firm and the address.

"I'll be there before noon," he said, and hung up. Instead of a dial tone, I found myself listening to a woman trying to make a reservation on a United Airlines flight to Chicago for the next day. I shook my head and put down the receiver.

I thought of telling someone in charge, Richardson or Huyett, that my friend would be coming, then I changed my mind. It would only give them an opportunity to object. If the bugs were from either one of them they wouldn't want a search.

The receptionist was just returning from a coffee break when I got back to the office.

"Are you going to be on duty in the next hour?" I asked.

"Yes, sir. Till twelve-thirty."

"In a few minutes one of the biggest black men you've ever seen is going to get off that elevator. He's about thirty-five, bald, and he must weigh three hundred pounds. The last time I saw him he was wearing thick glasses. He'll have a box with him the size of a steamer trunk. His clothes will look like he slept in them, because he did. Think you can pick him out?"

"Yes, sir."

"His name is Shelby, and he's working with me. He's to have free run of the place. Anywhere he wants to go, find a secretary or someone to show him around."

She swallowed. "You got it."

My next stop was the card index in central filing. Emily had several files of her own as a client, which wasn't surprising, considering how long she'd been with the firm. A very old one where we'd done a power of attorney for her. A ten-year-old file involving a traffic ticket. Another file, nearly as old, involving medical insurance problems. And a two-year-old file—Will.

The card index showed it as open but it wasn't in the drawer. Instead I found a red "File Out" card with a notation that the file was with Mister Richardson.

Margaret, his secretary, had her own office next to his. It had two windows, one of which overlooked Washington Square, and it was bigger than the offices of either of the associates. Her desk was bare except for a row of three pencils of equal length, all freshly sharpened. They were one inch from the edge, and exactly parallel. It occurred to me that I'd never seen her touch them.

"Good morning, Mister Garrett." It was as neutral a tone of voice as a human being could produce—not friendly, not fa-

miliar, not distant, not hostile. Not anything. But the narrowed
eyes gave her away. She was on her guard.

"There's another file I need to see, Margaret. The Voss will
file."

"I'll see that it's delivered to your office."

"I've already checked for it, thanks. It's signed out to Mister
Richardson." I could have added, "in your handwriting," but I
didn't.

"Then it must be in his office."

"Could you get it for me right away, please? It's important."

"He may be using it at the moment."

"I passed by his office. He's not even there."

"I'll have it brought to your office as soon as I can."

"Let's get it now, if you don't mind."

"Well, I—"

I leaned forward and put my hands on the desk. I hoped
they would leave big greasy smudges in the finish. "I need it
now, please."

The only movement was the tapping of her forefinger on
the edge of the desk, but I knew she was ready to explode.
"I'm not sure that Mister—"

"If you have any questions, perhaps we can take them up
with Mister Palmer or Mister Huyett. Otherwise I need the file.
Now."

"Yes, sir."

I followed her into Richardson's office. A stack of files nearly
two feet high was on the credenza. She ran her thumb along
the edge till she was two thirds of the way to the bottom, pulled
out a thin folder, and held it to her chest.

"You understand that the file cannot leave this office."

She sounded like she was speaking for an audience, and I
thought of the bugs. Or maybe she was just making the record
clear between us. I didn't care. "Fine. I just want to read it,
that's all."

I held out my hand. She gave me the file with all the enthusiasm of a mother giving up her only child for adoption.

It didn't take long. The file contained only five documents: a single sheet of notes in Palmer's indecipherable handwriting, dated two years ago; a receipted bill from the same time period, showing that Emily had received a fifty percent discount on her will; a receipt from the Register of Wills, showing that the will had been admitted to probate on Tuesday; and a photocopy of the will itself.

Richardson was the executor and the sole beneficiary. And now, a very rich man.

"Anything else, Mister Garrett?"

I looked up and realized I must have been staring at the will for a long time. "Would you happen to know when Tom will be back?"

"He's signed out till four."

"Where?"

She didn't need to consult his book. "The Register of Wills, plus lunch, and then a meeting of the bank board."

"I thought Roger handled the probate matters."

"Mister Richardson must have decided to handle one himself."

I handed back the copy to her. "This one?"

"I wouldn't know."

Like hell you don't. "Thank you, Margaret. Please tell him I'd like to see him when he has a minute."

I retraced my steps to my office. A catering service came by with a cart loaded with sandwiches, but I didn't feel much like eating. I didn't feel much like thinking about Tom and his two million dollars, either, but that's what I did. I'd practiced with him, been partners with him, for years. Was he capable of killing his mistress for money? Of course he was. With enough motivation almost anyone is capable of anything. It's just that most of us are lucky enough not to be deeply tempted to do anything really evil. Two million dollars was a lot of temptation—was it too much to resist?

I put together another scenario involving Emily. She suspects Richardson is taking out money. She doesn't want to confront him—or maybe she does, and doesn't get anywhere. She doesn't want to go to the other partners if she can avoid it, so she calls me. Perhaps for my advice or to act as an intermediary, perhaps to do an investigation. He finds out I'm coming—maybe a message slip was left lying around, maybe my name was written in her appointment book, maybe she even told him. But instead of scaring him off, the news pushes him over the edge.

It was tight, logical, and consistent. And it worried the hell out of me.

Chapter Seventeen

Thursday, Noon

For the moment, with everyone unavailable, there was nothing else to do within the office. I decided to try another lead.

"Delaware County Prison." It was a male voice, hoarse, and in the background I could hear the clanging of steel doors.

"I need to pay a visit to one of your inmates. When are visiting hours?"

"Are you his attorney?"

"No."

"Law enforcement?"

"No."

"Are you on his visitors' list?"

"We only met once. I doubt it."

"Immediate family?"

"Sorry, no."

"Sir, if you don't fit into one of those categories, we don't let you in at all. Sorry."

"If I came out, could I at least get a message through to him?"

"That much we can do for you."

"I'm calling from Center City. Before I come out, can I be sure he's still there?"

"Okay. Give me his name."

"Johnson Bentley."

"Just a minute . . . DOB?"

"Can't help you. But he would have been brought in by Radnor Township either Tuesday night or Wednesday morning. Charges were probably Aggravated Assault, Criminal Attempt —Homicide, and a UFA."

A pause. "Sorry. We don't have him."

"You've got to."

"You say he came in Wednesday morning?"

"Most likely."

"Let me check yesterday's roster. Yeah—here we go. He was arraigned Wednesday morning. Bail set at one hundred fifty thousand by JP Miller . . . petition for reduction of bail submitted to court . . . order entered reducing bail to seventy-five thousand dollars . . . ten percent bond not allowed, per Judge Cahill. Cash bail posted same day. We released him yesterday."

I wondered how cold the trail would be. "What time?"

"He was transported to the courthouse for posting of bail at three."

"Can you give me an address?"

"We don't have that here."

"How about the surety on the bail?"

"Once they're released, we don't maintain anything up here, sir."

"If bail was set by the court, then it would have been posted at Clerk of Courts, right?"

"Yes, sir."

"Thanks for your help."

Unfortunately, knowing that the information was in the Clerk of Courts office didn't help me. Despite every plea I could muster, the second assistant chief deputy wouldn't release it over the phone. I was on my way to Delaware County after all.

Media, the county seat of Delaware County, is a beautiful, secluded little town of narrow streets lined with old shade trees, only fifteen miles from Center City. Unfortunately for me, the reason the town was so secluded was because it was impossible to get there. Going west out of Philadelphia on West Chester Pike left you with the choice of either going all the way out to Broomall and then doubling back, or tackling miles of beep-and-creep on Route 1. A variation, if you knew the back roads, involved going west on Walnut to the Cobbs Creek Parkway, which was just a glorified name for a two-mile stretch of 63rd Street, and fighting your way through the beep-and-creep on Baltimore Pike. Commuters argued the fine points of which route was better, but as far as I was concerned it was just a choice of which traffic jam you preferred.

I decided to try the Cobbs Creek–Baltimore Pike route. I can't say if it was a mistake or not. It took me an hour and ten minutes to cover the fifteen miles—it might have been even longer the other way.

When I reached the Clerk of Courts office, there was no doubt who the second assistant clerk was. I'd met a hundred people like her in government, mostly women, but some men, too. The kind of person who was born middle-aged, doing their job, and hating it.

This particular one was gray-haired and bony. Her skin looked like it hadn't seen the sun in years, and her mouth was set in a permanent frown. It deepened when she saw me at the counter.

"Afternoon. I'm Dave Garrett, the investigator who called about Johnson Bentley. About an hour and a half ago, from Philadelphia." I tried not to make it sound like too much of a barb.

"Well?"

"I'd like to see Mr. Bentley's file, please."

"If you're not with the court, I can't do that."

"You told me that the problem was you couldn't give out the information over the phone."

"Well, there's a second problem. As you see."

"You let me drive all the way out here knowing you weren't going to let me see it when I got here?"

"How was I to know you were coming?"

"I told you how important it was."

"We don't change our access policy because someone made an unnecessary drive, sir."

I counted to five, slowly, to keep myself from saying anything I'd regret. It didn't help. I had to go all the way to fifteen.

"Who *can* have access, if you don't mind?"

"The district attorney's office, the press, personnel of this office, the defendant himself, and his attorney." She smiled coldly.

"Thanks very much."

I scoured the corridors of the courthouse, looking for a lawyer I knew. My plan was to give him a dollar's retainer to represent Bentley, but I did better. As I passed by a row of courtrooms, a familiar face emerged.

"Jim!"

"Dave, good to see you again."

Jim was a stringer for the *Philadelphia Inquirer.* I'd helped him with a couple of stories over the years, and he'd done a feature about my disbarment that would have moved a stone statue to tears. It fell way short of moving the state supreme court, but that wasn't his fault.

"Busy right now?" I asked.

"I'm covering a trial, but we're in recess for twenty minutes."

I took him by the elbow. "I need a little favor . . ."

The clerk from hell wasn't pleased to see either one of us.

"Hi, again," I said cheerfully. "I'd like to introduce you to James Hess, a member of the Fourth Estate in good standing."

"I know him." She might as well have been wearing a sign, I'M MEAN, BUT I'M NOT STUPID.

Jim spoke up. "I'd like to see the bail papers on Mr. Johnson Bentley. I understand he posted bail yesterday."

She looked at him, then at me. "Is he doing a story on him?"

"That, madam," I said, "is none of your fucking business."

She stiffened. "We don't tolerate rude language in this office."

"Tolerate it or not, I don't care. I've got a job to do and you've been wasting my time. Just get us the file, or get us your boss."

We stood at the counter and looked at the file, such as it was. I looked for the criminal complaint and didn't find it. Then I realized that the only thing heard by the court so far was the bail reduction—the criminal complaint would still be with the district justice for Radnor Township. The petition for reduction of bail wasn't in the file, either. I didn't know whether it would be sent back to the district justice, or whether it was in the Clerk's office but hadn't been filed. I certainly wasn't going to ask her for it. But the bail piece itself was there, and it gave me all I needed—Bentley's address. 942 Jansen Avenue, Essington, Pennsylvania 19029. I made a note and we handed back the file.

Jim and I went into the corridor. "Where the hell is Essington?" I asked.

"It's an old residential-industrial area on the Delaware, just south of the airport. Near the Tinicum Marsh."

"Thanks a million, Jim. I owe you one."

"No trouble. Good luck. And be careful with this guy."

We shook hands and I headed for my car. I'd wasted a big chunk of the day getting the address and I was anxious to see if it panned out. I headed straight south on 252, heading for 95. There was probably a more efficient way to get there, involving secondary roads and cutting through backyards, but I just followed the state highway, up and down over the hills covered with manicured lawns and precisely pruned shrubbery. Nothing was allowed to get out of control in lower Delaware County, at least not this part of it.

I went past the Springhaven Country Club. Despite the drizzle the crews were out mowing the rough and raking the sand traps. A lot of effort went into golf, for no benefit I'd ever been able to appreciate. If all the golf courses were plowed up, could they raise enough to feed the poor in our country? And the rich could get some honest exercise like tennis, instead of driving their golf carts around. Of course, it would never happen that way—the food would rot in some grain elevator after being stored for years at government expense, and the rich would probably play cards if they couldn't golf. That was the trouble with good intentions. They never seem to quite translate into bettering things. Hell, World War II was started by a man who thought his intentions were good.

I reached 95, headed north, and got off at the Stewart Avenue exit. The sign indicated that Essington Avenue/Route 291 was dead ahead; and after half a mile of driving through a wasteland of scrub and broken concrete, I found that it was right. I made a left and headed north.

Essington was close to the Springhaven Country Club only by the crudest geographic measure. The outskirts were the kind of industrial uses no one wants in their backyard—meat packing plants, scrap yards, and truck repair facilities. The town itself was grimy and shabby, with empty warehouses and rows of poorly maintained bungalows. The commercial district featured pizza parlors, hoagie shops, and bars. I didn't see a home that looked less than thirty years old. Most of the buildings seemed to date from right after World War II. It was probably one of the towns, like Levittown, thrown up in a hurry in our national pride and ambition after the victory parades were over. We'd whipped the world in war, and now we were going to whip them in peace, with our shipbuilding and our cars and our electronics. And our good old-fashioned—what did they used to call it? I hadn't heard the term in years—American know-how. It seemed so very long ago. My own war had been Vietnam.

I was almost through town before I found Jansen Avenue. When I made my left I was at the 400 block. It was as seedy as the rest of the town, but people were making an effort. Most of the yards were fenced and mowed, and all of the parked cars looked to be runners. I hadn't gone more than a couple of blocks when I realized something was wrong. I still had five blocks to go, and dead ahead, no more than three blocks away, was the raised bulk of U.S. 95, at least thirty feet above me. I hoped the road might curve and parallel the freeway, but I was wrong. After three blocks the road stopped, ending in a chain-link fence with a gate. Beyond the fence was an access tunnel, big enough for one-way vehicle traffic, leading under the highway.

I got out of my car and went up to the fence. The thunder of traffic above me on 95 was physically painful, but I could see that the gate was unlocked. A padlock ran through a chain, but it had been damaged. Shot off with something big, and repositioned afterward. The metal was shiny where the bullet had cut through. It hadn't happened very long ago.

I pushed the gate open and drove into the tunnel. It was unlighted except for my headlights, a giant storm culvert with pavement. When it stormed, water must flow through this thing, one way or the other. Otherwise it would have been a refuge for the homeless. The concrete walls were bare, not even any graffiti, and the roadway was clear.

I came out the other side. In front of me was an expanse of tall weeds and scrub trees—Tinicum Marsh, I realized. For years developers had tried to drain it off, but the environmentalists had fought them to a standstill and had the area declared a national wildlife refuge. No cars. No people. No houses, especially no 942 Jansen Avenue.

I stopped the car, wondering what to do next. Then, almost obscured in the tall weeds, a couple of hundred yards away, I saw a small dark building. Driving slowly along a muddy track, I moved closer. I stopped about fifty yards away and got out. It was a weatherbeaten shed, not more than ten by ten, with a single front door and window and a corroded tin roof. The roar of traffic was still loud, but not overwhelming. The marshland around me was dotted with some rusted fragments of car bodies, but otherwise there was no sign of human life.

I saw no power or phone lines running to the shed. No

smoke from the chimney. No movement at the window. I moved closer along the track, keeping to one side so I could throw myself into the brush if I needed to.

I came up on the shed on a blind side and stood with my ear against the wall. The traffic made it difficult to hear, but I couldn't detect any noises inside.

I edged around the corner and looked through the window. The room was dark, but I could see that it was bare except for a chair. Someone was sitting in the chair. I couldn't see very well, but I had a bad feeling from the way he was sitting.

I knocked on the door. No response. I stepped back, kicked it as hard as I could, and jumped back to one side, out of the way.

I didn't need to bother. When he'd signed his bail papers, Johnson Bentley had promised he could be located at 942 Jansen Avenue, and would not flee the jurisdiction. At least once in his life, he'd kept a promise.

Chapter Eighteen

Thursday, 4:00 P.M.

As soon as I realized he was dead, I decided to do the most important thing any civilian can do at a crime scene. Nothing at all.

I stood perfectly still in the doorway. When the police got here, a fine-tooth comb would be the crudest instrument they would use. This shed would be measured, photographed, vacuumed, checked for prints, and subjected to every other test the forensics people could think of. Touching or handling anything could be doubly dangerous—not only might I destroy evidence, but I could also leave some trace to implicate myself. I was sure to be a suspect, at least until a time of death was established. After all, the man had tried to kill me two days before, and the police knew that I wanted to meet him.

The first order of business was to think about my own alibi. But for when? It depended, of course, on the time of death. Bail was posted after his transportation to the Clerk of Courts at three. He must have been released before five, when they closed. Say four o'clock, plus an hour to get here. So Mr. Bentley and his friends who'd posted the bail were probably here by five.

They probably got him here willingly enough—he'd given the 942 Jansen address at their suggestion. He thought he was going to be lying low for a few days. Maybe, he was told, until someone else took care of me. Without me as a witness, the only charge likely to stick was carrying a concealed weapon. A pleasant thought. I would need to be on my toes.

The room was bare, except for a wooden chair with arms. No curtains at the window. No lantern, flashlight, or candles. They wanted to learn if he'd told me or the police anything. It was just a question of how much time they had for the job. The autopsy might show something, but there was no way for me to tell if they'd worked him over or not. Whatever they'd done, I was sure it had happened inside, in the privacy of this room, and that it had happened in daylight. They wouldn't have worked in the dark, and they wouldn't have shown light at the window without curtains. So they worked on him from five till no later than six, and killed him and probably left before it got completely dark. All right, then. The Greek woman in the deli, Susan, and the waiter at the restaurant were my alibis.

The body was tied to the chair with duct tape at the wrists and ankles. The tape was stretched where he'd struggled against it, but it still held firm. He was wearing the same clothes I'd seen him in, except now they were thick with dried blood. I was no expert on bloodstains and I certainly wasn't going to touch it, but I figured that even a big puddle like this one could dry in twenty hours, especially since it could soak into the wooden floorboards.

I saw two possible causes of death. One, a friend of Mr. Bentley's had slashed his throat all the way across, from one point of the jawbone to the other. Protruding from the slash was his tongue. Whoever did this had reached in and left his tongue hanging out. A friend of mine in the DA's office in Manhattan called it a Brooklyn necktie, a warning not to inform. I hoped that they'd at least waited till he was dead. Of course, I had no reason to think they had. Two, there was a small black hole in the center of his chest, the size of a cigarette burn. It didn't look like much, but when I went around behind him there was a bullet hole in the back of the chair. Someone had shot Bentley from a few feet away. It didn't look like the muzzle had been pressed against his chest. A friend of mine had given me a tour of the Medical Examiner's office once, and the contact wounds I'd seen had been a lot bigger. I figured it was done right here in the room, once they'd finished with him. It made sense. Why bother to take him outside and make noise?

I stepped out of the doorway and turned around. The soil around the shed was moist, but sandy, and I doubted whether the police would be able to get any useful casts of my footsteps. Just to be on the safe side, I retraced my steps as carefully as I could, being sure to step exactly where I'd stepped before, except now going in the other direction. I backed my car straight up the tire tracks I'd come in on, for the same reason.

I headed north on 291 till I found an automatic car wash and told them to give me the deluxe job. The attendant looked at me oddly. Maybe he was wondering if the plastic sheet taped over the driver's side window would leak, or how to plug the bullet hole in the door. Or, most likely, why anyone would pay anything to have this wreck cleaned in the first place. But he took my twenty dollars and smiled. A quick trip to the washroom to scrub the soles of my shoes and I was ready to do my civic duty. I drove to a pay phone up the road, out of sight of the car wash. I called in the discovery of the body to the Tinicum Township Police Department and was off the line before they could run a trace.

When I got back to the office Shelby was sitting on the sofa in the reception room. There was no room for anyone else. In front of him was a big black case, sitting on a mover's dolly.

"Shelby. Good to see you."

He smiled, showing a motley set of discolored, chipped, and broken teeth. "How you doin', man?"

"Okay to talk in my office?"

He smiled again. "You bet it is."

I led him down the hall, attracting stares as we went. When

we got to my office he stayed standing; I realized he didn't trust the chair to take his weight.

"You've kept me busy, friend," he said.

"Let's hear it."

He pulled a small plastic bag from his pocket and gently poured nine small black objects onto my desk. Each of them was about the size and shape of a pencil eraser. A pair of tiny wires sprouted from the base of each one.

I picked one up. "Where were they?"

"There was one in each of the lawyers' offices, one in the bookkeeper's office, one in the restroom, and one in here."

"Let me guess. These look too small to have batteries. They were attached to a power source and drew their power that way."

"A different one in each office. In one office, it was a desk calculator. In another, a wall clock. Desk lamps. In one office there's a fish tank, and they drew juice off the filter pump."

"How were they mounted?"

"A quick and dirty job. Right to the power cords. You know how most cords have a little plastic gizmo so you can wrap up the cord if you need to? He taped the mikes to that. Not a bad concealment job, considering."

"Amateur or professional?"

"Definitely a pro."

"Because of the quality of the equipment?"

"Nah. It's decent stuff, but it's standard catalogue issue. But you use this number of bugs, ain't easy to get any use out of it. You got nine sets of conversations being transmitted, you need nine receivers and nine voice-actuated tape recorders. And people to listen to it and let you know what's worth knowin'. If it was an amateur, he has a hell of a big family helping him out."

"You wouldn't happen to recognize the work, would you?"

He smiled and stroked his chin. "Now, what makes you say that?"

"Let's say it's a small town."

"Yeah," he admitted. "I do."

"Who?"

"Let's just say it's a guy in the area who runs a security business. It wasn't me; if it was, I wouldn't have taken your money."

"How about a name?"

"If I tell you his name then you're going to go ask him who his client was. Just tellin' you the name ain't worth the breath."

I knew when to stop trying. Shelby had done two years in Graterford rather than give the state police a name. "Any idea how long the bugs have been in place?"

He shook his head. "This model is a couple years old. Some of the wiring on the ones near the floor looked a little dusty. Could be a year; could be three weeks. I don't think much longer than a few months—somebody'd unplug something and see it, sooner or later."

"The conference rooms were clean, right?"

"That's right."

"Whoever did this was interested in what the lawyers said. Not the staff, and not what the lawyers said to clients."

"Right again."

I looked at the row of little black microphones. "Doesn't tell me a hell of a lot, does it?"

He smiled broadly. "You're three for three."

Chapter Nineteen

Thursday, 5:00 P.M.

I stood in Richardson's doorway, trying unsuccessfully to keep my composure. "Tom, I left word I needed to see you right away."

He didn't look up from his work. "I'm very busy right now, Dave."

"So am I." The words were simple enough, but something in my tone made him stop and look up, startled.

I wanted to confront him about my suspicions about him and Emily, but I didn't trust myself to rush into that subject. "In a couple of hours," I began, "I'm going to be a suspect in a murder because of this case."

"Whose murder?"

I closed the door and sat down. "The second gunman was bailed out of jail and then killed. I found the body this afternoon."

He squinted at me through his trifocals. "Why would anyone think you'd be involved?"

"Because I've got at least one motive—revenge. Plus, if the police think I had some kind of relationship with these people that made them come after me in the first place, that would be a second one. I asked the police to let me see him Tuesday night, and earlier today I asked after him at the jail and the courthouse. He was already dead by then, but that doesn't help much—they'll think I was trying to set up my own alibi."

His voice was very soft. "David, did you kill him?"

"Hell, no. I wanted to talk to him, not kill him. He was my only lead to whoever wants me dead."

"Are there more of them?"

"Absolutely. I couldn't guess how many."

"You said you needed to see me."

"Yes. I need your help."

"Anything you need. Just tell me."

"You can start by not lying to me anymore."

He didn't move or change expression, not at all. I could hear the clock ticking behind me.

His voice was mild, and a little vague. "That's a pretty rough thing to say, David." He sounded like my high school counselor, which in my book wasn't a compliment.

"Shove it, Tom. The game's over."

"David . . ."

"David, *what*?"

He spread his hands in a slow, open gesture, palms up. "There's nothing you don't know. We've been friends a long time, and—"

"Don't you dare! You say you want me to get to the bottom of this. But every time I uncover something, you want to trade on our friendship so I won't ask any awkward questions. It's bullshit. If you want my help you'll start telling me the truth."

His lips were compressed into a fine line. "So that's the way it is, is it?"

"Yes."

He was expecting me to say something more, but I didn't. The single word just hung there in the air between us.

"I talked to Margaret," he said at last. "So you know about the will."

"And I talked to Emily's sister."

"Oh." It was barely audible.

"Come clean, Tom."

He looked at the bookshelves across the room. "This doesn't look very good for me, does it?"

"It looked bad enough at the start. What makes it worse is all your lying."

"I've never really lied. I just kept some things to myself. I never thought they needed to come out."

"You expect me to give you a medal? I've been dodging guns for the past two days because of you."

"I didn't know about her money, David. Not when we started seeing each other, not when we used to talk about whether we should do something more . . . formal about our relationship. She told me she wanted to rewrite her will in my favor. I referred her to Roger, of course. It wouldn't have been ethical for me to handle it myself. I didn't like the idea of someone in the firm knowing—I'm sure he wondered about it—but Emily didn't tell him about us, I'm sure of that."

"The will is two years old. When did you learn about her money?"

"Only a few months ago. We went away to St. Thomas for a few days at Christmas, and that's when she told me. She said it was my Christmas present." He stopped. "That doesn't look very good, either, does it?"

"What about your own will?"

"A few charitable bequests, everything else to my children in equal shares."

"Nothing to her?"

"It's the same will I made after my wife died."

"What's your net worth, right now, without your inheritance?"

"Well, you have a lot of nerve—" He saw the look in my eyes and stopped. "Maybe three hundred thousand."

"That's not a lot to show for thirty years of practice."

"Not enough to live on when I retire."

"We were having some pretty good years, eighty-three to eighty-nine. What happened?"

"A bad real estate investment, the stock market, problems with the office with high overhead." He smiled a little. "I guess I'm a lot better at helping other people with their money than I am with my own."

"Why would Emily change her will?"

"She was in love with me."

I let out my breath slowly. "I don't think you made this entirely clear to me that last time we talked."

"No, I didn't."

"Were you in love with her?"

"No. It was a warm, close relationship, but what I told you the last time was true—it wasn't love, not on my part."

"I read a little of her diary. You made quite an impression on her."

"She was never in love when she was eighteen," he said. "It was her time."

"What was she expecting from you?"

"Nothing beyond what we already had, and when she told me about the will, she said as much. I was very touched, of course, but I never saw it as her trying to pressure me."

"You didn't?"

"We'd talked about marriage, very openly, long before the will business. We were both uncomfortable with the idea. We were both content to let things go on the way they were."

"Are you sure about that?"

"Emily cared for me, and I for her. But I've lived by myself for some years, and she'd lived on her own her whole adult life. We both valued our independence."

"That sounds more like you than her."

He considered. "I suppose it does. Yes, I think she would have married me if I'd asked. But it takes two, you know."

"I want you to look me straight in the eye and tell me you didn't do it."

"What for?"

"Because if you lie to me about that, I swear to God I'll prove the truth and get myself a ringside seat at your execution."

He swallowed, hard. "I can't believe you think I'd really do such a thing. It's monstrous. After all the years—" He stopped himself when he saw my expression. "No, David, I swear, I had nothing to do with her death. Nothing at all."

For a long moment I just studied his face. I wanted to believe him unconditionally, the way we'd practiced law together for years, but I couldn't. His words were just one more witness statement, to be filed away and compared with the rest of the evidence. Kate's warning came to my mind again.

I didn't want to end our meeting on that note. I was glad I had something more to say. I pulled a small black object out of my pocket. "Look familiar?"

He squinted at it. "No."

"This is a microphone, and a tiny transmitter. A bug. Nine of these were found in the offices today. Know anything about it?"

"What offices?"

"Every lawyer's office, Emily's office, and the restroom."

It took him a moment to collect his thoughts. "Is the firm under investigation?"

"Not by the government, at least I don't think so."

"By a client?"

"Maybe. I can't imagine why, though. Most likely it's someone in the firm."

"Well, it's certainly not me."

"Can I believe you this time?"

"I guess I deserved that. Yes, you can."

"Did Emily mention this to you?"

"No, never." He glanced down at a sheet of paper he was holding.

"What's so interesting about that?" I asked.

"It's a memo from Huyett. He's calling an emergency partners' meeting for six."

"To discuss what?"

"It doesn't say."

"You mean, you're the managing partner and you don't know?"

"No."

"Come on, Tom."

He hesitated. "I don't know what to think."

"When people say that, they usually do. Emily warned you about this, didn't she?"

"She said she didn't trust Huyett or Palmer."

"And you told her, very politely, to mind her own business."

"It was a partnership matter," he said stiffly.

"You know how ridiculous that sounds?"

He looked around the room. "Now I do."

Neither one of us wanted to talk about it, but nothing else seemed worth saying. I listened to the clock, and then looked at my watch.

"It's five till six, Tom. Time to go."

He nodded and stood up slowly, like he was awakening from a deep sleep. Which in a way was true.

"I don't think this is going to be more than a few minutes," he said. "I'd appreciate it if you could wait for me."

"All right. I have some more things to do around the office anyway."

He walked down the hall stiffly, deliberately, like a man going to his own execution. I saw him stop at the door to the main deposition room, go in, and shut the door behind him.

I didn't know how long the meeting would be—my guess was no more than half an hour. I went to the offices of everyone but Richardson to collect their appointment books. Flora's book wasn't in his office, and as far as I could tell, his secretary didn't keep a duplicate. But I located the books for the others easily enough, and within fifteen minutes they were back where they belonged and I was back in my office with photocopies.

I started with Susan's. Nothing except what I expected to see—two days marked off each week for appointments in Upper Darby, and indications of which nights she'd worked late, presumably for the edification of her supervising partner. A couple of the days had deadlines for research memos penciled in. Nothing for the Friday afternoon before Emily died. Five appointments for the following Monday.

Next I picked up the photocopies from Palmer's book. On the surface he looked to be as busy as he claimed. One appointment after another, eight till six, and something nearly every evening. I counted three separate appointments with "Ross." No other name, no information on the case, no indication if it was a settlement, a client conference, a negotiating session, or something else. On the assumption that Ross was a last name, I checked the client index. No client by that name. I checked the adverse party index—we weren't in litigation with anyone by that name, either. Then I looked at today's page for ten in the morning. A one and a half hour meeting with Ross. Back at eleven-thirty, they'd said.

I looked at Huyett's schedule—the same appointments with Ross, including the one this morning. Comparing the two books side by side, each of them also had two appointments at the same time with a "Roland" and one with a "Long." Again, nothing in central filing or the adverse party index, and nothing explaining what the appointments were about. I went back to Susan's book. There was no overlap on any of the suspicious appointments with either of the partners, Palmer or Huyett.

I checked the weekend surrounding Emily's death. The two of them had left the office at three to see "Long" and apparently had not come back. Saturday Huyett had played golf. Palmer's book indicated a half-day's preparation session for contract negotiations with a client whose name I recognized. Neither had anything for Sunday. On Monday they saw "Roland" together in the morning; each had different appointments in the afternoon. Nothing for Monday evening for either one.

It was clear now, at least in part. If Richardson was telling me the truth, I was willing to bet that Huyett and Palmer did the bugging—or rather, Huyett did, and Palmer was willing to go along or at least close his eyes to it. Emily hadn't called me about any financial irregularities—as far as I could tell, when she'd called me a week ago, there weren't any. She called me because she found a bug in her office, and because she knew Richardson wouldn't listen to her suspicions. She wanted me to help prove to her lover that his partners were plotting against him.

Like most insight, it came far too late. Richardson entered without knocking, his face a blotchy combination of red and white. He shut the door behind himself and paced back and forth in front of me. "Damn! Damn!" he said.

"The firm is breaking up," I said.

"The sons of bitches called an emergency meeting when they knew damned well Vince couldn't be here. Not that it would have made a difference, anyway."

"Just what happened?"

He stopped pacing, but didn't sit down. "They voted us out. They're paying us off and kicking us out!"

"I'm sorry, Tom."

"And you want to know the worst of it?" The sarcasm was heavy. "According to *modern management principles* it's better if the *departing members* of the firm make their *exit* as soon as possible."

"What does that mean?"

"I guess this is what I get for sending him to all those modern management seminars—to be kicked in the—" His voice broke off and he teetered on the edge of a complete breakdown.

I tried to keep him focussed. "When do you have to be out, Tom?"

"Tomorrow at close of business. And you, too. They don't want you poking around *their* law firm any further."

"Fine. I'll tell them I'll be out by then."

"She tried to warn me, you know."

No purpose would be served by telling him what I'd been thinking, at least not right now. "Sometimes women have a better sense of these things."

"She cared about me. She really did."

"Of course she did."

"I never—realized—" That was as far as he got. He collapsed into the chair and tears began streaming down his cheeks. At last, Emily Voss received a proper mourning.

Chapter Twenty

Thursday, 8:00 P.M.

I could have stayed and worked at the firm, but after talking to Richardson I needed a change of scene. As much as Tom needed consolation, I had less than twenty-four hours to solve the case. I decided to work in my own office, a ratty second-story walk-up in a bad part of West Philadelphia. The front door was reinforced with sheet steel, all the exterior windows were barred, and the offices all had double or triple dead-bolts. We still had break-ins at least once a month. One of the other tenants, a Korean who ran a check-cashing agency, had been so frustrated he set up a shotgun and set it to fire if someone jimmied the door. He made it a point of going to a couple of the local bars and warning everyone. When he came in the next Monday his heart nearly stopped—the door was ajar. He pushed it open, afraid of what he'd find. The shotgun had been stolen.

I parked directly in front of my building. It was a loading zone, but it was directly under the only working streetlight on the block. It was a sad commentary on my neighborhood that my battered old Honda was a temptation to thieves. It occurred to me that I was going to have to replace the side windows

right away, even if I didn't receive payment on this job immediately. The sheets of plastic I'd taped onto the window frames
were too much temptation. What was that New York joke? A
fellow had a NO RADIO sign in his car window, came down in
the morning to find the window broken and a note on the seat,
"Just checking."

It was raining lightly, but not enough to drive the hookers
off the corners. Two of the regulars stood in front of a bar at
the end of the block, their raincoats hanging open to reveal
skirts that barely covered their panties—if they were wearing
panties at all, which I doubted. They waved at me and I waved
back. One of them had only been working the block a few
weeks. The other was an old-timer. She went back five, maybe
six months. She was white, which was unusual in that area. But
even from half a block away I could see that she didn't have
much time left. Between the two of them they didn't weigh as
much as one healthy woman. The younger one leaned against
a lamppost, zonked out on something. The older one was pacing back and forth with her hands crossed over her belly. For
fifty dollars I could probably have had them both, with syphilis,
gonorrhea, AIDS, and hepatitis thrown in at no extra charge.

I put my key into the upper deadbolt lock. The key turned
freely, but I couldn't feel the bolt moving. I pushed harder and
the door swung open. Inside was a foyer, which was dark except for a sliver of light escaping from under the door that led
into the reception area.

I stepped back into the street and considered my options. I
discarded the possibility that one of the tenants, or the cleaning
people, could have left the door unlocked. No one who lived
more than twenty minutes in West Philadelphia would leave
anything unlocked, ever. Even if they were inside they would
have locked up behind themselves. So I was dealing with a
break-in. What were the odds that the burglars were still inside?
Very slim. Once they got in they generally followed the same
routine—a tour of the petty cash drawer, an inspection of the
offices, a quick look around for office equipment that might

have some street value, and they were gone. Ten to fifteen minutes. No, not likely anyone was still inside. I went back into the foyer and pushed open the inside door.

I was wrong.

It wasn't burglars. I knew that right away. They were the wrong age, wearing the wrong clothes. Three middle-aged white men in polyester suits with badly knotted ties. Two were sitting on a broken-down sofa and the third was on the receptionist's desk. "Evening, Mr. Garrett," the one on the desk said. The choice of words was casual but the tone was clipped and businesslike. He had the bearing of a man with long military experience. I looked at his black shoes and saw that they were spit-shined.

"Evening." I made a show of keeping my hands at my sides.

"I'm Detective Martin, Philadelphia Police," he said. He didn't offer to shake and neither did I.

I indicated the door behind me. "You guys working on the burglary here?"

He shook his head. "I'm with Homicide."

Neither of the homicides had occurred in Philadelphia, and I wasn't even supposed to know about the one in Tinicum, so I kept my mouth shut. The silence stretched out. Finally one of the men on the sofa spoke. "I'm Detective Cassidy, from Radnor Township. And this is Sergeant Risser, Tinicum Township." Cassidy was older, at least fifty, with graying temples and a pot belly. He sat with his hands together across his stomach like the great placid Buddha of law enforcement. Risser was another matter. He was years younger, solidly muscled, and coiled at the edge of the sofa with his head down like a tackle waiting for the snap. I was glad we had the desk between us.

"Pleased to meet you. I guess you know who I am."

"You weren't at home, and this was the only other address we had for you," Cassidy said. He looked around the room with distaste. I knew exactly how he felt.

"It's my office." I shrugged.

"Times must be hard."

"Hard enough."

Cassidy paused. "The door was open when we got here."

"Very convenient."

Martin's face turned red. "You have a problem, Garrett?"

"You mind if I go upstairs and see if you—if somebody's tossed my office?"

Martin said no, but all three of them accompanied me upstairs. No one was taking a chance I'd hunt up a gun or go out the back. I opened the door and checked inside. "Everything looks okay to me," I said.

"Mind if we all sit in here?" Martin asked.

"Yeah, I do. This is my private office. If you have any business with me you can do it downstairs."

Martin muttered something to Risser as we went down the stairs.

I sat in the receptionist's chair and put my feet up on the desk. "Well, gentlemen, what can I do for you?"

Risser, the Tinicum cop, spoke first. "You can tell us where you were yesterday."

"What time?"

"Does it make a difference?" he wanted to know.

"Yeah, it does."

"Then suppose you tell me where you were all day."

"Suppose you give me a time," I countered.

He stood up and crossed his arms across his chest. He stayed where he was, a good six feet away, but the threat was clear enough. "Let's just suppose I don't."

I looked at Martin, the Philadelphia cop. "Is this when I learn about my right to remain silent, or are you boys just going to be satisfied with some fruit of the poisonous tree?"

Martin flushed. If he gave me my *Miranda* warnings he was afraid I'd shut up. If he didn't, anything I said might be inadmissible in court. Of course, maybe he didn't care if it was inadmissible so long as it was useful. "You want your rights?"

"I'm not free to leave, am I?" He didn't answer. "And I'm the subject of a focussed investigation, right? So why shouldn't I get my rights?"

Martin looked at the floor. "We're not certain you did it."

"Did what?"

It happened so fast I didn't have a chance to react. Risser rushed me, grabbed my legs, and pulled me, feet first, out of my chair and across the desk. I hit the floor on my back, my arms splayed out, with Risser holding me up by the ankles. My bad shoulder took the impact, and pain shot through my right arm.

I didn't know if he planned to use me for a pogo stick, but he never got the chance. I relaxed my arms, let my shoulders take my weight, and pulled back my legs. Risser was strong, but not strong enough to hold my full weight. I twisted, and one leg came free. He leaned toward me and kept the other pinned against his chest.

That was a mistake, and it was all that I needed. I pulled back on the trapped leg, then kicked out toward his face and snapped his head right into the kick. The heel of my shoe connected solidly with his chin. He flew backward into the wall and fell heavily to the floor. A framed picture of the Liberty Bell, the only decorative item in the entire room, fell off the wall and hit him on the head.

"You fucking son of a bitch!" His hand went behind his back, whether for his gun or a blackjack, I couldn't tell, and he started to get up. I stayed put on the floor. If he wanted to work me over, I wasn't going to give him the excuse of self-defense. But before he made it to his feet, Martin stepped between us.

"Break it up, both of you! I'm too old for this shit." Risser got to his feet, but his hands stayed in sight. Whatever he was carrying in the small of his back stayed where it was.

I picked myself up and sat on the desk. "If you think I'm going to kiss ass, you're going to wait a long time."

Martin put up his hands, palms out. "Okay, everybody, just

take it easy. This isn't getting us anywhere." He dropped his hands and looked at me. "So, where were you?"

I wasn't going to play their game, even if it meant another ride across the desk. "I was lots of places. I told you, give me a time."

Risser answered for me. "Yesterday, five till seven, you were killing a man in the marshes."

"No, I don't think so."

"Then what's your alibi?"

"Who says I need one?"

"You were seen leaving the area this afternoon."

"Why would I go back, if I killed him yesterday?"

"Suppose you tell us."

"I wouldn't. I'd be nuts to do that, as a matter of fact."

"So give—what about five till seven Wednesday?" Risser stepped toward me in a way I didn't like.

"At five I was in Center City, working on a case. There's a Greek woman in a deli on Spruce who can vouch for me. From six until about ten I had a dinner date."

"Must have been slow service."

I shrugged. "We went to her place afterward."

"You get laid last night?"

I looked him in the eye. "Did you?"

He turned red and gave me a look that warned me to stay out of Tinicum Township the rest of my life. "I want her name and address."

"Susan Minnik." I could have given them the office address, but that would have made tracing my client one step easier. Instead I found a telephone book on the floor and gave them her address and phone number. I gave them the name of the restaurant for good measure.

"And where were you this afternoon, about four-thirty?"

"I think you already know."

"Don't give me any shit, Garrett."

"I don't get off on answering questions when you already know the answer."

"You were at the shack in the marsh," Risser said.

"And I found Bentley's body."

"What did you do?"

"Nothing. I know better than to disturb a crime scene. I looked around without touching anything, got out of there, and called it in."

He produced a notebook and started writing. From there we went over everything I'd seen, one fact at a time, while he took notes. Eventually he ran out of questions, looked over his notes, and flipped his notebook shut. He turned to the Radnor Township detective. "When you're done with his .357, we'd like to let our boys take a look at it."

"You know damned well that gun couldn't have been used on Bentley," I said. "It was locked up in Radnor's evidence locker before he ever got out of jail."

Risser turned to me. "When I meet a citizen with an attitude I like to be careful about giving him a gun."

"It cost me five hundred bucks."

"It'll be in good hands."

"When do I get it back?"

"When your attitude improves."

I decided not to ditch the Hi-Power after all.

It was the turn of Martin, from Philadelphia. "What kind of a case you working on?"

"Sorry. You know that one of the things my clients get is privacy."

"We can put a tail on you and tap the phones, but we don't want to bother unless you make us."

I sighed. Maybe I could at least control the damage. "Okay. I'm doing an investigation for a law firm in Center City." I gave them the name and the office address. "The firm's bookkeeper was found dead Tuesday. Fire in her apartment—"

"Voss, right?"

I nodded.

"I reviewed the paperwork. Looked accidental to me."

"It may have been. I still don't know."

"So what's your case got to do with these two guys? Bentley and Washington?"

"I wish I knew. Honest."

"If Voss was a homicide, any leads?"

"No," I admitted.

He looked at the other two, who shook their heads. No one had any more questions. They stood up to leave.

"One thing," Martin said. "You seem pretty calm for someone who's a suspect in multiple homicides."

"I'm not a suspect."

"What makes you say that?"

I smiled. "You never read me my rights."

He glowered at me and stamped out.

Chapter Twenty-One

Friday, 8:00 A.M.

Tom and I had breakfast in the coffee shop in the first floor of the building across the street. By "breakfast," I mean that I nursed a cup of coffee and Tom tore his napkin into tiny pieces.

"Remember when we used to have office breakfasts once a week?" he asked. "The old Horn and Hardarts?"

"The food was awful. The only thing good was the coffee."

"You younger people never appreciated the place. It had a sense of history to it."

"Especially the sweet rolls. You couldn't cut them with a knife and fork."

"I called Vince last night, after the meeting, at the rehabilitation center."

"How did he take it?"

"He didn't say much. I called him again this morning. He's still stunned, if you want my opinion, but at least he didn't start drinking. He said he'd sign himself out for a few hours and see to packing up his things. Oh, and there is one other thing that came up at the meeting last night."

"What's that?"

"Huyett admitted that he'd planted the bugs. He said he wanted to know how much we knew. Imagine it. Eavesdropping on your own partners. God, am I glad to be rid of the man, even this way."

I drank my coffee and watched the early commuters go by. Everyone in such a hurry, even this early. "Have you considered taking Susan?" I asked. "I've been dealing with her a lot these last few days and I'm impressed."

"Maybe. There's a couple of weeks of hard work just disentangling the clients and the cases. Then I can start thinking about the future. Anyway, Vince is going to be out for a month. I don't want to make any decisions without him." He looked down at the bits of paper in front of him. "This is going to sound odd, Dave, but if Emily had to go, it's just as well it happened before she had to see this. The firm was her life. She was here nearly thirty years. It would have been like the child dying before the parent."

"I've got some news in her case."

"I thought you'd given up."

"Not for a minute. After today I won't be much use to you —without the police involved, there's no way to get to the bottom of this without the firm's cooperation—but you've still got me for today, till five."

"What do you think you can accomplish today that you haven't been able to do the last three?"

"Because I got a piece of luck in this morning's *Inquirer*." I pulled a clipping from my briefcase.

Entered into rest on March 13, in Radnor Township, Pennsylvania, Taylor Washington, of 2109 Turner Street, Philadelphia. A memorial service will be conducted at the Light of Hope Baptist Church, 1317 Oakdale, Philadelphia on Friday, March fifteenth at ten A.M.

He passed it back to me. "Who's Taylor Washington? What's he got to do with this?"

I put away the clipping and smiled. "I didn't have the pleasure of knowing him well. We only met once, as a matter of fact. He wanted to demonstrate what a sawed-off shotgun will do at three paces. I demurred."

"You don't seem to be bothered by the experience."

I drained my coffee cup and set it down harder than I meant to. "It bothers the hell out of me. I don't like killing people. I'd be a psychopath if it didn't bother me. It's the worst thing about this job, that twice this year already I've had to do it. But I've got a job to do. For you. And I don't have the luxury of really dealing with it right now."

"Are you going to go to the funeral?"

"No. I'm going to go to his house."

"But—won't everybody be at the funeral?"

"That's what I'm counting on."

"This sounds like something I don't want to know about."

"So don't ask."

Whatever else I thought of Huyett, he didn't waste time. When I got to the office at nine the firm's sign had already been taken down for repainting and a neatly typed notice hung in its place, announcing the offices of Palmer, Huyett & Ross. Listed as associates were Ellen Fitzpatrick, Susan Minnik, and Michael Flora. I was prepared to wager that Ross was tall, with blond hair, and that Fitzpatrick was short and carried a big briefcase.

I went to my office and found the door closed. When I opened it, the room was covered with drop cloths.

" 'Scuse me, buddy."

A pair of painters were right behind me, carrying rollers and brushes. I stood there stupidly for a moment.

"Sorry, bud, but they want this one done right away. A lawyer gets this first thing Monday morning."

"Sure. Where's my files?"

"They're in the big office around the corner. Mr.—uh— Richardson's. That's where we were told to put everything."

"Thanks."

As promised, the files were in his office, on the sofa in a neat pile. I didn't need them at the moment, and anyway, I didn't have time to waste getting mad. Mainly I just needed some privacy.

I opened my briefcase again and took out some jeans, tennis shoes, and an extra-large sweatshirt. I locked the door, stripped down to the body-armor vest that covered most of my underclothing, and changed quickly. I took out the Browning Hi-Power I'd lifted the day before and gave it a close look. I didn't like the prospect of relying on a strange gun I'd never even had a chance to fire, and I wanted to look it over as carefully as I could. I'd seen pictures of this type of gun before, but I'd never actually held one. It was a single-action weapon, which some say made it obsolete as far as combat handguns go, but it had a thirteen-round magazine and fired the 9mm cartridge, a powerful round but a lot less kick than a .45. This particular gun was a beauty—a gold trigger, black-checkered grips, and a stainless-steel finish instead of the standard blue. I ejected the magazine and pulled back the slide. A round jumped out of the chamber and landed on the floor. That answered my doubts about the intentions of my friend from yesterday. It handled differently than my .357, and when I tried pointing it at various objects around the room I found myself aiming high. There was an adjustment on the rear sight, but I didn't bother with it—I wasn't getting ready for a fifty-yard target shoot.

I took the remaining eleven rounds out of the magazine, checked the tension on the spring, and replaced the clip in the gun. I did some dry firing and decided that the trigger pull was acceptable. If someone had been fooling around with the trigger pressure, at least it wasn't bad enough to give the gun a hairtrigger. After that I reloaded. The barrel was too big for my revolver holster, so I shoved it into my belt at the small of my back. When I checked in the mirror, the gun was hidden completely by my sweatshirt. I was as ready as I'd ever be.

It was raining again as I drove north on Broad Street, and water ran in from the bullet hole onto my left pant leg. Traffic was heavy, and there was time to watch the slow deterioration of the city as I traveled north. In the City Hall area, at the foot of North Broad, the city was fresh and hopeful. The deteriorated buildings were coming down as fast as cranes could work, and blocks that had been parking lots as long as I could remember were filling up with stores, restaurants, and office buildings. The level of new construction thinned out once I crossed Vine, and stopped after Spring Garden. North of Harper, about a mile from City Hall, it started getting rougher. The fast food franchises petered out first, then the large retail stores. The parked cars were older, and more poorly kept. Fewer people were on the streets, and most of the ones I saw were women with young children, or retired people. No young men to be seen.

I drove nearly as far as Temple University and took a left on Cecil B. Moore Avenue. The first couple of buildings were fraternity houses. They were covered with overlapping graffiti in half a dozen colors as high as a child could reach, and the lower windows were barred. I hated graffiti. Nothing made a neighborhood look like shit faster. Back in the days when I was drinking heavily, right after the divorce, I'd been at a party with a woman artist who argued with me interminably about how graffiti was community art, an expression of the artist's assertion of control over his environment, and ought to be encouraged. I excused myself, went to a hardware store, and spray-painted her car.

Broad Street hadn't exactly been Club Med, but it didn't prepare me for what I saw the farther I drove from the University area. The buildings themselves were impressive, in a way —row upon row of three- and four-story dark brownstones, the same vintage as Emily's. Many had elegant curving stairways and broad, imposing entranceways. But the stairways sparkled with broken glass and the entrances were choked with unbagged garbage. I saw very few parked cars, and except for a few men obviously guarding their cars, no one was on the street. The only unattended vehicle I passed had no windshield and was sitting on blocks.

I began to see vacant lots, some of them fenced and others not. No evidence of old foundations, at least nothing obvious. Some of the lots had saplings that had to be ten years old. No signs about No Trespassing or warnings to stay off. If there had been signs, I assumed they'd been stolen. Some of the lots were being used as garbage dumps, but others were nothing more than patches of weeds. How could you have vacant lots in the middle of a metropolitan area of five million people?

The 2100 block of Turner Street was worse. Some of the buildings were boarded up, and not one building on either side of the street looked like it had seen any exterior maintenance in years. I counted three vacant lots and two blackened shells of burned-out buildings. The only person on the street was a young black woman in a soggy dress that had gone out of style ten years ago, pushing a baby carriage. She moved steadily up the street, paying no attention to the rain.

None of the buildings had numbers. I parked at the end of the block and got out.

"Spare change, Mister?"

A skinny black youth—he could have been anywhere from eight to fourteen—was speaking to me from a doorway.

"No."

"I ain't et since yest'day."

His limbs were hidden in clothes that were too big for him, but there was no mistaking the sunken eyes. "Where are your parents?"

"Mama in Muncie. Aunt Lucille take care of me."

"It doesn't sound like she's doing a good job."

"She been sick."

I nodded at him and turned away. From behind me, I heard his voice again. "Guard your car, Mister?"

"Like hell."

"Jus' a dollar."

I'd never had the muscle put on me before by a kid weighing less than seventy pounds, and it took me a minute to decide how to handle it. "I'll make you a deal, kid. I'll buy you a good lunch if you work for it."

"Sure."

"What's your name?"

"Jason."

"Mine's Dave. You know where Taylor Washington lives, Jason?"

"He dead."

"I know that."

He was sizing me up, paying attention to the inflection in my voice. "I knowed him."

"Where?"

He pointed to one of the better buildings on the street, on my side, a few doors away. "Third floor rear."

"Fire escape?"

He shook his head. "Crackheads come and cut it up."

"Okay. Stay here."

"Oh, Mister?"

"Yeah?"

"Watch your step. The floors is weak."

His advice was unnecessary. Once I got to the top of the outside stairs, every step was an adventure. The steps themselves were fairly clean, but the landing was more than half blocked by a pile of garbage. I hurried past into the alcove, but that smelled worse. It reeked of urine, and once I stepped on something soft that I hoped was just old newspapers.

The interior door had several locks, all broken. I pushed on it and it swung open on one of its three hinges. The other two were broken away from the jamb. Inside was a hallway. I saw several overhead fixtures, but none had any light bulbs. How much could you get for a used light bulb, for Christ's sake?

Leaving the door open behind me for light, I moved across the hall to the stairs. The smell of urine was even stronger in the enclosed space, but at least the floor was clean. Under the

slashes and circles of spray-painted graffiti I dimly saw a delicate patterned wallpaper. The junkies hadn't figured out what
to do with used wallpaper, for what difference it made.

A radio was playing somewhere on the second floor, but no
one came out to challenge me. As I started up to the third floor
I began to sense a heavy, cooking smell, like frying. It became
stronger as I moved upstairs.

There were only two apartments on the third floor. A glance
told me that the front one had no door and no furniture. From
the damage to the walls, it looked like the junkies had even
stolen the wiring.

I took my time before I went any farther. The rear apartment
had a door, a peephole, and a battery of locks that would have
protected Fort Knox. A light was burning in the middle of the
hall, and another one was right above the door. The flooring
leading up to the door had been torn loose so it would squeak
when someone walked on it. Just to the right of the door was
a hole, about two inches across, at waist level. Either a loophole
for shooting, or a pass-through for drugs. Or both, depending
on the visitor. No graffiti on the door—nobody wanted to mess
with whoever lived there.

Moving cautiously, I went up the stairs to the fourth floor,
which was also the top. Both apartments on this floor were
empty and doorless. At the rear of the landing was a window,
frozen shut but with no glass. Immediately below was the roof
of a three-story addition to the rear of the building. Part of
Taylor Washington's apartment. I stepped over the sill and put
my foot on the roof. It was slick with years of accumulated
pigeon shit, but it held under my weight. Taking my steps carefully, I went to the edge and looked over.

I was in luck. The junkies hadn't been able to get the top
of the fire escape, and a ladder led down from the roof right
by a rear window. The ladder was pulled loose from the building on one side, and it ended just below the level of the window,
but it still looked safer than going in through the front door. I
drew my gun and started down.

The ladder began to sway the farther down I went, and I wasn't out to test how long it could support my weight. As soon as I reached the window I crouched down and looked inside. No curtains. I was looking at the kitchen. An enormous black woman between fifty and sixty was tending a kettle, several saucepans, and a large skillet. Through the glass I could hear her humming to herself as she worked. I could hear another sound, too, the high, constant wailing of a baby crying.

I shoved the gun back into my pants and fished out my black plastic folder that contained a large silver badge that said, if you looked closely enough, CITIZEN OF PHILADELPHIA. Then, holding the gun and the folder in one hand, I tapped hard on the glass with the muzzle.

She looked up immediately. She looked at me with curiosity, even surprise, but there was no fear in her eyes. I gestured with the gun, being careful not to point it at her, and she opened the window for me. The smell of frying was stronger now. It made me hungry, even though I'd just eaten. She stepped back to give me some room and I climbed inside. I wondered what sights she'd seen that allowed her to take my entrance so calmly.

"My name's Garrett. Sorry to have to intrude like this."

"You lookin' for Taylor, you too late. He's with the Lord."

"What makes you think I'm looking for him?"

"A man who comes in the way you do, he looking for Taylor."

"Are you his mother?"

"His wife's momma."

I shoved the gun back into the small of my back. "Is this your place, ma'am?"

She shook her head. "This is a place of the devil." But she said it with sadness, not anger. "He was a good man before the devil got into him. Who are you, Mister? You a bondsman?"

I chose my words carefully. "What makes you think I'm not a cop?"

"I never seen one cop alone 'round here."

I paid attention to the baby's cry. It wasn't a normal cry—it was steady and insistent and half wild. The cry of a crack baby. "Is that your grandchild in the other room?"

The sadness reached her eyes. "Yes, she is."

"Her mother at the funeral?"

For the first time, she wouldn't meet my eyes. "Her momma on the street. Been on the street for months."

"You take care of your granddaughter?"

She raised her eyes again. Her voice was full of quiet pride, and resignation. "Ain't nobody else to do it, Mister. I's raised her from a baby and now I's raisin' her baby, too."

"What did Taylor do for a living?"

"Nothin' good. The devil's work is what he did."

"Was he involved with drugs? Crack?"

She wouldn't say the word, but she nodded. "The work of the devil. Took them both away from me."

"Did he work for somebody or did he sell out of the apartment?"

"He did his work outta here a while. Then he went to work for the man."

"Was he a user?"

She nodded again.

"What did he do for the man?"

"Whatever he had to do."

"Where?"

She looked out the window angrily, not just at the ratty backyard but at the ruin of half a city. "Corner of Lewis and Twenty-fifth."

"Thanks."

"If yous got nothin' else on your min', I gotta lotta cookin' to do before noon." She paused. "You can leave by the door this time, if you want."

I returned to my car. The boy was sitting on the hood, throwing pebbles at a tin can on the sidewalk.

"Car's all okay for you, Mister."

"Got another job for you." His eyes brightened. I wondered

how long it had been since an adult had paid any attention to him. "You know where Lewis and Twenty-fifth is?"

"You want to go there?"

"I want you to come with me."

He shook his head. "I ain't goin' inside there."

"Neither am I. Get in."

"Mister?"

"Yeah?"

"You the man that shot Taylor?"

"What if I am?"

"I ain't goin' down to Lewis unless you is."

"Well, then you better get in."

The first few blocks were as blasted a chunk of urban terrain as you would find anywhere outside of the South Bronx, but the neighborhood started to improve as we rolled west on Turner. It wasn't as nice as lower North Broad or even the area near Temple, but people were trying. No garbage. Some window boxes with flowers. People owned cars, and were even willing to park them on the street. The few vacant buildings were neatly boarded up.

Then we made a left and went one block south to Lewis.

I stopped at the corner and took a long look. It was like a bomb had hit the neighborhood. It was worse than anything I'd seen on Turner. Nearly all of the buildings, other than the corner property, were vacant. The street was lined with FOR SALE signs. I counted half a dozen kids doing nothing but watching —some on steps, some on rooftops. Kids of ten, even eight, carrying pagers. Men sat on steps in the rain. If they knew they were outside, they didn't care. Young women were in the street, trying to flag down passing cars. They moved like zombies, sometimes walking into the path of traffic. I couldn't imagine anyone wanting to have sex with the poor half-dead creatures, but every so often a car would stop, a girl would get in, and they'd ride away together.

I looked at the corner building. Three stories, brick, heavily barred windows and doors. The funny thing was, the place generally was in good condition. No broken windows. Paint in good shape. It even had its gutters and downspouts. Whatever had happened to this place had happened fairly recently.

I reached for the door handle but Jason grabbed my arm. "Mister, don't get out."

"It's okay. I'm not going inside."

"Be careful, hear?"

"I hear you."

I got out, slowly, and crossed Lewis in the general direction of the building. That was all, but I might as well have fired off a machine gun. The minute I started to move, things went into motion. The men lounging on the staircases started shuffling off. The women stopped hailing cars. The kids disappeared completely.

I had to walk past the building to find what I was looking for. And I found what I expected; swept into a neat pile were several hundred tiny clear plastic vials, the kind of thing you might see with perfume samples. They were empty now, but there was no question what they had contained. I kicked at the pile with my foot and turned back toward the car.

When I passed by the stairs the door opened and two men slipped out and stood at the top of the stairs, looking down on me. Their arms were crossed across their chests and their feet were wide apart in shooting stances. Out of the corner of my eye I saw that one of them was wearing a red beret.

None of my choices was very desirable. I could break into a run and take the chance of a slug in the back. I could draw my own piece and shoot it out against them and whoever else might have me covered from the windows. Or I could just stare them down. I stopped and turned, very slowly, my hands on my hips. They couldn't see it, but my right hand was a little farther back, on the grip of the pistol in the small of my back.

The three of us looked at each other without moving. We were ten feet away, and worlds apart. Black against white, poor against middle class, local against outsider. Shootings took place in front of crack houses every day in Philadelphia, and this one was on the very edge of happening. All it needed was the slightest nudge for potential to become reality. I could imagine the story, buried on page ten, about three men being shot in front of a crack house in North Philadelphia. An everyday story, except one of them would be me.

It seemed like forever, but it couldn't have really taken very long. The man in the red beret tapped his companion on the arm and the two of them drew back inside. I never saw the door open. One minute they were there and the next they weren't. I stayed facing the door until I heard it latch.

I got back in the car and started the engine. Jason didn't say a word.

"Hungry?" I asked.

"Ah . . . I guess so."

"Well, let's go to the nearest chicken place and get us a couple of chickens. One for now and one for you to take home to your aunt."

"Okay."

I didn't tell him, but the plan also included a drink for me. Just one, but I needed that one pretty badly.

Chapter Twenty-Two

Friday, Noon

I entered Susan's office without knocking. The adrenaline was starting to wear off and I wanted to sit down, but the chairs in front of her desk were covered with books and files. Her desk had been full yesterday—now it was jammed.

She looked up. "My God, Dave, what happened?"

"It's been a busy morning."

"You look like you've been through a war."

"Not exactly, but close enough. Look, I need your help."

She gestured at the mess in her office. "This isn't exactly the best time. We're in the middle of trying to sort things out, you know."

"I see you're going with them."

"I haven't made up my mind. The sign in the lobby is the way it is because I haven't said I'm not going with them. If Mr. Richardson wants to make me an offer I'd be happy to consider it."

"I'm glad to hear that. Things are moving fast. Can you help? It could make the difference in wrapping up the case."

"I thought it was all over."

"I have till five to try to finish."

"Oh. That's not much time."

"So I need to make the most of it. Can I count on you?"

She gestured at the piles of paperwork surrounding her. "I'll do what I can."

"Check with the tax assessment office about the owner of the property at the northwest corner of Lewis and Twenty-fifth. Then go to the Recorder of Deeds and get the deed in to that owner."

She indicated her legs. "You understand, I usually call a title company to check things like that."

"Fine. Call them. But however you do it, I need it ASAP."

"I'll see what I can do."

When I left her office I saw Ron Wolfe, the accountant, waiting for me, his hands crossed patiently in front of him.

"Jesus, Ron, I haven't looked as happy as you do right now since I first got laid."

He swallowed, but grinned even broader. "I got it!" he said, waving a piece of paper over his head. "It's right here!"

I took his arm and leaned close. "Quiet down," I said. "A killer could be listening to you."

That sobered him up in a hurry. We went into the restroom and checked that it was empty.

"So tell me what you've got."

"Good Start. It's a Pennsylvania corporation. Originally incorporated four years ago. I've even got an address for them. Twenty-four North Merion Avenue, Bryn Mawr."

I grabbed a sheet of paper towel and wrote it down. "Good job, Ron. Now, who incorporated them?"

"CT Corporate Systems, over here on South Broad."

"What the hell is it?"

"They're a servicing company that forms corporations for people, registers out-of-state corporations, things like that."

"But CT didn't form the company for the hell of it—they were doing it for somebody."

"Well, they signed the corporate papers. Actually, they are the incorporators."

"Okay. So what about the officers?"

"I tried. CT won't say, and the Corporations Bureau won't give out that information except on written request."

"Shit, fax it up there. Or call somebody in Harrisburg to run it down personally."

"I've already done both. And I called to follow up the fax. They say they're working on it."

I slapped him on the back. "Good job. If you work hard enough, someday you can be making fifty dollars an hour as an investigator, too."

The rain had stopped by the time I reached my car, but the sun showed no signs of breaking through. There were two ways to get to Bryn Mawr from Center City: the direct but slow route right out Route 30, and the long way round on the Schuylkill Expressway. The trouble was, if traffic was heavy on the Schuylkill, I'd be stuck—especially if the jam started anywhere west of Belmont. Philadelphians didn't call it "the sure kill distressway" for nothing. I took a chance on the Schuylkill and luck was with me. Traffic was heavy but it moved fast—almost too fast for my tired old Honda. I watched my rearview mirror, but as far as I could tell I was alone.

Bryn Mawr isn't the sleepy college town the name implies. The women's college of the same name is there, well off the main drag, but the school is too small to impart a tone to the entire community. The town is pretty enough, and the side streets have lots of old shade trees and well-kept houses, but it's also in the middle of the commercial strip of the Main Line, with its full ration of car dealers, fast food joints, banks, strip malls, and all the rest.

As I approached Merion Avenue I wondered exactly what Good Start would turn out to be. Some kind of savings and loan? Real estate? A mutual fund? Whatever it was, it was important to the case and I was closing in on it. I felt my heart beat a little faster as I got closer.

Twenty-four North Merion was a small office building, painted a cheerful red, white, and blue, with MAIL BOXES ETC.

across the windows. I pulled to the curb and stared out my windshield. A mail drop. I slammed the door a lot harder than necessary.

Inside, both walls were flanked with metal boxes, similar to post office boxes. In the rear of the store was a display of packing supplies and a counter where a plump middle-aged woman in a store uniform presided.

"Yes, sir, can I help you?"

"My name's Dave Garrett. I'm an investigator." I showed my license and gave her a business card. "I need some information."

"Yes, sir?"

"There's a corporation that used this office as a mailing address when it started up. The name is Good Start. I need to know who's behind it."

"Sir, I'm sorry, but we can't give out that information. This is private."

"I'm investigating a murder. I think that whoever formed the corporation is the killer, or at least he knows who is."

She bit her lower lip. She'd been trained to sell packing tape and rent mailboxes, nothing like this. "I'm sorry."

"It's very important."

"I understand that," she said. "But I just can't."

I'd learned a trick many years ago, as a teenager, for dealing with situations like this. I just kept asking.

"The police have decided it was an accident, not a homicide, so it's up to me to solve this."

"I understand, sir, but I can't help."

"Somewhere out there is someone who's getting away with it."

She nodded.

"And the only way to find them could be in your files."

"I understand, really I do."

"If you can't help me, I have nowhere else to turn. This is our only real lead, right now."

"Well, the company policy is very strict."

She was distancing herself from the company. It was all the opening I needed. "This doesn't have to involve them," I explained. "I don't need a written report—just tell me, verbally, what's in the records."

"I really shouldn't do that."

"The company is never going to know about this."

"Oh, I don't know . . ."

"The family would be grateful, knowing that you helped."

That was enough to put me over the top. "Wait here," she said, and disappeared into the back.

When she returned I didn't like the expression on her face. My first thought was that she had changed her mind.

"I'm sorry, sir, but I can't be of much help."

"How do you mean?"

"We have a forwarding order. Any mail we get, we send on to a post office box in Philadelphia."

"Can you give me the box number? Maybe the postal authorities will cooperate."

"That, I doubt. But I can save you the trouble."

"Oh?"

"That P.O. box number, I recognize it. It belongs to one of our competitors, Executive Services."

"Who are they?"

"A mailing service. Someone doesn't want to get mail at their regular address, they arrange for the mail to be sent there. The person picks it up there, or they forward it somewhere else."

"Let me get this straight. Mail to Good Start comes to you, then you send it to this P.O. box."

"And then it goes Lord knows where. Maybe Good Start picks it up there, maybe Executive Services forwards it to Good Start, maybe they send it to another mailing service."

"Somebody's going to a lot of trouble not to be found."

"Yes, sir."

"Do you get paid by check from them, by any chance?"

"That's right, especially in a situation like this. We photocopy all checks, for our own records, and I looked. There's no return address on the checks."

"The customer must have an address."

"Right. The P.O. box we forward mail to."

"Look, I need one more favor. He filled out an application or something when he opened his account, right?"

"Yes. It was before my time, though."

"Could you photocopy that application for me?"

"Why?" Her tone was sharper now.

"You won't get in any trouble. I just want to have a sample of his handwriting."

This was getting beyond our deal. She eyed me suspiciously. "You sure about that?"

"Just mask everything on the application but his signature when you make the copy. No one will know where it came from."

The signature was bold, slanting sharply to the right, with strong angles. It was a long name, and I couldn't begin to make it out. The first letter of the first name was a T and the last name started with a K and ended in an O or an A. Everything else was a jumble, like the graffiti in North Philadelphia.

I was in a black mood as I drove back toward Philly. I'd started with such high hopes and ended with a photocopy of an illegible signature. And time was running out.

Ron Wolfe was in the waiting room, with his coat on, when I came in. "Dave, I'm glad you showed up. I was just about to leave."

I didn't follow him. "Getting some lunch?"

"No, they told me they'd be bringing in their own person on Monday to take over, so I could just let things go for now."

"Let me guess. The new person is a woman with an Italian name."

"They didn't say. But I've got something for you this time." With a flourish, he handed me a fax. "This ought to blow the case wide open for you."

As I looked at it, I wondered where he learned expressions

like that. It was two pages, the first being a cover sheet from a law firm in Harrisburg I'd heard of. The second page was a copy of the corporate filing application of Good Start. The same strong, illegible signature. And underneath, a typed name.

"There you go, Dave. Thaddeus Kosciuszko. It's a pretty unusual name. You ought to be able to track him down with no problem."

I was about to say something cruel, but the look on his face stopped me. "Ron, thanks very much. I really appreciate the efforts you've made this week. It's made a real difference to me."

"Glad I could help, Dave. And let me know how it turns out."

"If I can, I will."

We shook hands and I was alone. Three hours to go, and my only help, such as it was, was gone.

I went back to Susan's office. She was going over a list and eating a cup of yogurt at the same time. I remembered that our only refrigerator was through a narrow door. Every time Susan needed to put something in or take it out, she needed to ask for help.

"How you doing?" I asked.

"These guys are *nuts*. There's no way we can separate things by Monday. All five of us could spend the whole weekend here and not do it."

"Well, I'll tell you something to cheer you up. You're Polish, right?"

"Uh-huh."

"I tracked down the man behind the Good Start corporation. I even have his signature. We can prove he was up to his neck in the whole thing."

She stopped eating and looked at me. "And?"

I held up the fax. "Actually, Ron deserves the credit for tracking him down. It's Thaddeus Kosciuszko."

"This is a joke."

"No. Well, it is a joke, and it's on us."

"He was the guy who fought in the Revolutionary War, wasn't he? Isn't his old house on Third?"

"The very same. But Ron thought he had a hot lead."

"Jesus, one more screwup."

"I know you're busy, but what did the title company say?"

"Shit! I forgot to call. I can do it in a few minutes."

"Don't bother, I can take care of it myself."

"It wouldn't be any trouble."

"I might as well go. I can't think of anything else to do."

"I'm sorry," she said. "I can do it."

"No, this place is giving me the creeps. I'd just as soon get out. And by the way, don't bother checking with the Register of Wills—I have the information I needed."

"Okay. Uh—Dave?"

"Yes?"

"Today is really your last day on the case?"

"As of five, I'm working for some *ex*-partners. The new firm is entitled to bar the door to me, and they've done it. So the answer is yes."

"So you really were working on Emily's case after all."

"That's what I told you."

She picked up a pencil and looked at it. "I'm sorry about the other night."

"We've already covered that."

"Sort of. You were super and I acted like a jerk."

"Don't be so hard on yourself."

"I'd like to make it up to you, if you'd let me."

"You don't have to."

She looked up from her pencil. "Would you like me to?"

"I just want you to be sure you really want to."

"The next couple weeks are going to be a mess, but could we have dinner again after that?"

"I'll give you a call."

She gave me a big smile before she turned back to her work.

Chapter Twenty-Three

Friday, 2:00 P.M.

The Recorder of Deeds office in City Hall isn't what most people expect. It's not grimy, like most of the courtrooms, or bustling with activity, like the Prothonotary. Signs say NO FOOD OR DRINK, but the title searchers all have coffee cups. The staff wear sweatshirts and jeans. It has the atmosphere of the back room of a state college library: warm, cozy, a little shabby, but basically comfortable.

I took a number from the dispenser and sat down at the long gray Formica table that ran all the way from the doors to where the shelves began. The black and red "NOW SERVING" sign indicated a number three below mine. I took off my coat and tried to use the time constructively.

Teach us to sit still, T. S. Eliot said. I hadn't sat still for a moment in three days, and what did I have to show for it? A shot-up car and a headful of facts that didn't fit together. I had three hours left. Not enough time for any more running around. It was time to begin solving the case with what I had, if I could.

What had I learned? Well, for what difference it made, that everyone in the firm had lied to me, at least once. Richardson was the biggest liar of all—he concealed his affair with Emily, the will, the money, and the fact that he had seen her after Friday. Vince, in his own way, was worse. Like any alcoholic, he lied to himself. Could he have done something in a blackout? I liked and trusted the sober side of Vince, but the other side . . . Huyett—had he lied to me, or just been obstructive? I tried to reconstruct our conversations. He'd said he'd talked to the accountant when he hadn't. And of course he'd lied about why he'd had the books audited last month. But all of it was explainable by his desire to keep me from finding out about the impending breakup. Flora had lied so often that it was easier to keep track of when he told the truth. Susan. There was something she'd said that didn't quite add up. What was it? Nothing big, nothing even about the firm. But somewhere along the way there was something that didn't sound right. Palmer lied about the bugs, of course—he had to know that Huyett had planted them. Even Ron Wolfe, the accountant, had fed me bad information, though I was sure he hadn't intended to. If lying was the test of guilt, I'd run the whole bunch of them in.

I decided to think about the case in terms of time. If my theory about how she was killed was right, someone held her, starting on either Saturday night or Sunday, until late Monday night. And she'd called me with suspicions on the preceding Thursday. She sat on information about *something* for two or three days. Someone kept her alive for a couple of days. Why?

One at a time. Why keep her alive Monday? Maybe to buy time. If she was in the office Monday she might have seen the hundred-and-twenty-thousand advance. By Tuesday it was history, because the money was on the way in to cover it. Maybe. The people going through the books wouldn't care about the entries as much as making sure everything balanced out.

Why kill her? Either because she knew there was something wrong, or because it was inevitable she would have discovered it had she lived. I voted for number one—people who think that discovery is inevitable don't bother to put money back.

So what did she know? And why didn't she tell Richardson?

Or did she—not everything, but maybe something . . . something he hadn't paid any attention to.

Two title searchers moved past me, carrying stacks of folio volumes. "Just because it's filed," one of them muttered, "doesn't mean it's recorded." In other words, don't assume the job has been done right. Hmm. I'd been assuming something about Emily. That she was correctly *interpreting* what she found out. But why assume that? Being dead didn't give her any greater claim on clear thinking. Suppose she saw a big funny money check go out that was suspicious because she'd never heard of the file. Or that she found the bug in her office. Or both. And assumed that whatever she found was the work of Huyett and his pals. Maybe she didn't tell Richardson because she knew he didn't want to hear about the possibility of internal problems in the office. Maybe it never occurred to her that something else was going on—assuming that Good Start was something separate from the new firm Huyett and Palmer were starting.

I wanted to stop and rub my eyes, but at that moment a young Hispanic woman called out my number. I raised my ticket and she sat down across from me. Her perfume was overpowering, and she was wearing a loud yellow and green T-shirt that said something in Spanish.

"I need any information you can give me on the property on the northwest corner of Lewis and Twenty-fifth, here in Philadelphia."

She wrote down the streets on a scrap of paper. "You have the grantee's name?"

"No."

"Tax parcel ID number?"

"No."

"Grantor?"

"No."

"Date of transfer?"

"No."

"House number?"

"Sorry."

"Anything at all?"

I shook my head.

"Well," she said. "Nobody told me they'd all be easy."

Whether it was easy or hard, it didn't take her long. A couple of minutes later she was back with a tax map of the neighborhood. "Yes," I said. "That's the one."

"I figured. Let's take a look."

We went to a microfilm reader. She inserted a spool of tape, glanced at the index of deeds it covered, and jammed the machine on full power. Tape whipped through the gears and flew across the screen in a gray blur. Suddenly she hit STOP, and came to rest almost exactly on the deed she wanted.

"Here we go." She spun the machine around to give me a look and checked her watch. "Eleven minutes, five seconds, and nothing to go on."

"A record?"

"No. But close."

I took a look. The deed was dated eighteen months ago, and conveyed the real estate from the Secretary of Housing and Urban Development to Good Start, a Pennsylvania corporation. The price was two hundred sixty thousand dollars, and the address of the grantee was Twenty-four North Merion Avenue, Bryn Mawr.

"What's HUD doing in this?" I asked.

"Probably they guaranteed a loan to a former owner who defaulted, and they wound up with it in the foreclosure sale. But at this price, in that neighborhood, maybe it was a property they'd renovated. That's a lot of money for up there."

"Who financed this?"

"Give me a couple minutes." She was as good as her word. "No mortgage on record. It must have been a cash deal. Somebody really believes in North Philly real estate, putting that much money in."

"Maybe it's not their money," I said.

"Oh?"

"Just maybe. Thanks for your time."

I walked back to the office, trying to think as I went. Our firm wrote a big check to Good Start, which owned a crack house. And Good Start had money to burn *before* it got into the crack business at that location—they'd been able to pay cash when they bought it. But why pay cash for a building to use to sell crack? It didn't make sense. I was no expert, but from what I knew, crack dealers either rented, or used abandoned buildings. Why go to the trouble, and run the risk of losing your money in a forfeiture proceeding?

The more I thought about it, the less I liked it. The Good Start operation was a combination of a lawyer's care and passion for secrecy coupled with the money and ruthlessness of the drug trade. Except for the fact that blacks were running it, I was reminded of the Mafia. Well, could this be a joint venture of some kind? If it was, I was back to Flora. Or not.

As soon as I got back to the office I went to Emily's office. The photocopy of the funny money check from Mellon had arrived and was sitting on her desk in an envelope with my name on it. The signature was Richardson's, but even I could tell that it wasn't his handwriting. I took the check and the forged signature of Thaddeus Kosciuszko from the fax and compared them to the handwriting of each of the attorneys in the office. Except for Richardson, who had an upright, rounded style, the signature on the check could have been the work of anybody in the office. A documents examiner could probably do better, with enough samples of handwriting and the cooperation of all possible suspects, but I knew that it was never going to happen. It was up to me, with whatever I knew or didn't know, and whatever time was left on the clock.

I sat at a table in one of the conference rooms, looking at the photocopy of the check. Not a single idea came to me. It was time to let up for a minute and get a fresh grip on it.

DeAndrea came into the room, without knocking, wearing a tattered plaid sports shirt and jeans. His movements were tentative, like someone who's surprised to find himself still alive after a natural disaster. He shook my hand and stretched out into a chair. He was pale and tired, but his eyes were clear.

"You're looking a lot better today, Vince."

"You mean, for the first time I look like I give a shit."

I gestured around at the office. "You're taking it pretty well."

"Exactly which disaster did you have in mind?"

"I was thinking about the firm."

"My tie is to Tom. Huyett and the others can go piss up a rope."

"Vince, I want you to know, I've got a lot of respect for you for agreeing to get help. A lot of guys go a lot longer."

"I kidded myself about being able to do just one more, hang on a little bit longer. I was lucky it wasn't worse."

"What are you going to do now?"

"After my thirty-day rest cure? I don't know yet. Maybe I'll use the time to read the Uniform Commercial Code. I hear it's fascinating fucking reading, better than a Tom Clancy. I'm done with trying cases, that's for sure." He stopped for a second, and when he resumed he seemed to forget I was there. "You know, the things you do, they either make you stronger or they make you weaker. For a long time I liked trying cases, as much as I may have bitched about it. But somewhere along the line I turned the corner and it started to eat at me. I need to get out while there's still some of me left."

"Are you and Tom going to stay together?"

"Of course. As long as the two of us can stand up, we'll probably practice together. What else do we have left?"

"You've still got time to build a good firm again, if you stay off the juice."

He shrugged, as only he could do. "The new firm? Eh— who knows? If it works, fine. The main thing is, to try."

"Good luck," I said, and meant it.

"I wish you could be a part of it."

"Me too."

"Seriously. If something ever happens, you get some suck

with the Supreme Court and get yourself readmitted, there'll always be a place for you."

"That's good to know."

"Take care of yourself, Dave."

"You too."

We shook hands, hard, and he went out the door.

I shut it behind him, turned off the lights, and sat alone in the half-dark. When he left something went out of that room that was more than just a middle-aged man in jeans that were too tight. Without him, the room was drab and bare. Nobody but me at home.

I looked at the check again. It gave me nothing back.

Chapter Twenty-Four

Friday, 4:00 P.M.

O ne hour until I had to clear out. I did what I do best when I don't know what else to do. I ask for advice.

Kate answered on the first ring.

"How do you get to the phone so fast?"

She sounded distant. "Oh . . . I was right by the phone."

"Did I wake you up? You sound like it."

"No, I was in bed, just resting. I still don't feel very good. Some kind of twenty-four-hour bug with a slow watch. But you didn't call to ask about my digestion."

"Are you going to a doctor about it?"

"If it's not better by tomorrow, yeah."

"All right, then. And yes, I need your help. I've got just the rest of the day to solve the case and all I have is more questions." As quickly as I could, I went over what I'd learned. I left out the details of the confrontation at the steps of the crack house—there was no point in worrying her.

"David, I think you're in an impossible situation. They want you to find the killer. To be logical and detached and objective. But you have some kind of emotional involvement with every single person there, except for Flora."

"Well, maybe it is Flora."

"Maybe it is. But from what you tell me, everything that happens points away from the Mafia, not toward it. What you've got is a connection to a black cocaine ring. That's the only lead you've got and that's what you ought to follow."

"Let's put Flora to one side for a minute. You don't think I can see Huyett objectively?"

"No. You're not as good as you think you are in handling people who don't like you. You try to ignore it, but I can tell you resent him."

"He's lied to me like crazy."

"Sure, but I think the lies were all to protect his plan to set up the new firm. He didn't want you turning over any rocks before he was ready to turn them over himself."

"You're right," I admitted. "And we can skip Palmer, too."

"Mmm . . . wait a second, though. He's the lawyer who handles the estates, right?"

"Yes."

"What if he'd been borrowing against client funds, and needed money in a hurry to pay off to an estate?"

"Yeah, but the check was made good almost right away."

"So maybe he needed the money just for a couple of days, till he could cover things from somewhere else."

"The accountant couldn't find anything tying him to the money."

"He and Huyett fired the accountant," she pointed out. "Maybe he would have found something if he'd had a little longer."

"Well, maybe. I don't know what to think." I sighed. "You've made your point I'm the wrong person for the job. But I'm in it, and I'm almost out of time."

"I'm sorry. I should be helping instead of throwing in garbage you don't need. What do you think of Flora?"

"He's a scavenger, not a killer."

"And what about Susan?" she asked.

"Now it's my turn to question your judgment."

"How do you mean?"

There was always a lilt in Kate's voice when she was concealing things from me, and I was hearing it now. "You're jealous of her," I said.

"I don't have the right to be jealous. I'm married and the two of you are single."

"That doesn't mean you're not jealous."

"All right," she admitted. "Let's go on, though."

"If she's in this, she has to be a hell of a rich associate."

"Well, maybe she stole a lot more money than the hundred and twenty and the money for the building."

"She didn't steal it from the firm. Everyone assures me the books are tight—Emily watched them like a hawk. Ron can't find anything wrong. Huyett's accountant did a full review a month ago and found nothing."

"So what if she stole it somewhere else?"

"Then there's no motive to kill the firm's bookkeeper," I pointed out.

She couldn't think of an answer for that one. "Then what about Richardson?"

"Either he's an evil genius or he's being set up. And I know him well enough to know he's not an evil genius."

"There's a lot pointing in his direction."

"I can't believe he would have killed her," I said.

"Maybe something got out of control. We both assume that no one in the firm did it personally. Maybe his instructions weren't obeyed."

"I can't see him taking a risk of her being hurt," I said.

"Maybe you just don't want to see it."

"Okay, so he's getting close to retirement, whether he's willing to admit it or not, and until Emily died he didn't have the money to retire. But he could have married her—two million would have been plenty for both of them."

"How do you know marriage was an option?"

"Because—" I stopped myself. "Because Richardson told me so," I said slowly.

"Do you have any proof she wanted to marry him other than that?"

"You're tough."

"I have to deal with some pretty tough people in Frank's business. So, all we have is his word?"

"And the diary."

"But how do we know he was the man in the diary?"

"We don't," I admitted. "For all we know he was *jealous* of the man in the diary."

"If the man existed at all," she mused.

"There's still the photo of her in the café. At least it shows they were together outside the office."

"It could have been taken by anyone," she said. "Like maybe the man in the diary."

"So how did Richardson get it?"

"The first time you saw it was *after* Emily was killed. Whoever did Emily for Richardson could have picked it up and given it to him."

"She wouldn't have called me in if she suspected him."

"Well, maybe she was wrong," Kate said.

"I sure hope she wasn't."

Neither of us said anything for a while after that. It was a painful silence. Finally Kate broke it. "So what do you think about your friend DeAndrea?"

"When he drinks he's capable of being mean, even violent. But I sure don't know that he's capable of it."

"You seem to think you know him pretty well." There was skepticism in her voice.

"I'm not being as blindly trustful as you think. If he somehow went to her apartment and murdered her in a drunken rage, he couldn't have concealed everything so clearly. This was done by people who planned everything very carefully. And he wouldn't have done it sober. Never."

"So we're back with nothing, except maybe Richardson."

"No, not exactly. You've given me a thought."

"Tell me and we'll both know."

"We've got a lot of facts. But we keep circling around what we *don't* know. What we *do* know—about the killing, about Good Start—doesn't tell us anything because we can't imagine who it connects with. We don't need to understand any more about the crime—we need to understand the people better. And the only people I don't understand are Flora and Minnik."

"It's nearly five." I couldn't tell if she agreed with me or even if she was following what I was saying.

"I know it. Call you later. 'Bye."

I went to Flora's office. He'd left, his secretary explained, an hour earlier, but I went in anyway. I dug his appointment book from under a stack of unread mail and checked the entries for last week. There were a surprising number of appointments, all of them short, and notations for every evening. Monday it was dinner with Aunt Marie; Tuesday, a basketball game at home—cousin Tony was playing. Wednesday night he was out with a real estate agent looking at houses in Elmwood. Thursday night was dinner with Huyett and Palmer—he didn't have the imagination to hide it. Friday night simply said "Home." Saturday had a notation, "Aunt Becky's Fiftieth—five o'clock." Nothing for Sunday. Monday night, the night Emily died, was "home—pick up VCR."

I flipped back through the weeks; one was very much the same as another. If he'd dummied up his activities in the few days before her death, he'd been careful about it.

His secretary, a thin brunette in her early twenties with oily skin and dangling gold earrings, was just putting the dust cover on her word processor when I came out. "I know it's after five, but can I just ask you a question or two?"

She was putting on her coat, but said, "Yeah. Sure."

"Worked for him long?"

"Ever since he got here." The accent was pure South Philadelphia, broad and flat.

"Did he have much to do with Emily?"

"Not that I seen."

"Did he have any contact with her the end of last week, like Thursday or Friday?"

She shook her head and her earrings shook. "Nope."

"You sound pretty certain."

"There's no need to see her unless you need checks. Anytime he needed a check, he asked me to get it."

"What about last Friday?"

She looked puzzled. "What about it?"

"I heard he was out all day."

"No. He was here. I remember, 'cause Roger yelled at him about not telling him that something was urgent."

"What time was that?"

"Right after I got back from lunch. Maybe one-thirty."

"You sure it was Friday? Not Thursday?"

"I'm sure. Roger was yelling about how Mike had screwed up his weekend for him, 'cause there was no more time to get it done during business hours."

"Thanks for your time. Have a good weekend."

"Hope I was some help."

"Oh, you were."

It was nearly five-thirty and I'd clearly overstayed my welcome, but I went back to the conference room I'd been using anyway. I shut the door, closed my eyes, and tried my best to be still.

I was missing something—not so much a clue as the right attitude to take toward the case. I was seeing lots of trees without having a sense of the forest.

Susan had lied to me about Mike being away on Friday. Why? And it wasn't the first time she'd tripped up—I tried to think of what she'd said. Something about her family. Her brothers. Her three brothers and how she used to lock the bathroom door. Why did that strike me as odd? I opened my eyes and opened Susan's personnel file. The article about the accident in Pittsburgh. It mentioned three brothers—but as survivors of the girl who died. Could both people in the car have identical families? The odds were against it. Still, it was possible. Maybe Kate was rubbing off on me—I was being too hard on Susan. I looked at the photocopy carefully. It looked genuine to me, but I'd never seen the *Post-Gazette* before, and anyway, someone with a desktop publishing program and a scanner could create anything they wanted.

And there was something else she said. While we were in bed.

I called her old law firm in Pittsburgh, but no one answered. Then I studied the clipping again.

I called Directory Assistance and found the number for the *Pittsburgh Post-Gazette*. I got through and asked for the Records Department. The phone rang a dozen times and I began to worry that they had shut down for the evening, too. But finally I got an answer.

"Records Room." He sounded like I'd woken him up.

"This is the place to call for old papers, right?"

"Right."

"I need a photocopy of an article from four years ago."

"Where are you calling from?"

"Philadelphia."

He sounded bored. "Copies of papers up to ten years old are available at the University of Pennsylvania Library."

"This one can't wait."

"It's our policy not to respond to requests where the information is readily available in the requestor's area." The voice had a measured, singsong quality, but underneath there was an edge.

"Is there a fax machine there?"

"Yes, there is."

"My name is Dave Garrett. I'm working for a law firm, trying to solve a murder. I'm a private detective. I'll give you the fax number here. Give me your name and address. If the fax is here within half an hour there's fifty bucks in it for you."

"Cash? To my house?" He sounded shocked; I'm sure it was against company policy.

"Sure. No checks, just cash."

"How soon do I get it?"

"I'll put it in an envelope before I leave the building."

"Okay, buddy; you're on."

I sat down to wait. And hope. And hope, too, that I was wrong.

Chapter Twenty-Five

Friday, 8:00 P.M.

It took Susan a while to answer the door. For a long moment we just faced each other, she in her chair and I standing in the doorway. She was wearing a string of pearls and a long-sleeved black dress that went nearly to her ankles. The material looked heavy and thick, like velvet. She backed up her chair, turned, and went into the living room. I sat on the sofa across from her.

"I know," I said.

She avoided my eyes. "I was in the library," she said. "I saw the fax coming in." She spoke slowly, as if getting out the words was an effort.

"You want to talk about it?"

"It doesn't matter now. It's all going to unravel."

"You sound like you don't care."

"I'm not a lawyer, but I know what I'm facing. A life sentence and maybe even the death penalty, for Emily. Add a few years more for embezzlement. And you want to know the funny thing? No one was supposed to get hurt at all."

"Go on."

"Nothing was supposed to happen to Emily. They were just

supposed to go in on Saturday morning when she wasn't there and get something. They were supposed to make it look like a burglary."

"Let me guess. They held her over the weekend and made her call in to the answering service on Monday. Then on Monday night they poured a bottle down her throat and waited till she passed out. They put her in bed, filled the biggest pan they could with grease, turned on the burner, and got out of there."

"I suppose. I didn't ask and they didn't give me the details."

"So what did Emily know?"

"She didn't know anything—the plan was to keep her from finding something out. I took an advance on the firm's line of credit with a funny money check. A big one, nearly a hundred twenty thousand dollars. The bank sent out an acknowledgment that got to our office on Friday afternoon. I didn't have the cash to cover it myself until Monday morning."

"So what could you do about it then?"

"The account I got the advance on, I'd prepared a ledger card myself. It wouldn't show the advance and it wouldn't show the deposit. The whole thing would wash. All I'd have to do after that was wait till the monthly bank statement came in, and destroy the funny money check. It had Richardson's name, but I wanted to be sure they wouldn't try to use it to figure out I was the forger."

"Wait a minute. The bank statement itself would still show both transactions, wouldn't it? And if you destroyed the bank statement, she would have just called for a duplicate."

She shook her head. "You don't understand. I wasn't going to destroy the statement. I didn't care if Emily had a deposit and advance she couldn't account for, as long as she couldn't trace it back to me. It would just be a mystery that wouldn't really matter because the books balanced. Like I said, a bank notice acknowledging the cash advance came in on Friday. I saw it in her office, but I couldn't sneak it out. She wasn't feeling well and didn't walk around the office much. I looked for it after she went home Friday afternoon. That's when I realized she must have taken it home. I had to keep her from figuring out what it meant."

"So what went wrong?"

She took a long breath and focussed on my eyes. "David, I have no reason not to tell you the truth anymore. None at all. No, I didn't trust them. But they said the business with Emily was making the best of a bad situation. When they got there, she had the cash advance acknowledgment right in front of her. If the bank hadn't been so conscientious, the whole thing would have worked."

"These guys sound pretty tough."

"I didn't realize how tough till it was too late."

"They were from the crack house?"

"Yes."

"What did keeping her alive on Monday have to do with anything?"

"They never called me while they were holding her. The first thing I knew, she was already dead. What they told me was, they made up their minds on Saturday they were going to have to kill her. Once she was dead, somebody would go over the records. They decided to give me Monday to make the deposit so at least there'd be no cash discrepancy."

"Very considerate of them."

"I never wanted anything to happen to her, I swear it."

"Not that it matters now, but it's funny how they fell all over themselves to turn a burglary into a murder."

"Huh?"

"If they killed Emily, that gave them a better hold on you. Blackmail."

"Scared people do stupid things, especially when they don't have time to think. And I was scared."

"The same people who did Emily came after me."

"I didn't call them. I swear it."

"How did they know I was on the case if you didn't tell them?"

"They didn't trust me to keep them informed. They had

their own people watching the firm, seeing who came and went."

"A couple of hundred people go in and out every day."

"But you did a lot of criminal defense work right here in Philadelphia. They recognized you. They made some calls and found out you were a private eye. They were watching the building. They followed us to the restaurant and then followed you home."

"You knew they were following me."

She shook her head. "No, I only learned about that after they tried to kill you. That was the first I knew about it."

"If all you did was some embezzlement, and immediately replaced the money, and if all you tell me about Emily and me is true, what are you so worried about? I mean, you're going to have a record, but a good criminal lawyer could cut you a hell of a deal. The DA would have a lot of trouble proving a conspiracy case against you beyond a reasonable doubt."

She laughed softly. It was a sour, unpleasant sound, and I was glad when it stopped. "You think I hired people like that, with all the risk, because of a little check-kiting? If I was ever prosecuted they'd find a heck of a lot more than that."

I didn't understand what she meant by *if* she was prosecuted, but I kept going. "No matter what else is in your background, if it happened as you say, the worst you're guilty of is conspiracy to commit burglary."

She looked down at her lap. Suddenly she looked very tired. "My luck with the legal system hasn't been very good. I've taken my own measures."

"Even in a worst case, and I mean worst case—conspiracy to murder, arson, burglary—there's no way they'd give you the death penalty. You'd have a shot at parole in a few years."

For the first time her voice showed some animation. "Because the jury would feel sorry for a cripple?"

"I've always been honest with you, even when you didn't return the favor. And the answer is yes."

"It's good to know there's some advantages in being fucked up."

"Your problem isn't in your legs. It's in your head."

"You have a lot of nerve saying that."

"The rest of the people in the firm, they're weak and stupid sometimes. They're capable of big mistakes. But you're the only one who's capable—"

"Of what? What are you going to call it? Before you start judging me, you ought to know what happened to me."

"I know a few things about you. When you doctored up the newspaper article you just changed the names and transposed the captions of the pictures. The whole story is there if you just change back the names. Your real name is Marjorie Axell. The other night at your place you said you were twenty-seven, which is right—but Susan Minnik would be thirty-one now. And you were a real estate paralegal for a firm in Pittsburgh when you had your accident. The real Susan Minnik was killed in that accident. When you got out of the hospital you moved here and took over her identity."

"What do you know about the accident?"

"Just what was in the article. The real version, I mean."

"They kept the details out of the papers. I'd been reviewing papers for a settlement at a title company. It was just before Christmas. Susan was supposed to handle the settlement. After all, she was the lawyer and I was just the assistant. She showed up late and she was pretty drunk. She'd been at a couple of office Christmas parties. After the settlement my car wouldn't start and she said she'd give me a ride back home. I asked her if she'd let me drive, but she insisted. She ran a stop sign right into the path of a truck."

She folded her hands in her lap. "I suppose you think I should have just put it all behind me and been a good sport, huh?"

"I didn't say that."

"I could have lived with the accident, if that's all there was.

It was stupid and needless, but it happened, right? It was the rest of it."

"The rest of it?"

She closed her eyes and cocked her head to one side. "Picture it, David. I'm an honest, hardworking little kid who clears two hundred dollars a week and has to pay part of it to a shitty medical plan. I get out of rehab and they give me a stack of medical bills for nearly a hundred thousand dollars. I say, give them to Workman's Comp. The comp people turn them down —they say I wasn't on the job. I hire a lawyer to fight for me. He loses and sends me a bill of his own for three thousand dollars. I hire another lawyer, on a contingent fee, and sue my law firm. The case gets thrown out; the judge says it wasn't my firm's fault they'd hired a drunk. So the lawyer sues Susan's estate. Guess what?"

"She was driving without insurance and had no other assets."

"And I get a bill for a thousand dollars from my second lawyer for his costs advanced."

"Did you have insurance of your own?"

"You mean, uninsured motorist coverage? Of course I did. Little people like me were always so careful to do everything we were told. But my insurance was high because I lived in a bad neighborhood, and all I could afford was the minimum. Fifteen thousand dollars."

"Did you collect at least that?"

"Not a damned cent of it. The lawyer charged me five thousand dollars for making the phone call to the insurance company. And even after my medical insurance paid their share, I still owed nearly twenty thousand, so the hospital took the other ten. You know what happened next? Fucking hospital calls up and wants to know how I'm going to pay the balance. Do you think they care that it wasn't my fault, that I was out of work six months, that nobody is giving me a penny for being crippled for life? No. All they want to know is, can I afford five hundred dollars a month, and that collection proceedings will start if they don't hear from me by the first of the month."

"That's when you decided to get even."

She didn't respond right away, and I thought she was falling asleep. But then she opened her eyes. Her voice was soft, but clear. "You're damned right I did. If that was how the system worked, I was going to make it work for me. I already knew how to run a real estate practice. I knew more than a lot of lawyers know. I'd done hundreds of settlements, title searches, lien searches. So I took Susan's name and moved as far away from Pittsburgh as I could get. I just started using her Supreme Court number and paying her bar dues. Nobody checks that stuff, you know. I used my computer. Desktop publishing—changed around the news story just a little and had instant background."

"Why Philadelphia?"

"It was easier to lose myself. I move to a small town, I get noticed. Maybe someone mentions me to someone who knew about Susan. Here, lawyers are a dime a dozen."

"So you started a dummy corporation as part of the scam."

"Know the joke, 'What do you call five hundred lawyers at the bottom of the ocean? A good start.' That's where the name comes from."

"What does any of this have to do with the money you borrowed from the firm?"

"That was just the tip of the iceberg. A tiny little temporary cash crunch. Four years ago I was up to my neck in debt. Now I'm rich, for what good it did me."

Her attention was wandering, like she was drunk, and I had to work at keeping her focussed. "Want to tell me about how you did it?"

She leaned back in her chair. "It was so simple, and no one ever suspected. Do you ever do any real estate?"

"Once in a while. Not in a long time."

"I was juggling settlements."

After three days, the little bulb in my head finally came on. I'd found the money trail. It was a simple enough scam, if you had trusting clients and enough nerve. Your client says he wants to buy a house for a hundred thousand dollars and he's prepared to pay cash. No finance company, no title searches. The property is presently mortgaged to the ABC mortgage company for eighty thousand. At settlement you get a check from your client for a hundred thousand. You give the seller his twenty thousand and he goes away happy. But instead of giving ABC its eighty, you keep it. And with a little luck, ABC doesn't find out. They don't have people driving around interviewing their customers to see if they've sold their homes. As long as they get a mortgage check every month, what do they care? Of course, it's coming from you instead of the seller, but nobody is likely to notice that, so long as the checks clear.

"You can only do this with people who pay cash."

"Right. But there's more of them than you think. That office I worked with in Upper Darby. I ran it all myself. A lot of the real estate transactions are cash, and with people who know each other. Even within the same family. Lots of old ethnic families that hang together. Two brothers buy out dad's business, father gives a row house to his daughter and son-in-law as a wedding present, adult children buy the house of their aged parents to keep Welfare from getting a lien—I did lots of deals like that."

"How many properties you juggling?"

"Right now, about thirty, thirty-five."

"How do you make the monthly mortgage payments?"

"Out of the money I hold back."

"How do you handle it when the new owner sells? You have to pay off the mortgage then."

"I kept a slush fund to pay off mortgages. Didn't happen too often." She laughed again. "Just once too often."

"But sooner or later aren't all the properties going to be sold and you're going to have to clean up all the titles?"

"Sure. What I did's just a way of raising money for short-term use. It's not permanent. But if you can get a high enough return off your investment you can get rich."

"How rich?"

She smiled lazily. "I was five or six years away from being able to retire. I have a little more than six hundred thousand of real estate money out right now. I have about a hundred of my own invested on top of that. Plus, I normally keep a hundred in ready cash in case I have to pay off any mortgages. The seven hundred is earning an average of twenty percent a year."

"Not legally."

"Actually, a lot of it is. Mostly I own apartment buildings and I have a corporation that does some trading in the stock market."

"And a crack house."

"And a crack house. I'm not proud of that one."

"How did that come about?"

"I owned the building. It was apartments, and it was hard to rent for enough to make it cash-flow. They sent word to me through the super that they would pay ten thousand a month if I would kick out the other tenants and keep my mouth shut."

"So you did."

"I didn't have a choice. How could I have explained how I had enough money to be the owner in the first place?"

"So what exactly went wrong?"

"Like I said, a cash crunch. I had to pay off a mortgage a month ago. That drained my reserve. Two weeks ago, I had to satisfy the mortgage on the biggest single property I'd been juggling. I needed a hundred and forty and I only had twenty. So I used the firm's money."

"Why not go to the loan sharks?"

"I didn't trust them not to blackmail me."

"You should have known you were dealing with some pretty rough customers at the crack house."

"I was dealing with them anyway. And besides, I knew about them. I had something on them if it came to that."

"You've come a long way from the girl in Pittsburgh who was such a victim."

She was quiet for a while. Then she shook her head and roused herself. "David, would you help me transfer to my bed?"

"I think we ought to be seeing the police, don't you?"

"There isn't going to be any police. This is as far as it goes." She smiled a little. "This is a good dress to die in, don't you think?"

I made the connection. "You've taken something."

"Every downer and tranquilizer and sleeping pill in the house. And there were a lot of them."

"How many?"

"Bottles full. It won't be long now."

I stood up. "Jesus, we have to get you to a hospital."

"Why? So I can spend the next twenty years in jail?"

"You don't know what you're saying."

"No, you're the one who doesn't know what he's saying. What, exactly, do I have to look forward to?"

"You can't do this to yourself."

"If I was a dog with nothing to live for . . ." She didn't finish her thought. "Why do I have to suffer?"

"Emily suffered."

"You're not thinking about her, you're thinking about how you're going to make your case without me. Well, it's all written down. It's all here in my papers and on the computer. You don't need me."

"I could have been killed."

"Saying I didn't want that to happen doesn't help, does it? Actually, I liked you. Really I did."

"As much as you like anybody."

"Yes, that's true." She yawned. "I'm getting pretty sleepy. Will you help me transfer to bed? I'd hate to go in this damned chair."

"Why should I do that?"

"Because you're a good man. And because somebody owes me."

"Who?"

"Nobody. Everybody. But you're the one who's here, and it's not much to ask, is it?"

It was the kindest, the best, and the most irresponsible thing I'd ever done. I knew it was wrong at the time, and if I had the chance, I like to think I would do the same thing again.

I wheeled her into the bedroom, laid her out, and propped her up on some pillows. I pulled down her dress all the way to her ankles and took off her shoes. I sat on the edge of the bed with her and held her hand. It was cold.

"David? You ever in Pittsburgh about five years ago?"

"A few times, yes."

"Would've been nice."

"What's that?"

"To have met you then. Maybe things would've worked out different."

"Maybe."

"David?"

"Yes?"

I had to lean close to catch the words. "Talk to me."

I held her hand and told some stories. I can't remember now what they were, or how I picked them, just that it seemed better to have her go hearing a human voice than going out on her own. A couple of times I felt a return pressure from her hand. Then it went completely limp and she was in a deep sleep. I watched her chest rise and fall, a little slower each time. She was right; it didn't take long. I kept talking until I was sure it was over.

I took away the wheelchair when I left the room. I think she would have liked that.

Don't miss Neil Albert's next
Dave Garrett Mystery,

CRUEL APRIL

coming soon in a Dutton hardcover edition.

Chapter One

Tuesday 10:00 P.M.

I picked up my second Wild Turkey and looked at my reflection in the glass. I wondered how many people were studying themselves in bar glasses around the country at that very moment. I thought of how much bourbon I'd dumped into my poor liver in the last twenty-five years. Middle-aged thoughts. Maybe it was that I had a whole new reason to worry about my health.

I looked up past the glass at the bartender. He was a grandfatherly Italian with a big smile and thick horn-rims. He leaned over the bar. "So, you meetin' your girl?"

"It's that obvious?"

"A man don't look that happy waiting to pick up his momma." He pointed at my hand. "And you ain't wearing no wedding ring."

"You're good. You ought to be in my line of work."

"Whatdya do?"

I looked at my drink again. "I used to be a lawyer. Center City. Now I'm a private detective. My name's Dave." We shook hands over the bar.

"Mine's Tony. So what's it like, bein' a private eye? You catch crooks, like in the movies?"

"The cops get paid to do that. I mostly do investigations. Missing-persons cases. Take statements from witnesses. Surveillances, things like that."

"That how you met your girl?"

"Her name's Kate," I said after a moment.

"Irish?"

"Oh, yes. Red hair and green eyes. And a real redhead's complexion. She lives in Miami, and she has to put on gobs of sunblock before she can go outside."

Tony pulled out his wallet and handed over a picture of a round-faced woman with short, frizzy hair, standing in front of a small brick row house. Her body hid most of the house. She could have been anywhere from sixty to eighty. "Your wife?" I asked.

He beamed with pride and tapped the picture with a stubby forefinger. "Thirty-seven years we been together, six children, three grandchildren."

I handed back the picture. "Kate doesn't look anything like that. She's straight up and down. Has to run around in the shower to get wet."

I could see him struggling with the concept of a woman like that being attractive, and failing. "You two—getting married?"

Tony had a knack for asking good questions. "Maybe. I'm not sure. Things have been happening pretty fast between us. I only met her a couple of months ago. Tonight will be the first time I've seen her since then."

He shrugged. "Things happen fast, slow—if it's right, it don't matter. Angie and I, we have three dates, all with chaperones, then we decide to get married. And look at us now. Say, Dave, you got any kids?"

"No. She has two from her first marriage. They're both in college now."

"College? Boy, nonna mine made it that far."

"Education runs in the family. She teaches English at a community college down there."

"Hey, smart lady." He hesitated before he asked the next question. "Say, if you don't mind me asking, how old is she?"

"I'm not exactly sure," I admitted. "I think just about my age, forty-four."

"Angie was a grandma by the time she was forty-seven. You know, it's nonna my business, but you want to have a family, you better start pretty soon."

"I'd like that," I admitted. "When I got divorced," I said, "I figured that was it for me, as far as getting married or having kids, I mean. This is like something falling out of the sky for me."

He became very serious. "Dave, you can't take it that way. It won't last."

"How do you mean?"

"Life ain't no lottery and there ain't nothin' free worth havin'. You only get to keep what you earn."

"That's an interesting philosophy."

He spread his arms wide, gesturing around the bar. "I'm just a guy stretching out his Social Security a little. I ain't no philosopher. But I know what I know."

"Don't you believe in just plain good luck?"

"For small stuff, sure." He shook his head sadly. "But family . . ." His voice trailed off and he rubbed an imaginary spot on one of the glasses. "So, she as excited as you are?"

"I talked to her from the Miami airport just a couple of hours ago, right before she got on the plane. Yeah, she sounded excited." I looked down at my glass, which was nearly empty. "But there are some complications."

He gave a rich, robust Italian laugh. "The two of you are old enough to be grandparents, you've only met this girl once, and you say there are *complications?*"

"She's still married. They've been living in the same house, but separate lives, if you know what I mean, for a long time. They were planning to divorce when the youngest got out of college."

"Same house?" he repeated.

"It's not as uncommon as you might think."

He shook his head. "Hard to imagine."

"When we first met she told me she was divorced. It was only later that I got the whole story."

Tony started wiping the bar, which was already spotless. "Dave, I like you, but I gotta say this. You two have to come from behind. You started with a lie."

I was startled. "I thought you would say that God will forgive."

He leaned closer, as if imparting a secret. "God don't run the whole show. Things happen that got nothin' to do with Him."

"Like whether you earn things?"

"Yeah." He held my eyes for a moment, then his expression relaxed and he was just a jolly bartender again. "Hey, Dave, sorry to get so serious on you. This isn't like me to be getting so personal. Let me give you another on the house."

I held my hand over my glass. "Thanks, but I have to run. Her plane's due in right now."

I found the gate just as the plane pulled in. A vendor across the corridor was selling oversize Mylar balloons. I bought one that said "Welcome Home" in big pink letters and found a spot right at the head of the stairs. "Welcome Home" seemed a little silly—she'd never even seen my apartment—but it was either that or "Bon Voyage." Besides, if things worked out it would be her home from now on. Our home.

The door to the ramp opened and a stream of suntanned passengers came through. Most seemed to be college students coming back from spring break. I saw a pale, slender woman with short red hair, but when I looked more closely I saw that she was younger than Kate. Then some tired businessmen and some equally tired businesswomen, most of them burdened with luggage that looked heavy.

Some more college students went by, and then a few older couples. Retirees moving up north for the summer, I guessed. It was easy to tell the ones who were still in love and those that weren't. After the old folks was another rush of college students—evidently the retirees had been holding things up. Then no one for a minute, then a few more retirees. Then no one at all.

After a couple of minutes one of the flight attendants came slowly up the stairs, a short brunette wearing too much makeup. A black bag on a little baggage cart trailed faithfully behind her like a dog. She looked hardly older than the college students, but she was barely putting one foot in front of the other. I wondered how long she'd been working.

I caught her eye, but she didn't stop until I sidestepped and blocked her path.

"Excuse me. My—fiancée was on board and hasn't gotten off."

Her face was impassive behind her makeup, but her eyes were bleary. "Sir, all of the passengers have deboarded."

"That can't be."

"It's part of my job to check, sir. There's no one on board but the flight crew."

"She has to have been on the flight."

She closed her eyes and rubbed her temples, but her voice stayed level. "Perhaps she missed it, sir."

"Would you mind if I went on board, just to make sure?"

"I've already checked. Even the lavatories, we always do. There's no place to hide on an airplane."

She was right about that. "Can you please—"

"Sir, all I can tell you is that there's no one on board. Perhaps she never was aboard."

"Look, I know you're tired, but I'm really worried about

her. Would it be such a problem if I went down and took a quick look?"

"I'll tell you what I'll do for you, sir. I'll go back and check one more time, okay?"

"I'd appreciate it very much."

She left her bag with me and disappeared back down the ramp. About five minutes later she came back, shaking her head. "Sorry, sir. There's nothing I can do."

"Please, miss. I need your help."

"If the flight was overbooked, maybe she accepted an offer for a free ticket or something and she'll be on a later flight."

I shook my head. "She would have called."

"Well—did she have checked baggage?"

"I'm pretty sure."

"The one thing I can tell you is to check the baggage claim. If a passenger voluntarily gives up their seat, we try very hard to make sure the bag doesn't go without them. If the bag is there, well, I don't know what to tell you."

It was a sensible suggestion. "Thanks for your help. Very much." She nodded at me and disappeared into the crowd.

By the time I found the right carousel, the bags had all been unloaded and reclaiming was in full swing. The college students were shoulder to shoulder around the carousel, pointing and shouting at their friends as familiar bags traveled past. The older people mostly hung back, except for one tiny woman who'd cleared a prime space for herself with the aid of an umbrella and a no-nonsense expression.

As the crowd began to thin, the rest of the older passengers began to come forward and claim their bags. I saw some familiar faces, but not the thin woman with red hair. I only saw a couple of the business travelers, but then I remembered that most of them had carry-on bags. Then the retirees thinned out, leaving four items behind.

I moved and took a look. After a while, I saw a gray suitcase, packed to bursting. I'd seen it before, in her room in Lancaster. And the tag had Kate's name and address.

I watched the bag circle slowly around until it was out of sight. I realized I'd been holding on to the balloon. I let go and let it bounce off the ceiling twenty feet above. I wouldn't be needing it now.